ANGEL DOWN

Richard Totino

This book, my first to be published, is dedicated to two women. First is my late sister Barbara. She once, following another of the often-trying events, described my life as a "living soap opera". In hindsight, her description was correct. I have led anything but an ordinary life. And throughout all of these events, she was right there as my sister and more importantly, as my friend supporting me and lending an ear whenever needed.

The second woman is my wife Sharon. For some reason, the good Lord led me to this woman at a time when I was finally old enough and smart enough to understand and appreciate her value and her love. Our years together have been the most exciting of my life. We have shared so much together. She has given me the solidity that I lacked, the love that I sought and the companionship only dreams are made of. For all of this, I am completely devoted to her.

And finally, to our children. Our combined tribe of eight with another seven grandchildren have brought me so much challenge and joy my cup truly runneth over. Thank all of you. Your contribution to my life is far more than you will ever know.

Contents

Part I

A Rude Awakening

Chapter One

"Hello," the gravelly, half-asleep voice gurgled into the cold, white plastic mouthpiece. A man struggling not to sound as if he had been abruptly awakened from a sound slumber-pretending to be one who never slept, instead always awake, always at the ready.

"It's down!" the voice at the other end of the line blasted, out of control, hyperventilating, trying to manage his words by squeezing them into the tiny holes in the phone's mouthpiece, forcing them into the thin wires and air vapor connecting him to the man he had just startled awake.

"Down! What's down? What are you saying? Who is this?"

"It's down-lost!"

"What's down? What's lost? What are you talking about, and who the hell is this?"

"I... it... it's Davenport, sir. It's down, sir... the president's plane's gone!"

"What!?"

"Lost! Radar lost it! It just disappeared!"

"What the-" shocked by the words fighting to filter into his consciousness, the White House chief of staff exploded into full awareness, blood rushing into parts of his brain he hadn't even known existed. He threw the covers back and erupted from his bed, eyes wide open and bulging, face flushing red before his feet could find the wide-plank floors of his newly-restored early American home. "Where are you, Davenport?"

"I'm at Andrews," responded the quivering voice, sounding fearful and confused. "I'm in the tower."

"Andrews? What the hell are you doing there?"

"I was assigned here for his return, the president's return. I was to meet his plane and handle the normal stuff. You know, press and TV. The report came in from Air Force One just as I got here. Just before it turned around."

"Turned around? Hold it! You just told me the president's plane was down. That it was lost. What do you mean, turned around?"

"Yes, sir! I mean, no, sir! I mean-" The young assistant press secretary was shaking so hard he felt his legs weakening beneath him, ready to fold and collapse on the floor. His face scrunched in agony as he tried not to piss in his pants.

"Okay! Hold on, Davenport. Settle down, son. I know I'm coming at you fast and hard, but I've gotta know what's going on. Just calm down and breathe. Now, you just told me the plane was down. What are you trying to tell me? What the hell time is it, anyway?"

"It's 2:40 a.m., sir! He wasn't on Air Force One. He—"

"What! Did he fly a commercial? Shit! Is the whole damn-? We have civilians? How many dead? What about-?"

"Damn it, sir! I'm trying to tell you. If you'll just give me a second, I'll explain what happened."

Davenport held his breath and let it out slowly, trying to get a grip on his emotions. He felt his heart pounding against the inside of his shirt. He felt the pressure of being on the scene of the loss of the President of the United States of America.

"The president wasn't on Air Force One. He was with his daughter. She flew to Halifax and met him after the E... Eleventh conference. She wanted to show him her new twin-engine plane. Once she got him to the airport, she started talking him into flying with her. She was practically begging him. You know how he is with her—can't say no. She's his little girl. So he gave in without the slightest struggle or concern for himself. Said he'd fly to Quebec City with her and ordered Air Force One to go ahead. They were going to fly as far as Quebec City for dinner at their favorite place in Old Quebec, then board Air Force One for the flight to Ottawa and the president's meeting with the prime minister. The Secret Service objected as strongly as they should have and as strongly as he knew they would. They tried to get him not to do it, but he dismissed their concerns and ordered them to go ahead. 'After all,' he said, 'I'm flying with my daughter.' Anyway, they scrambled to get things organized before the president and Ms. Richardson took off. Air Force One was to fly at forty thousand feet over top of them. They were supposed to circle overhead and maintain radar and radio contact the whole way. She was airborne for about an hour when the plane just disappeared from the radar. Everybody lost them—Air Force One, Portland, Halifax, St. John, Quebec— everybody lost them from radar. The civilian airports confirmed with Air Force One within seconds. Just gone! Within seconds."

"Where?"

"Over the mountains, sir."

"The mountains? Which mountains?"

"Maine, sir. The mountains of northern Maine!"

"You're sure?"

"Yes, sir. I'm afraid so."

"Wait a minute! What time did all of this happen? What time did she take off?"

"About eight o'clock."

"Eight o'clock? Last night? That was over six hours ago! Why the hell wasn't I told about this earlier? Why didn't I know about this at eight oh one?"

"The military and Secret Service expected them to reappear on radar right away. They thought it was a fluke and that they would show up any second and it would be over. No crisis."

"Everyone is sure it's down? Not just a loss of radio signal or something? Maybe some piece of equipment went bad? Maybe they flew behind a mountain and it blocked out her equipment? Are they sure?"

"Yes, sir. Air Force One turned around and went back over Ms. Richardson's flight path. All the way back to the beginning and, then turned around again and flew all the way to Quebec City. No signal, no sign of them. Besides, enough time has gone by. She would have made it all the way to Quebec by now, and we would know they were okay."

"Shit!"

"Yes, sir."

"Could they have been shot down?"

"No, sir. No sign of anything like that."

"Shit! What fucking idiot let him get in that plane with her?"

"I don't know, Mr. Wilson. But I do know that the Secret Service put up real strong objections. It's like I said, he can't say no to his daughter. I know there are two agents with them. They insisted and at least won that concession from the president. And Air Force One was to monitor them all the way. But they lost them. That's it. That's all I know."

"Jesus Christ! Who else knows about this? Is there press out there at Andrews?"

"No, sir. All the press is on Air Force One, traveling with the president. The only people who know anything are the tower crews here and in Portland and Halifax and Quebec, and the crew, of course. The flight crew on Air Force One."

"What about the press on Air Force One?"

"They're still on the plane. The Secret Service hasn't let them off yet. I'm sure they're getting pretty pissed off by now."

"Cell phones. What about their cell phones?"

"Taken away. I know that for sure. Part of the new security policy. The head of the service detail took them all away before they even boarded the plane. He's holding onto all of them until he's given new orders."

"Good! Oh hell, are you talking to me on an open line?"

"Ah... yes. Yes sir, I am," Davenport replied sheepishly. "Oh shit. Tower crews. Flight crew. Every CB and shortwave radio freak, ham operator, and airport tower within earshot of a radio."

"No, sir. I don't think so. They were on a closed frequency. Military channels. Exposure should be limited. Very limited."

"Keep it that way, damn it. Lock this down, Davenport. I've got to get it under control before it hits the fan."

"Yes, sir. But how, sir?"

"I don't care how you do it. Just do it! Keep it quiet. Keep it buttoned up. Take every cell phone, blackberry, raspberry, and any other kind of berry that's out there. Arrest people if you have to. Gag 'em! Shoot 'em! Throw 'em in the fucking tower of London if you have to, but keep it quiet. Don't speak to anyone but me until I tell you otherwise. Refer everybody to me and to me only. And stay right where you are so I can find you. Monitor everything. I want to hear from you every thirty minutes, come hell or high water, beginning at... three thirty. Less than an hour from now. I'll be in my office by then. I'll expect your first report at that time. Make sure you keep everybody off the air. Threaten them with their lives if you have to. Got it? Am I clear?"

"Yes, sir." The line went dead before Davenport's response could sneak by his vocal cords. Once again, he found himself wishing he had taken the position in the family business that his father had offered him.

Back in his Georgetown home, Bob Wilson began dressing like an automaton on fast forward, unconscious of his motions. His mind and body were racing independently of each other. His brain flooded with all that lay ahead of him and the country. The next few hours would seem like a lifetime.

He suddenly realized that he was being watched. His wife was sitting upright in bed, her mouth hanging open in shocked disbelief, an explosion of questions only seconds away, blocked for the moment by the thinnest layer of fear and confusion.

He thrust his finger in her face. "Not a word," he spat out with all the threat and authority of his official government position, not in the mode of a husband of thirty years. It was the top assistant to the president of the United States ordering her. "Not a goddamn word to anyone, most of all your sister. Especially your sister. I'll have her killed if you say one word to her," he bluffed. "Have I made myself clear?"

She nodded numbly at this live-in stranger who, moments ago, was her husband. She watched as he jumped from their bed, seemingly landing in his pants and shirt in one motion, raced to his car, and sped off into the pre-dawn darkness. The weight of his office, his job, was suddenly clearer to her than ever before. She was hurt by the way he spoke to her. She was sad because of what lay ahead of him. The fun and games of being at the center of power were over. This was for real. The President of the United States of

America. The most powerful man in the free world, the leader of the greatest country on earth, was missing. His airplane was down. He was probably dead. She had to call her sister.

Chapter Two

Bob Wilson needed solitude. The sight of the stream tumbling down the rocky creek bed along the Rock Creek Parkway in the middle of the nation's capital helped to calm him. The wet, cool fall air washed his skin. It was quiet this time of night. Probably the only quiet time of day around here.

The world was in a crisis and didn't know it, at least not yet. He knew that once he reached the White House, the scramble would begin, and the entire world would be turned upside down.

As he drove, he made a mental list of actions to be put into motion the second he reached his office. Oh yeah! The scramble would be on. All the little dogs would quickly join in the hunt to feed upon the unfound corpse. Every last one of the faithful nipping at the opportunity to come out of this as the new Big Dog, the King of the Hill.

Through all the crocodile tears and long faces, the dogs would be in the hunt, every opportunist claiming a deep personal loss. All looking for the way and the words to make this all about them. A near family tragedy. The loss of one is regarded as almost a brother. All were looking for "closure." Looking for some way of realizing political gain. Fighting through the tears. Phonies all, every fucking one of them!

By the time he arrived at his office, he had begun to get his thoughts under control. Organized, at least to some degree. He flopped into his office chair. The burden suddenly dumped on him weighed heavily. He had not bargained on this. No matter what happened from this moment on, no matter who stepped up to take command, he had not bargained on this. He wasn't elected to any post. Only those who were would ever be seen and acknowledged. But he would have to do it all, have to handle all the crap. All the hysteria. Who would ever have seen this coming?

He lifted the telephone to call the first person who needed to know. The one person, ready or not, who had to step up to the plate for the very first time. "Here goes," he muttered as he pressed "O."

"Good evening, Mr. Wilson," came the calm, trained voice of the White House switchboard operator, totally unaware of the situation about to explode across her console.

"Good evening, operator. What is your name, please?"

"Mrs. Shultz. Mary Shultz," she responded in her most professional voice, silently wondering why he had asked for her name. She was about to find out.

"Mrs. Shultz—Mary—we have an emergency. I want you to clear all other calls from your station. Advise your supervisor. You are to be available exclusively to me and to this office until further notice." He knew that the security clearance she held by being a White House operator did not require him to tell her that everything was to be treated as classified.

"If your boss has any problems with this, send her up here and I will instruct her personally. You are to be available to handle only my outgoing calls and all incoming to me are to be routed through you. All calls are to be electronically scrambled. I also want every call recorded. You are not to go off shift without my releasing you. You are to stay on the line and listen in on all calls. And you are to monitor every conversation no matter whom I might be speaking with."

"You want me to listen in? To listen to your telephone calls?"

"Yes, Mrs. Shultz, and to record them all. You're about to be put into the middle of some heavy-duty shi-stuff. Am I clear?"

"Yes, sir," she answered, fighting to control her voice. The unknown crisis she was being dragged into suddenly electrified all her senses. She could feel the tension created within her just from hearing the voice on the line giving her instructions. She wiggled upright in her chair and braced herself for whatever was coming next.

She had been trained to deal with just such a situation. But no one—not her, not one of her peers—ever expected it to really happen. Not to them. The prospect, the idea, of such an experience excited them during their training; it made the boring day-to-day stuff bearable. Only it would never really happen, would it? But now? My God! Oh my God. Was this another 9/11?

"Good. I need your help, Mrs. Shultz. I need you to be at the top of your game. Stay calm and alert. If you hear or sense something, write it down and call me. Don't be shy about it; speak your mind. There's going to be a lot going on all at once, and I'm going to need your ears and brain and your intuition.

"Now, the first thing I need you to do for me is to call the vice president. I don't know where he is. Find him. His aide will answer at this time of day. So when you get his aide on the phone, tell him to hold and call me back when we are connected. Okay?"

"Yes, sir."

Wilson hung up the telephone, leaned back, and lit a cigarette, his first since the call that had interrupted his sleep well over an hour ago. Reaching for a yellow legal pad and a pencil, he began to list the people who had to be contacted. The list was long.

Each person on the list had to be brought into the inner circle. Some for action and support. Some out of political necessity. Some just because their egos demanded that they be considered among those within the inner circle. Some because they considered themselves essential. In reality, the order in which each would be notified would fit their true status.

The cabinet members, the Speaker of the House and key representatives, the Senate leadership on both sides of the aisle, the Joint Chiefs, the Chief Justice—on and on went the list.

But no wife! Thank God for that. No wife. The president was a widower—how long had it been? Nine years? All he had now was his daughter. And she was with him, also missing.

The president's daughter was better, stronger, more supportive, more dedicated, and more protective than any wife could ever be. His beloved daughter. His goddamned, beautiful, pain-in-the-ass, wonderful, fucking airplane-flying daughter.

The phone rang. "Mr. Wilson, please hold for the vice president's aide," Mrs. Shultz announced with a new level of command and authority.

"Okay," he acknowledged, as he heard the metallic electronic clicking of the voice scrambler being engaged by Mrs. Shultz on the White House end of the line.

"Go ahead, Mr. Wilson. Okay, Captain, Mr. Wilson is on the line."

"Hello."

"Captain, this is Bob Wilson, White House Chief of Staff. What is your name, please?"

"This is Captain White... Charles White, U.S.M.C. I'm the military aide to the vice president."

"Good, Captain White. Will you please put the vice president on the line?"

"Uh... b... but Mr. Wilson, he's napping."

"Wake him up."

"But, Mr. Wilson, he's asleep."

"Captain, I assume that if he's napping, he's asleep. Now wake him up and get him on the phone."

"Bu... but..."

"Shit, I don't have time for this. Listen up, Captain White. I don't give a damn if he's back on the farm in Iowa fucking his favorite goat, get him up and get him on the phone and do it now!"

Thud. The captain must have dropped the phone, or Wilson's words had knocked it out of his hand. That was the language the military understood and reacted to. Four-letter words always cut to the chase. Wilson smiled to himself. The captain was probably wondering if the vice president really had sex with goats. Wilson waited impatiently, tapping his pencil on the yellow pad for what seemed hours.

"Hello."

"Mr. Vice President?"

"Yes, Bob. What is it?"

"Sir, this call is being scrambled on my end. Will you please engage the equipment on your end?"

"Bob, what is it?"

"Sir, the scramble, please."

"Okay. Hold on a sec."

It took only a minute for the scrambler to be hooked up. It was always kept close by. Now, no one, either by design or by accident, could eavesdrop on either party in the conversation.

"Okay, Bob, it's engaged. What's going on?"

"Sir, the president is missing. His daughter met him in Halifax, Nova Scotia. She somehow persuaded him to fly with her in her new twin-engine plane. Air Force One was to monitor their flight along the route and meet them in Quebec. Shortly after reaching altitude, they disappeared from both onboard and ground radar. Contact was completely lost.

"They're presumed down and lost somewhere in the mountains of northern Maine or possibly in the wilderness area of western New Brunswick. Two agents were also on board. That's all I know right now. Information is still coming in. I'll be receiving an updated report in just a few minutes. I have a man in the tower at Andrews. He's monitoring all information and will relay it to me."

A loud, long silence vibrated like thunder through the telephone line. "Who else have you contacted?"

"No one, yet. You are the first."

"Good. Don't. Where are you now?"

"At the White House, sir. In my office."

"Stay there. I'll be there in less than half an hour. Put together a list of everyone who needs to be brought into this."

"I've already done that."

"Good! I'll be there as soon as I can. Then, we'll decide how to proceed, Bob?"

"Yes, sir?"

"Contain it. No matter what, contain this. We've got to know more before it breaks. I don't need to tell you what's at stake. I don't want panic on our hands here or abroad. I don't want anybody getting crazy ideas and trying to take advantage of this situation. We've got to maintain control. No matter what. Understood?"

"Yes, sir."

"Bob? Until we've got him back, you work for me. I'm going to need your help."

"Yes, sir, Mr. Vice President. I understand," Wilson replied, remembering his own words spoken to Mrs. Shultz a short while ago.

"One more thing..."

"Yes, sir?"

"Get coffee in there. Lots of it."

The vice president's voice was calm. Controlled. Betraying, nothing. Nothing except authority and command and confidence. Maybe he was more than Bob Wilson had given him credit for.

Maybe he wasn't as young and ill-fit for the job as many thought. Maybe he was more than just a no-questions-asked guy, blindly and totally loyal, more than just a handsome face and friend to the president. Maybe there was some substance there after all. Wilson would soon find out. He and the rest of the Washington establishment and the rest of the world. It wasn't official yet, but like it or not, Dennis Carson was now, or soon would be, the president of the United States.

Part II

Thinking Outside the Box

Chapter One

8:17 p.m.

The vice president of the United States arrives at the White House. He makes his way to the Oval Office to find senior White House staff already present. The unofficial information network has somehow alerted them that something is up and they've all scrambled for their places. No one wants to be left out.

The vice president immediately takes charge, exhibiting a level of self-confidence and ability far beyond anything previously credited to him in his short career in politics. Those around him who had their doubts no longer had a choice. Right or wrong, right side up or upside down, he is now the man who sets the direction they are to follow. Whether they like it or not, he is now head of the country.

By the grace of God, Vice President Carson expands instantly into his new role, putting everyone on notice that he is in charge. Each question, each issue that arises, he meets head on. He issues orders and directions with the calm assurance necessary to wrest control away from the political opportunists who could so easily let things get out of hand. The White House staff, the government, and the country will now be looking to him, and only him, to tell them what to do and how to do it.

Bob Wilson has instructed the Secret Service to step up the vice president's detail to the next level. Security around the White House has been increased until everyone is sure of what has happened to the president and verified that he and his daughter aren't in the hands of anyone who poses a threat to the vice president or the country. The events of September 11, 2001, have resulted in a whole new checklist of things that have to be addressed, and the potential for a terrorist act tops the list.

Leaders of both houses of Congress and both political parties have been called in, along with the Speaker of the House and Secretary of State, who have both suddenly been raised one rung up the ladder of ascension to the presidency.

The Senate Majority Leader, the Cabinet, the Joint Chiefs of Staff, the Chief Justice of the Supreme Court, the heads of the FBI, NSA and CIA, and all the military intelligence services are present. The governors of the New England states and New York have all been simultaneously notified by a communications up-link via satellite because their states were within flight range of the president's daughter's new aircraft.

These states, along with Canada's eastern provinces, will become the focal point of the search activities already underway. They will be asked to supply the needed support to the military and law enforcement groups from within their respective states. The prime minister of Canada, the president's host at the Halifax conference and a longtime personal friend have already been contracted, advised of the events of the past few hours and officially asked to lend support to the efforts to locate the president.

Bob Wilson's long list is now complete. Everyone has been contacted, advised, or informed in accordance with the "Ego Scale" of importance. The situation is in hand; the big wheels of big government have been set in motion.

This will be a military operation, and once the military takes over, operations of this scale are almost scary, with the massive amount of manpower and equipment that can be set in motion with a single telephone call. And only big government can do it.

Chapter Two

Information began to trickle in during the hours it had taken to call the roll of officials. Sydney Richardson, the president's daughter and only child, had filed a flight plan to Quebec for 9,000 feet. Her intended path would take them from Halifax across the Bay of Fundy, over the city of Saint John in New Brunswick, then west toward Mt. Katahdin and Baxter State Park in central Maine, and finally, northwest toward Quebec City over the vast wilderness timberlands owned by the paper and lumber companies.

The Secret Service had ordered the civilian radio towers to clear the entire route of all aircraft. The Canadian authorities in Halifax had requested and received authority for the flight plan from both the Canadian civil and military flights. All flights of all aircraft, large and small, were to be re-routed before Ms. Richardson left the ground.

Her new plane was capable of flying a lot higher. It could be pressurized to reach altitudes that would easily clear anything in her path. But it was far more fun and exciting to fly lower and dip and dive through the mountains that lay just beyond the thin skin of the aircraft. Their massive power radiated to those who loved the out-of-doors while the expanse of lush green timberlands mesmerized and calmed.

President Donald Richardson loved his only daughter, his only child, to a fault. He trusted her as a pilot without reservation. She was highly qualified, with more hours in the air than her youth would lead any critic to believe, having learned to fly years before she was old enough to be licensed for either an airplane or a car.

Sydney Richardson would rather fly to the grocery store than jump in behind the wheel of a brand-new sports car.

The president took advantage of every opportunity to spend time with his daughter, even if it was upsetting to his staff. It was difficult—almost impossible—for him to refuse her anything, anything at all. Not only his child, she was his friend, his companion, and his advisor.

At critical moments, he would turn to her for input, reviewing with her all the options that had been placed before him. Many times, she said nothing, only listening, letting him talk his way through to a final decision. She was there when no one else was or could be. She was a window to the people; she brought him a sense of what was really going on out on the streets and in the countryside. She brought him down to earth when all others treated him as "Mr. President." Since the death of her mother, she filled the void in her father's life. They became inseparable, and anyone foolish enough to try to come between them was doomed to pay a terrible price. She worked tirelessly to make up for her mother's dying prematurely, leaving the two of them alone.

Sydney Richardson was not simply the First Daughter: she had become the First Lady and a better one than most presidential wives. She was at her father's side through the toughest times, the person he turned to when deciding if he would run for president. She campaigned with him. Set up the White House living quarters for him. Interviewed and selected the staff. Reviewed the menus for official functions. Tried to be sure he kept a balance in his public and private lives. Even tried to fix him up with a couple of dates.

Although she lived her life her own way, she always remembered her place in his life and in the eye of the public, never forgetting that her errors in judgment and her human slips in behavior would reflect on her father and his office. So, she kept the men in her life away from the probing eye of the camera and reporters. If a man wished to date her, he did it her way or no way.

She truly loved her father, enjoying his companionship far more as a friend than as a parent. She understood and accepted him as a man and his office as one to be respected. She would not—could never do anything that would embarrass him. They respected each other, emotional equals giving and receiving joy and love from each other. If they hadn't been father and daughter, most would have seen them as the perfect couple. Sydney could not actually be the First Lady, of course, but she was very often, and not so fondly, referred to as "the first Britch." Britch was the staff's way of combining brat and bitch. And security referred to her as "Daddy's little angel." And Angel became her code name.

Out of the public eye, she was the president's protector. She demanded loyalty and service to him or, in no uncertain terms, she'd cut your balls off. She never intruded into his politics, but she made no bones about running his house. Many were those who kept waiting until she checked what her father was wearing. Was it the right color for the occasion, was the tie right, the shoes right, his hair right? She drove the staff crazy, keeping important people, reporters, legislators, and even ambassadors waiting until she gave the okay. The president tolerated all of it. She was his baby and he loved her blindly. His little secret was that he enjoyed her doting on him. He needed the attention. Bereft of his wife, she was the only female in his life and his closest confidant.

So, when she asked him to fly with her, it was natural to say yes. No one who knew them would have expected anything different. He simply brushed aside the objections of his staff and the Secret Service. The justification was simple: she asked, he went. Besides, she was an excellent pilot, licensed the first day she became eligible under FAA regulations. She was checked out and qualified in a dozen different types of aircraft, including small jets and helicopters. The weather was good. Her aircraft was brand-spanking new. The president agreed to have two Secret Service agents in the back seats. Air Force One was to monitor the route, fly over them like a big babysitting mother duck, and meet them in Quebec. There was no good reason not to grant his daughter her wish. It's not in either of their minds anyway. End of story. No further explanation is required. Load up! Let's go!

Then they just disappeared. No apparent reason. No explanation. No bang. No blast. No flash. No nothing. Just—gone!

Chapter Three

It was now nearly noon. Those on Bob Wilson's list who were within driving distance had all gathered, some sitting, some standing, according to status—always according to status and the "Ego Code." The communications uplink with those farther away was being completed. Everyone would soon be online and able to participate as if they were right there in the situation room.

Entering the room, with Bob Wilson leading the way, the vice president stepped up to the microphone and began to speak in his newfound voice of control and authority, almost as if it were all practiced.

He presented available information, however sketchy, speaking with an ease that made it comfortable for everyone to speak up, to feel a part of the meeting and provide valuable advice and assistance. The vice president clearly asked for all the help that could be provided.

"We've come to this point, ladies and gentlemen. It has been only a matter of hours, but the president is missing and very possibly dead. That's the reality. Until we know more, I will assume the office of president as set forth in the 25th Amendment. We have matters of national security and law that must be addressed. We've got a country that will have a strong emotional and political reaction to these events. I'd like... I'm asking for your advice and certainly, your help and cooperation. I'm asking that we set politics aside for a while. This is not a time for political games and infighting. We need to stand united and face the country and the world as a strong government in control. The floor is open. Bob

Wilson will monitor those who wish to speak. I encourage you to speak freely."

"Mr. Vice President," a deep male voice called from the far end of the room. "What about the press? They're already buzzing, wondering why the president has not arrived in Quebec."

It was the most obvious of all questions, one that would ultimately lead to others, from the press, the American people, and the world. After a brief discussion, it was agreed that Bob Wilson would hold an emergency press conference to make the initial announcement.

The vice president insisted that the truth be told. There would be no attempt to hide or twist the facts. However, it was also agreed that if the vice president were to make the announcement, it would look as if the president were indeed dead, and there had been a transfer of office. Not yet. It was agreed that this could not appear to be happening yet. There had to be evidence that the president was indeed dead before any change of office took place.

Wilson would say that the constitution and the law were clear—the vice president assumed the duties and responsibilities of the office. He'd leave it at that for now. He would tell the world that the vice president was in control and would be addressing the nation once there was additional information about the situation and the welfare of the president and his daughter.

The Wilson press conference would also take the lid off the search effort and free law enforcement agencies, the National Guard, military reservists, even the Canadians, to join military units already in place. An all-out effort visible to the public would help assure the nation that everything possible was being done to find the missing aircraft and its four occupants.

It was debated whether the vice president should appear on national television later in the day. Even if there were no further details, his appearance would allay fears and assure the public that the country was in good hands and under control. It was decided to wait and see how events played out over the coming hours.

The Chairman of the Joint Chiefs recommended that all military bases be placed on the highest alert status. Agreed!

The Secretary of State recommended that all embassies worldwide be placed on the highest level of security and alert. Agreed!

The Secretary of Homeland Security recommended that all intelligence services be fully alerted and activated. Agreed!

The Director of the FBI recommended that an investigation be launched immediately to determine if there was any foul play involved. Agreed!

The Director of the CIA recommended that all field agents in all countries around the world be directed to determine if any other government had any hand in this. Agreed!

A voice came in over the satellite link suggesting that Vice President Carson take the oath of office.

"No!" he responded firmly and loudly with no hesitation. "I will not accept this suggestion. My friend is alive. I can feel it. I will not accept his death. I will not accept his office. I am here to serve him and my country and I fully accept that responsibility. But I will not accept his death. Not yet. Not until I see his body. Bring me his body, and then I will take the oath. Not until then."

The room fell completely silent. His profession of faith and loyalty stunned everyone. Here was a man few of them really knew. Few had worked with him before this day. In a few brief seconds, in a few short words spoken as tears welled up in his eyes, he rose above them. Separated himself from them. Became better than them. Some wondered if his words were sincere. If they hadn't come too quickly... too practiced.

Another few seconds passed before the voice of the Chief Justice pierced the silence. He supported the vice president from a legal point of view. He advised that the vice president could not assume the presidency, could not be sworn in until or unless the president was either found and confirmed dead or sufficient time had elapsed whereby he could legally be declared dead.

The tension of the moment was broken. The matter is set aside. More questions were raised, and each was addressed and answered. Another thirty minutes had been absorbed by the time the last question was asked.

Chapter Four

Nothing! Almost three days, and still nothing. The greatest Air Force in the world, the best-trained Army, the Marine Corps, the National Guard, police, forest rangers, search-and-rescue teams, firefighters, every shape and size of uniformed employee in every city, town, and village. Boy Scouts, Girl Scouts, Brownies, even the friggin' dog catcher and still nothing.

People from all the New England states, New York, Nova Scotia, Quebec, and New Brunswick, thousands of people searching a fifty-mile-wide strip. From Halifax to Quebec, land, sea and air units using every available technology, and nothing. A brand new sparkling-white twin-engine aircraft with four human beings aboard just disappears. No radio signal, no fire, no oil slick, no smashed trees, no pile of twisted metal and fiberglass. Not a word from any terrorist group anywhere in the world. Just nothing. Not a friggin' thing.

The ridiculous and absurd has begun to surface. There was absolutely no trace of Sydney Richardson's airplane.

So, they had to have been kidnapped. The CIA was behind it. No! It was an alien abduction. No. Bigfoot found them, dragged them away to some secret cave in the mountains and ate them. No, she made a mistake and flew south and ended up in the Bermuda Triangle. And the dumbest thing of all was that the media was putting these idiotic stories on the air. The nightly news was turning into Saturday morning cartoons.

Vice President Carson sat in a side chair placed in front of the president's desk in the Oval Office. He didn't want to be seen sitting at the desk. It would seem like a violation, an intrusion. He didn't want to appear too eager to take over the Oval Office. He had moved into, but did not occupy...

He couldn't. He couldn't accept that his friend might be dead and that his death would thrust him, Dennis Carson, into the office he had dreamed of for so long. It wasn't fear of the responsibility that would immediately fall upon him. It wasn't the job. He wished it were. He had lived for this moment his entire life. Dreamt of it as a kid. But not yet. He didn't want to risk a bad impression of jumping in too quickly at the expense of his friend and his young daughter while their bodies were still warm. Appearance... image... had to be careful.

He tried to sit at the president's desk, but couldn't. He was ill at ease thinking that it might appear that his loyalty to the president was pushed aside by opportunity. He convinced himself that he was only using the office because it was the nerve center of the country, of the world, and it projected an authority all its own, an authority that was needed in a crisis like this. Besides, it would make things easier for everyone else. Everything was right here at his fingertips. The situation demanded it. This was the right place to be.

He leaned back in the chair, arms dropped down beside him, neck stretched straight back until he was staring at the ceiling, his mind momentarily lost in the blankness above him. He was alone, and he could feel it. Right here, in the center of the world, he was alone.

The room was remarkably quiet. He was very tired. Not only had he not left the White House since he first arrived, he had hardly left this room. He was afraid to close his eyes for fear of falling asleep and tumbling to the floor in a dead heap.

He had showered and changed clothes several times. Caught a nap when and where he could, on one of the couches here in the office, head down on the arm of a chair, even leaning against the wall. Three hours was the longest he had been able to capture. And now he was really feeling exhausted.

He knew he would have to get some rest. He must remain alert. The first three days had been very demanding, very intense. But killing himself would accomplish nothing. There was nothing that would get done faster by his staying here. If he were needed, if something important happened, someone would awaken him.

He stretched and wiggled, contorting his body, searching for the one position that would ease the ache in his muscles and joints. Everything hurt, his skin, his teeth hurt—even his hair hurt. He searched for the energy to go on for a little while longer. Just a bit longer. At least until the new satellite photos came in.

God! It was quiet. So damned quiet. The soundproof walls. The carpeted floors. The bulletproof windows. Insulated in every way from the outside. The only sound was the muted drone of the TV news anchor and the crowd gathered behind him at some stadium. It was fall, and it was Sunday, and it was football. The population worried and felt badly that the president was missing and probably dead. But they also knew that the country would continue.

They were safe, and there would be a safe transition of power no matter what. This was the United States. We don't panic. We don't worry about who's running the government. It will all take care of itself, somehow. There'll be another president. Just give them time. But this was football season. Even here. Even in this office. The sounds of the sports ritual seeped out of the television, pressed back up against the wall. The volume was set barely high enough to avoid intruding into his thoughts unless he invited it in.

The pressure of the situation might demand that he not curl up on the couch and zone out while watching the game, but the man in him, the human weakness in him, demanded some satisfaction by knowing how his New York Giants were doing in midseason.

His sterile, oval cocoon was suddenly cracked by the buzz of the intercom. He reached for the telephone and lifted it to his ear.

"Yes?"

"Commander Lewis calling, sir," the secretary's voice announced.

"Okay, put him through please... Yes, hello, commander."

"I have the latest satellite overflight photos of the search area, sir. Nothing new, but I thought you would like to see them."

"Yes, commander; send them up, please."

"Yes, sir. They'll be there in a couple of minutes."

The vice president walked over to the couch and stretched out. He lifted the remote and sent a signal to the TV to update him on the score. The Redskins were moving down the field, but it didn't look good for them. The clock was running out. The Giants should be able to hold on and take a "W" back up north to the Big Apple.

He wondered if his clock was running out too. What play would he be able to call to pull things out with a big "W"? Was he the quarterback now? Did he have a game plan? Would the rest of the team follow him down the field for the big one?

"Sir?" a mild voice pulled him out of the television and back into the Oval Office.

"Yes?"

"The latest pictures the commander called you about, Mr. Vice President."

"Yes, Sergeant. Come in. Bring them over here if you don't mind."

A crisply-dressed Army NCO walked across the room and spread the photographs on the big desk. He stepped back and asked, "Shall I wait, sir?"

"Huh? Uh, yes, Sergeant... yes, please do," the vice president answered, half because he knew it would take him only a few minutes to go through the photos, half because he knew there wasn't anything for him to see or the place would be filled with staff before the pictures were ever brought to him, and half, three halves, oh well, he was tired, because he just wanted to feel the presence of another human being, one who wasn't firing question after unanswerable question at him and then standing around with their teeth in their mouth waiting for the obvious answer, or as if, because he had now been in this office for three days, he automatically had a ready solution to everything.

He studied the photographs as best he could with his untrained eye. The Sergeant peered over his shoulder, ready to answer any questions. The NCO had already studied the photos as a member of the evaluation team. And he, having a trained eye, knew there was nothing in the pictures and would be happy to assist his new boss in coming to that same educated conclusion.

Dennis Carson's shoulders slumped forward with the weight of the moment, as he slowly flipped through the black and white satellite photographs, one picture after another...remarkably clear. Not only could he see the trees, but he could count them. But each picture looked exactly the same. Trees, mountains, and more trees. But no sign of an airplane. No sign of people or a crash site. Just trees.

"Won't find them that way," the military man mumbled under his breath.

"What?" the vice president asked, as he turned to face the young man in uniform

"Sir!" the Sergeant snapped a formal response to his political boss.

"What did you say?"

"Nothing, sir. Just thinking out loud. Sorry, sir. I was out of line."

"No, no, Sergeant. What did you say?"

"Nothing, sir. I was out of line. Sorry, Mr. Vice President."

"No. Please, Sergeant, tell me. What did you say?"

"Nothing, sir. It was nothing."

"Damn it, Sergeant! I said it was okay. Speak your mind."

"Sir, Mr. Vice President, I'm only an Army NCO and I'd be way out of line, sir. The generals would have my ass."

"And until something better comes along, I'm your Commander and Chief—your boss. So, I'm ordering you. Speak your mind freely and start now or I'll have your ass. God knows, I need someone around here to shoot straight with me and stop kissing my butt, while waiting for me to be crowned president."

"Yes, sir," the young career soldier replied. "I said that they'd never find them this way. In my opinion, that is. Not unless there was a fire from the crash or they just happened to crash in the middle of a pasture or on top of somebody's cabin. Seems like none of those things have happened or it would be over by now. I just don't think they'll be found this way. Not from the air."

The vice president rocked back in the armchair and studied the young man in front of him. The Sergeant came to attention in response to the stare.

"Stand at ease, Sergeant. Forgive me for not knowing all the staff here, but what's your name?"

"Travis, sir. Staff Sergeant Daniel E. Travis... sir."

"Well, Staff Sergeant Daniel E. Travis, why won't we find them this way?"

"Mr. Vice President, it really isn't my place to—"

"God damn it, Sergeant! Shut up and talk. I'm making it your place and your business, so put the rank and military bullshit aside and talk to me. Man to man. No stripes. No bars. No stars on my collar. Got it? I'll appreciate it more than you will ever know. Now… what's your thinking?"

Hesitantly, the Sergeant took a deep breath and began. "Well, sir, they'll never find them this way. Not from the air. Not from a satellite or even from an airplane unless it was flying at only a couple of hundred feet. If there was a fire or an explosion and a lot of heat from the resulting blast, then the satellite would have already picked it up. If there was a fire, there would be smoke and a big black spot somewhere out there where there isn't supposed to be one, and we would see that easily as well. Either way, we would have seen the results, but we haven't. So, it isn't there and we won't find them from the air. No, sir, they won't be found this way."

"Why not?" The vice president was intrigued by this bright-eyed young soldier.

"You've got to be kidding, sir. Do you remember the Gulf War? The first one? Do you know why we kicked the shit out of the enemy in only a hundred hours? It's called superior power, and it works. But, do you know why we also killed so many of our own people on the ground? It's called overkill. Nobody in the world can do things better than the U.S. military, and nobody can screw things up better than the U.S. military.

"We had enough men, planes, and weapons to wipe them out five times over. Why? Because our on-theground intelligence sucked. So, to be sure we'd win, we had to overkill the situation.

Had we had half a dozen men on the ground in the country a year ahead of time, we would have been a lot better off.

"Same here. We've got thousands, tens of thousands, of men and tons of equipment in this operation. It won't work. We are at the point where everything gets in the way of the results, and the time and attention needed for the command of the effort that loses sight of the effort. It's like having a seat on the fifty-yard line for the big game, but the marching band is right in front of you. Overkill!" Travis stopped, thinking he had already gone too far and was up to his ass in trouble, spouting off like this.

"Go on, Travis... please." The vice president was fascinated by the energy and intellect of Sergeant Travis.

Travis sucked in a deep breath, raised his head, and said, "Sir, that's big country out there. Tens of thousands of acres. One small airplane just big enough to carry four people? Come on! I could hide the Queen Mary out there, and unless there was a fire on board or a big spotlight pointing straight up, no satellite, no high-flying spy plane taking pictures would ever find it in those woods. It would be purely accidental. Just good luck! Look at history. Remember the U-2 flights over Cuba in the early 1960s? Found those missiles purely by accident. This forested, mountainous terrain could swallow up a little plane without a burp."

Sergeant Travis was on a roll and figured he had nothing to lose at this point. He had probably already punched his ticket to an undesirable discharge or a transfer to the DMZ in Korea to stand guard duty in a pile of snow.

Leaning forward, emotionally spitting out his ideas as if he had been frustrated in the attempt by his relatively low rank in the grandeur of the White House, he continued. "Secondly, they don't even know where the hell to look. They're guessing. They don't know where the plane went down. A fifty-mile wide search area off of a small aircraft's mountain dodging, joyriding flight plan? Shit! A small plane in those coastal and mountain winds and thermals at dusk can bounce that little aircraft ten miles before the pilot knows what's happening and can reach for a radio mic. Ain't no way, sir. No, sir."

Vice President Carson, studying this man, realized he was way beyond his pay grade. He measured his words, his emotion and passion, his intensity. He felt the depth of expression. These words came from somewhere deep. They were knowing, drawn from experience, filled with conviction and confidence.

"Sergeant, are you suggesting that our people out there are just going through the motions? Are you suggesting that our generals, your bosses, are not directing our efforts correctly? Or are you saying you know more than they do?"

Travis stiffened before the acting Commander and Chief. "No, sir, that's not what I'm saying. What I'm trying to say is that we're trying too hard with too much. We're getting in our own way. Too many people trying to get there first and be the hero who finds the president."

Carson's patience was at a raw edge from lack of sleep. He jumped to his feet and was in the face of the stiffened

G.I. in a heartbeat. He fought to gain control of himself before he blurted out words or behaved in a way he might regret later. The lack of sleep and near exhaustion almost won out.

"Look! Dan, isn't it?"

"Yes, sir."

"Okay. Look, Dan, I'm tired. I'm so damned tired I can't see straight. I'm so damned tired, if it wasn't for the football game on TV, I'm not sure I'd even know it was Sunday. Most of all, Dan, I'm so fucking tired of the people around here. They don't talk straight, and they sure as hell don't answer straight. All they know is how to use more words to cover their ass, to say nothing they can be held responsible for. But they sure are good at blowing smoke and sand. Clear enough for you? I don't need that, Dan. Not from you. I've got enough of that from the professional bullshit artists outside that door. And remember something, soldier. I was in the Army too. I was a lowlife second lieutenant once, so I know where you are coming from. So first, sit down. Please sit down and relax. We're just two guys at the NCO club kickin' back and tipping a few. Got it?"

They took seats on opposite ends of the couch across the room from the television set. The Vice President continued, "Look, I need someone to talk straight, okay? If you've got something to say, say it and don't hold back because you're concerned about me or your future. I need to hear it, all of it. No rank. No nothing. Okay?" His raw, nervous energy created words faster than his tired mind could absorb them before they came pouring out of his mouth.

"Yes, sir."

"Okay. You impress me. I don't know why. I'll figure that out later. Right now, I want to hear everything you have on your mind."

"Yes, sir."

"Okay, shoot. Why do you feel this way about the search effort?"

"Well sir, it's like I said. That's big country out there. You can't understand how big it is until you get out in it. Not fly over it. Not look at some map. You've gotta get up to your ass in it, on the ground. Hundreds of square miles of nothing but trees and rocks and hills. One after another, hill after hill, leading to a bigger hill and more square miles. Climb one or go around one, and there's another one staring you right in the face. Every mile of bushwhacking cross country is the same as seven to ten miles of walking on a sidewalk in a city. Every three hundred feet of elevation change is equal to another mile.

"I was raised out there. I've camped, hiked, hunted and backpacked all over those mountains since I was a kid. Those mountains could swallow up that plane in a second. It would be like flicking a grain of sand on this carpet and trying to find it wearing a blindfold while you're standing on a six-foot step ladder.

"Like I said before, unless it caught fire, the trees and underbrush, the tall grasses, a lake or a river, could just flat-ass swallow it up. You wouldn't see it until you tripped over it. And that's exactly what you've got to do. You've got to get out there, on the ground, and search. We've got to trip over it and you don't do that from thousands of feet up in the air.

"Secondly, do you know the glide ratio of that aircraft, sir?"

The vice president shook his head. He was transfixed by Dan Travis, mesmerized. "On a bad day, it's probably five to one, maybe as much as ten to one, depending on air, wind and temperature conditions. That means that for every foot she had in altitude, she could glide five to ten feet horizontally. If she was only at 10,000 feet or about two miles high, she could glide that plane from 10 to 20 miles. And we don't know if she had full power, one dead engine, or two dead engines and no power at all. If she had only partial power, if she lost only one engine, God knows how far she might have gone before she had to set it down.

"Now, I've read every report that's come in since this all began. Nobody has studied the winds, altitude, or location. All they did was begin at point A, lay out her flight plan to point B, and draw a straight line between the two. Then they decided to stretch the line twenty-five miles on each side and said, 'Okay folks, that's the search area, they've got to be in there somewhere, now go fetch.' On top of that, they reduced it on both ends, east and west, saying,

'Well, she flew for this many minutes, so she had to travel further than this line, but she didn't have enough time to fly this far, so we don't need to look there.'

"So, Mr. Vice President, what have we got left? This narrow strip fifty miles wide cut off on both ends. No, sir. Sorry. Ain't no way. They ain't going to find them this way. It's going to take somebody who knows those mountains, knows the winds and how they curve and swirl around those hills. Someone who can study charts and maps and weather reports and reports from other aircraft that were in the area a few hours earlier.

"Even then, you've gotta have the balls to make an wild-assed guess, go with your gut, and get in there, down on the ground and smell 'em out like you was goin' rabbit huntin'."

For the next hour and a half the two men asked each other questions, looked at maps, photos, charts, weather reports, anything they could find that had anything to do with the search area and beyond. The vice president ordered in some food and drinks, as well as some additional reports that Dan Travis thought might be of help.

Eyebrows were raised as aides entered the room to find the two men standing, sitting, leaning over maps and charts, shoulder to shoulder. The new leader of the free world being lectured to by an Army sergeant... ain't too healthy for a career soldier.

As they talked, each man took the measure of the other. The acting Commander and Chief and the young Sergeant. A world apart in rank, position and responsibility, working together, blending, and equalizing their differences. Two strangers, working under an oval ceiling, learning to respect each other and the contribution each could make to the major problem at hand. Two men, one highly trained in the classroom of life and people and war, the other trained in a classroom of books and professors and politicians. Two men dealing with a situation that distilled time from years into hours, hours in which they became trusted friends.

Their conversation stopped abruptly. The vice president flopped back into the armchair, exhausted, his energy totally sapped. In an hour and a half, he had learned more than he had in days, maybe, in some way, in his whole life. He quietly studied the face of his new confidant. He stood and began to slowly pace the perimeter of the oval room, his eyes glancing back to Dan Travis with every step.

Travis remained silent. He followed the movement and the eyes of Dennis Carson. In his gut, he knew he had just punched his ticket to spend the rest of his twenty years guarding icebergs in Greenland or monkey shit in Africa until he was able to retire, probably as a PFC.

The vice president stopped at last and stood next to the big presidential desk. His arms were folded across his chest. He looked across the room right into the eyes of Sergeant Travis. Dan squirmed in his seat, mentally reviewing how fast he could pack his duffel bag with all the cold weather gear he would be issued for his new duty station.

"Dan, I need to know more about you. How old are you? Where are you from? Where did you go to school? Are you married? Everything. I need to know, and we don't have a lot to time."

Puzzled, Dan laid out his life for the vice president. Thirty three years old. Born and raised in a small farming town in the Hudson Valley of New York. Apple country. Local school, kindergarten through twelfth grade, all in one building. Big time local athlete, played all sports. Two years at the University of North Carolina on a baseball scholarship. Left school because of money problems back home. Dad was injured in a farm accident and needed him to run the farm. Once his father had recovered, he'd joined the Army for both a job and a chance to continue his education.

He now held a master's degree in political science. That's how he got the assignment to the White House. Served in both Gulf Wars. Wounded in the shoulder, nothing real serious. Turned down a commission to become a first lieutenant because he truly enjoyed being an NCO.

Single. Never been married. Got close once, but got shipped overseas and came home to find her engaged to another guy. No current love relationship, although he'd had his fair share of dating. Mom and Dad still live in the same house he was raised in. Mom a housewife who raised four kids. He was the only boy and the youngest. Dad still worked the farm and sometimes drove heavy equipment to bring in a little extra cash, especially in the winter.

He was assigned to White House duty six months ago. Before that he worked at the Pentagon. When a slot came open for someone at the White House with very high security clearance, he happened to be in the right spot at the right time.

Spent his leave time back home with his parents and sisters and their babies. Did a lot of hiking and hunting all over New York State and New England, especially the back country in Maine. Belongs to a Search and Rescue team back home. Gave him even more time in the woods. Even got sent out on a search last time he was home—couple of kids got lost while hiking. He had a reputation for being the best woodsman in town. Liked writing short stories. No special topics, whatever came to him.

The vice president didn't miss a word. When Dan stopped talking, the room was deathly silent once again. In what seemed to be slow motion, Dennis Carson reached for the telephone on the desk. "Get me General Helms. I'll hold."

Oh shit, Travis thought. The Chief of Staff of the United States Army was being called by the vice president because he couldn't keep his big fuckin' mouth shut. Shit! Shit! Shit! He stood and walked nervously toward the nearest cream-colored, wall hoping to find a crack in the paint he could hide in. Goodbye, northern Virginia...hello Greenland.

Looking up, the vice president said, "Sit down, Sergeant, you're going to need all the rest you can get." Turning his attention to the phone, he continued, "General, Denny Carson. Yes, yes, General, everything is under control. Yes, I figured you had heard by now. He's here with me. Now listen, Charlie, I want him assigned to me. Yes, Travis. Sergeant Dan Travis. No Charlie, right now. Effective immediately. Don't ask so damned many questions, Charlie, just do it.

"You owe me, remember? Last month's golf game? Yeah! Right. No, he has been a tremendous help, Charlie. He will be a special aide to me—no, make that officially a special assistant, and I want him promoted to Master Sergeant also effective immediately. And General, I'll be sending him on a mission. A very sensitive, highly-classified mission that I will also need your help putting together. He is to report to me and only to me. Charlie? I know I can count on you.

"Now please listen. I want you to arrange to have a two-seater fighter jet standing by at Andrews. The fastest thing we've got. Sergeant Travis is going to Maine without delay and with no interference. Clear the way for the flight to land in Bangor.

"Have one of your aides meet him at Andrews in an hour. He will have a list. I want everything on that list ready and waiting for him in Bangor. Everything, Charlie. Even if you have to go to Walmart to buy it. No questions. No exceptions. Anybody who gets in his way or slows him down answers to me. No politics and no bullshit... Good... Thanks, Charlie. I knew I could depend on you.

"I'll fill you in. Come and see me in an hour, and if I'm asleep on the couch, just give me a little shake. Bring coffee. A few donuts wouldn't hurt either. You know the kind. Yeah! Right, those. See ya, Charlie."

The vice president replaced the receiver in its cradle, and turned slowly to face a shaken, brand new master sergeant. "Did you hear everything I said to him, Dan?"

"I think so, sir. My head is spinning a little right now. But I heard it all. Just a little hard to believe."

"Believe it, Dan. I'm going on my instinct and sending you out there. I don't know why. It's either the dumbest thing I've ever done, or the smartest. We'll have to wait and see. If you find them, we'll both be heroes. If you don't... well, I'll be president, and you'll be here with some new stripes on your arm, kissing a bunch of political asses right along with me." He scribbled on a piece of paper and handed it to Dan. "Here, this is the number of a telephone that is with me 24/7. Only you, my wife, and my kids have that number. I've also written down the name of my very first dog. He died when I was nine years old. It's your code name. It's for you and me only. Use it if you need me, and I will drop whatever I'm doing and get to you." He reached out and took Travis by the shoulders. "Go find them, Dan. I'm giving you everything you need. When you come out of those mountains, call me. And when this is all over, we will get flat-ass drunk together. Anyway it goes, we'll both need it. Now get the hell out of here before I wake up from this daze I'm in and realize what I'm doing. Go find them and bring them back. You're on your own from this point on. I'll be waiting for your call."

"Yes sir!"

Part III

Into the Wilderness

Chapter One

The next twelve hours were a whirlwind ride through the world as seen and experienced only by those few who are lucky or selected: those who touch power, who dare to touch real power, because it takes that kind of power to make things happen the way Dan Travis had seen in the past few hours.

Doors opening. Generals clearing a path. Multimillion-dollar military aircraft standing and waiting. Stiffbacked aides saluting a staff sergeant. Oops. A master sergeant, who only hours ago they would have ordered to fetch whatever they might need. Civilian staff flitting about, practically bowing to the anointed one, the one touched on the shoulder by the new man in town, Dennis Carson.

The word had spread quickly. They, the civilian and military bloodsuckers who prowled the edges of power in Washington, had no idea what he had been touched to do. It really didn't matter. Just knowing that he had somehow been taken into the inner circle at the very top of the food chain made him special. Now they engulfed him, hoping that whatever it was, some of it would rub off on them.

A few hours ago, Dan Travis had been a standard issue G.I. with a slightly above average assignment. Now he suddenly had power, and he could feel it—a power he didn't understand and didn't particularly like. One telephone call from the Oval Office and he had been launched into a new world, one in which he felt very uncomfortable.

It had started with the presidential helicopter picking him up from the lawn of the White House for the short flight to Andrews Air Force Base. Waiting in the helicopter was a White House secretary who furiously took notes en route as Dan listed all of the supplies and equipment he needed to complete this crazy mission his big fat mouth had gotten him into. He had to include every possible thing he might need for an extended wilderness survival search and rescue mission that would include himself and four additional people.

Five people. He had to presume that he would find all of them alive, and that he was the only one who had any experience in surviving in the wilderness, in a cold and wet environment, with the need for food, water and shelter.

Four rookies, presumably dressed in street clothes and shoes like they were going to their next meeting or to a dinner party. Then add himself into the mix, five people trying to survive and return home in one piece from some of the roughest, most desolate territory east of the Rocky Mountains, territory inhabited only by deer, moose, black bear, mountain lions and an occasional logger working for one of the huge paper companies that owned or leased enormous tracts of land in this part of the country.

He listed food, but for how many days? How many meals? Sleeping bags. Clothes. Boots. Cooking gear. Tarps for shelter. Medical supplies, lots of them. What would he find? What kind of physical condition would they be in? Guns for hunting for himself and for the others. Hopefully, they would be able to help supply meat if it was needed.

On and on he dictated his list until he felt he would be able to feed, clothe, care for, and protect himself and four others, including the most powerful man in the world, in a remote wilderness and get them back home safely. He had to be equipped for survival, prepared for the expected and for the unexpected. But for how long? For how many? Would they be alive? Badly injured? How deep into the mountains would they be? How many miles from help? What would the weather be? The President of the United

States of America was out there. This was no day hike in the woods with his buddies. This was real.

When the helicopter landed at Andrews, he was escorted to a jet fighter. The high-altitude supersonic flight from Washington, D.C. to Bangor, Maine would take only a short time at Mach 2. The sensation of such speed mesmerized him. He never could have imagined how it would feel to fly in such an aircraft.

What a rush! It was wearing an airplane, like sharing its metal skin, like absorbing and being absorbed, becoming one with the entire machine. When one moved, so did the other. When one twisted, so did the other. This was flying, not riding in a bus with wings.

This was not the same as flying in a C-130 or C-135 or 767. This was...flying. He wasn't at the controls, but he could sense everything, feel the thrust, see the air split open as the needle nose stabbed through it, touch the cold as it kissed his new metal skin. Nothing, he knew now, nothing could ever be more exhilarating.

On the ground in Maine, another surprise was waiting. He was not met by a military escort as he had anticipated. Instead, he was met by the state's highest official, Melvin Adams—Governor Melvin Adams. Holy shit! *What the hell have I gotten myself into? Me and my big mouth.*

The governor's car pulled up to the jet, now parked on the tarmac. Travis exited the aircraft and was met at the bottom of the ladder, not only by the governor, but also by the commander of the state National Guard, Major General Gerstner. They led him to the long, shiny, black limo where everyone introduced themselves. The governor offered Travis a seat in the plush car. Travis entered in a daze, not knowing what to expect next.

The moment the door closed, the limo moved away from the fighter jet toward the airport's boundary fence, and a large gaping gate opened to allow them to exit. So far, no one in the limo had spoken a word to one another since names and handshakes were first offered.

The driver slowed the vehicle as the fence grew near. Travis turned in the direction of the governor and began to say something to break the tension in the car. The general grabbed Dan by the arm and shook his head, pointing to the driver with a silent shake of his head. His message was clear.

When the car finally came to a complete stop just beyond the fence, the driver turned off the motor and got out of the vehicle. He walked away, obviously under orders to leave the three men alone in the car to talk. Once, the driver was well away from the car, Governor Adams reached into his inner coat pocket, pulled out a set of folded papers, and handed them to Dan.

"Sergeant Travis, these are your final orders and instructions, signed by the vice president as Acting Commander and Chief. Sort of makes everything formal and official. Only he and I, and now you, will know the contents of these orders. The general here does not know what it contains. He only knows that you are on a very high priority mission, sent personally by the vice president, and that he is to support you in every way and to provide all the supplies you requested.

"The vice president called me on a scrambled phone as soon as you left the White House. He gave me my instructions and asked for my full cooperation. Of course, I agreed. He also spoke with the general and gave him the list of supplies and materials you requested and asked that the general comply without asking any questions. I'm sure you know what was said to each of us and that we are here to support you without any reservations or delays.

"Once we finish talking, the driver will take us back inside the fence to a building on the other side of the airfield, where the general's people are gathering all of the items you requested. Everything will be completed shortly. We weren't given much time.

"Vice President Carson said you would know everything else that needed to be done and would give us directions. Because of our location and seeing that you will be operating within our state, we will be providing the communications link between you and Washington. He told me that you two had a code name, but he would not provide it to me. He made it clear that it was strictly between the two of you. But he did tell me that your mission had been assigned an operational code name. It's called WAG. You are WAG 1 and he is WAG 2. He said he named it after something you said, something about a 'wild-ass guess,' or something like that."

Dan smiled.

"He thought you would get a kick out of that," the governor continued. "I think he wanted you to know that no matter what, he hasn't lost his sense of humor."

"We didn't have much time for humor back in D.C.," Dan said. "He's got a lot to deal with. A lot more than he bargained for when he took the V.P. job. He was awful tired when I left. Somebody needs to be sure he takes care of himself. He needs to get some rest."

"He'll be okay. His wife is with him now, and there is a whole staff surrounding him to be sure he does what he has to do. I've known him for many years. He's strong. He'll do just fine. Now, if you don't mind, I'm going to ask the general to step out of the car. I've got some issues to cover with you that he will not be involved with."

He turned to the general and said, "If you don't mind. As we agreed earlier, I need to speak to Sergeant Travis alone."

"Yes, sir. I completely understand. I'll go keep the driver company until you're ready."

Once he was out of the car, the governor turned back to Dan. "Now, with regard to you, young man, I don't know what you said or what you did back in the White House, but I can tell you that Denny Carson is banking on you one hundred percent. He's putting himself at great risk with this little operation of yours. His last words to me were to wish you good luck and Godspeed.

"He also said that something deep in his gut is telling him that somehow the right man has come along at just the right time. That's you, in case you were wondering. Like I said, I don't know what happened between the two of you, but I've never known him to jump into something or get behind anyone like this. He's much too cautious, much too smart to take this kind of a risk.

"Whatever it is, Sergeant, you impacted him very strongly. More than I think you know. I don't think you can appreciate the position he has put himself in if word of this mission gets out. Sending one man on a mission like this when he is acting Commander-in-Chief with the entire military at his disposal, quite frankly, it's crazy. He's got the most powerful military in the world at the end of a phone, and he sends out one man. He'll get his ass nailed to a cross on Capitol Hill if this gets out. Whatever you got, son, I sure wish I had some of it.

"By the way, I'm WAG 3. That's as far as it goes. There is no WAG 4 or 5—just the three of us. Be sure to keep it that way. Maybe it will help you understand how sensitive this thing is if you realize just how tight this is being kept. One man. What a gamble. What the hell is he thinking? What the hell can you do that an entire army and air force can't?"

The governor, it was clear to Dan, was thinking out loud. He seemed both resentful and concerned. Resentful of the position and trust gained by this young army sergeant and concerned for the potential danger to which his friend has exposed himself. Or was there something else? Something in Dan's gut turned upside down. Something didn't feel right. This entire meeting was completely unexpected and didn't sit right with him, including the general's role and dismissal from the conversation. The WAG code names and numbers didn't blend in with the conversation he'd had with the vice president. Dan was about to say something to justify himself and the operation when the governor began to speak again.

"The telephone numbers listed in your orders are mine and his. You can reach one or the other of us at any time, twenty-four hours a day. No questions. No delays. No staff clearing the call. Whatever I am doing, instructions will be given that I am not to be interrupted, and you will be put right through. Same for the vice president. I'd recommend that you call me first, since we're in the same state. It would make sense that way."

More gut signal! Telephone numbers in the orders? Not right! The vice president made it clear that only his family had access to that number and asked Dan to keep it that way! "Call me first because I'm in the same state?" Double whammy! Cell phones don't care where you are; all states are the same.

"The radios you requested," the governor continued, "will have limited use where you are going because of the lack of towers covering that whole territory. Particularly because of the mountains, and especially since I'm not even sure of where the hell it is that you're going."

A question or a statement? Dan pondered. "And there is no cell service up north of here."

Dan was increasingly uncomfortable with the things the governor was saying. He and Dennis Carson hadn't discussed any of these points. Question or statement? He felt sure he would find out sooner or later. "Once you are on the ground," Governor Adams continued, "and you release the aircraft that parachutes you in, we want you to switch to the frequency listed with the telephone numbers.

"We will be monitoring every day, twice a day at 0800 hours and again at 1600 hours. There's little chance the signal will reach us, but it's all we've got in the way of equipment that is small enough and light enough for you to carry along with everything else you'll need. Anything more powerful would be far too heavy to deal with.

"You can contact us as you get close to coming out of wherever you're going. There is also a list of frequencies you can switch to that will be picked up by our State Police, the Forest Service, and park rangers. Don't use them unless absolutely necessary. The more people you talk to, the more this mission of yours will be exposed."

Dan Travis listened silently to the man sitting at the opposite end of the wide back seat of the limo. More warning flags. What was he hearing? What was he watching? The governor was rattling on like a nervous Nellie. Where was he coming up with all this stuff?

Why all the changes to the things he and the vice president had agreed on before he left Washington? Why were things being covered that had already been set in place? Why was this man making changes and setting up new procedures? Call him first? Would he be easier to reach? Same state? Change frequency after you're on the ground? After you release the aircraft frequency can be picked up by the Forest Service. Operation held tight was now on the same frequency as the Forest Service? Radio with limited range? What are you giving me, two tin cans and a long string? Why not just a satellite phone? It would bounce off a satellite no matter where I was, plus I'll be as close to some areas of Canada as to the U.S. Why was the governor so fidgety, so nervous

Suddenly, Dan realized that this was just a man sitting there next to him. Just a man. A very nervous little man, one who really did put his pants on the same way he did, one leg at a time. Being governor didn't make him anything special. He wasn't Superman. It came to Dan in a sudden rush that he had been sent on a mission by the Vice President of the United States of America, and it was an equalizing moment upon which this meeting turned. Dan felt empowered. Not cocky; that wasn't him. But he also knew that only he and the vice president were setting the rules of this operation and that all he was now hearing was off-base bullshit! He didn't know why. Was it because the governor needed to feel part of this very important mission or was there something else? Dan's sensors were up and alert. Something wasn't right with this meeting, and his gut was hurting real bad. Then he heard the voice sneaking into his ear again.

"All the information you requested is in the building going to now: maps, weather reports, wind reports, everything from the National Weather Service and NOAA, every military and commercial plane that was in the area an hour before and after Air Force One lost contact. Everything that could be gathered in the short time available since we were asked to get it together. Ground station data and satellite reports."

He paused, taking a nervous breath, and reached into his coat pocket one more time. "Oh! And one more thing. The vice president asked me to give you this." He handed Dan a small flannel bag. Dan opened it to find inside a chrome object the about the size of a pack of cigarettes, but only half as thick.

"What is it?" Dan asked.

"It's a pocket hand warmer, sort of a good luck charm. The vice president wanted you to have it. It's from him. I always carry one when I visit the northern part of the state this time of the year… never know when the weather changes… we all hope you'll be back, uh… safely, before it gets cold enough for you to need it… just a good luck charm."

"Hey, that's great!" Dan exclaimed. "Tell him I really appreciate it. But how did he get it out here so fast? Before I got here? I was in a jet fighter!"

"Well, actually, I had it. He left it at my house last time we went skiing together." Why was the man so uptight again? "Now, let's get you into that hangar and start studying all those reports we got together for you. I'm sure you're anxious to get going. Time is critical."

"Yeah, I am. One question, governor."

"What is it, Sergeant?"

"Why so secret? Why is the vice president doing everything under the sun to keep this so hush-hush? I'd think he'd want everyone to know that he's doing everything he can, everything possible to find the president and his daughter. Don't get me wrong, I'm not looking to be front page news, but hell! I feel like I'm some sort of evil secret agent, a dirty version of James Bond or something like Dr. No. You know, James Bond, but with some kind of a contagious disease or bad breath."

For Dan to have missed the expression that flashed across the governor's face, he would have had to be sitting in another car in another state besides Maine. A mixed expression of anger, surprise and fear! Surprise that a mere low-life army sergeant would have the audacity to ask the motive of the Vice President of the United States. The audacity to not just blindly follow orders as they were relayed to him by the governor of (at least momentarily) the most important state in the union—the audacity to not just drink the Kool-Aid.

And the anger stemming from this same low-life military bug of a person who would offer any kind of a challenge to a man of such power and influence. For the governor to have to deal with this man, who could possibly be thinking for himself and not simply blindly following the lead of such authority.

And fear! Fear of what the answer to this question, or any question put forth by this low-life, might reveal? But this one most of all. The simplest, the most logical question of all. Why? So simple it was nearly impossible to avoid. Fear that the answer would somehow divert the soldier from his mission. Or that by addressing this most logical of questions, he might disclose something that this person, this pawn, simply didn't need to know.

Oh yes! All of this was printed across the face of the man in the car with Dan. And more. Much more. Dan's gut was screaming!

And all of it really did highlight the question: why? In spades, why? And what? What is it that this guy is suddenly so nervous about? Shit! It's not his fat ass that's about to jump out of an airplane into the wilderness of the great northeast to go looking for one man and a girl that thousands of men and woman with boatloads of the most modern equipment in the world couldn't seem to find, a wilderness that stretched in the east from the middle of the Province of New Brunswick to the middle of New York State in the west and from the St. Lawrence River in the north to Interstate 84 in the south.

It wasn't the governor's nifty three-piece, pinstripe suit that was about to be tacked to a giant wall to be shot at by every doubter in Washington, D.C. and everyone else in the world, for that matter, if part of this harebrained idea went wrong.

The expression was gone as quickly as it had appeared. But it had been there. But now replaced by the molded plastic, frozen facade learned in Politics 101, to rapidly repair the crack, exposing the presence of doubt. This was followed by the vocal tones perfected in Politics 201, the vomiting of the measured response. "The press, Sergeant. Of course, he wants to do everything possible to find the president... and his daughter."

And his daughter! An afterthought, Dan sensed. Governor Adams went on. "But, like I told you a while ago, he's taking a great risk. How do you think the press would handle this situation if they found out that he was sending one man, all alone, equipped to the teeth, on what looks like nothing more than a wild goose chase, more like wild goose guess, while the country's entire military under the direction of generals with far more experience than you are using every bit of modern equipment to do the same job.

"If you get lucky, Sergeant, real lucky, he will come off as being brilliant and you will be a hero. If you fail, which you more than likely will, well, young man, you fail alone. If you even survive this little trek of yours, if you come out alive without the president, the vice president will be the new president. You will be off to some army outpost you've never heard of before, and he will in no way be connected to this crazy mission. This mission would never have taken place.

"Pure and simple, Sergeant. That's the way it is. Political risk reduction. Room for plausible denial. You succeed, he wins. You fail, you fail alone. Your career is over, not his. Hope you don't mind my being so blunt."

"No, sir. Not at all. I appreciate your being so honest. Only one more question, if I could. In your eyes, which is better, if I succeed or if I fail?"

He never got an answer. What he got was a kiss from his sister, a political two-step that leaves you on the ballroom floor with your arms wrapped around smoke.

Chapter Two

The Governor practically jumped out of the car, shouting an order to the driver to take Dan back to the hangar. This guy was going to leave Dan with nothing to grab onto. No one would be around if he failed. If he came back alive and with the president alive, well...

In the maintenance shack, Dan found a senior National Parks Ranger and an Air Force meteorologist at a table big enough to seat twelve for Sunday dinner. The table was loaded down with USGS topographical maps that covered every inch of Maine and the surrounding states and provinces, as well as weather maps from the Navy and the Air Force, hiking maps of the Appalachian Trail, and even an Exxon road map.

While the supplies Dan requested were being loaded on an airdrop platform, the three men studied all the available data. For four hours, they worked and shared each other's notes and ideas.

When they were done, Dan found himself aboard a Maine Air Force Reserve C-130 heading north to a GPS location on a flat piece of paper. No trees. No rocks. No water. No weather. No dirt. Just a few numbers that he had picked out of every other numbered spot on the globe. Little black numbers on a flat map that he hoped, that he believed from experience and intuition, would point to a clue in the wilderness that would lead him to a small airplane carrying two Secret Service agents, a young woman, and Donald Richardson, the President of the United States of America.

Dan was now alone on the cargo deck of the transport. Two skids loaded with equipment and supplies were topped off with huge cargo parachutes that would be deployed to lower their loads as gently as possible to the ground. The skids were identical. Each had exactly the same supplies, equipment, food, clothing, and weapons. Normal govern- ment overkill. If one is needed, send two just in case. But in this case, there was a good reason. He was going alone. If there were only one skid and the chute failed, he could be in serious trouble. If neither failed, he would have enough stuff to survive, build a log cabin, and retire to a nice quiet mountain retreat at the government's expense.

The rear doors of the aircraft were beginning to open, exposing the exit ramp. The deck crew was filing down the ladder from the upper cabin, strapped into their safety harnesses. The crew chief signaled Dan to ready himself. At the appropriate moment, the pilot would signal the crew chief, and his men would push the two skids along the rollers built into the floor of the aircraft until each spilled over the trailing edge of the ramp and fell into the emptiness below.

Then, when the crew chief signaled, Sergeant Dan Travis would follow the second skid. With trust in the training he had received and the equipment he had been given, he would step into the void. The great green mountain below would try to suck him down into its womb. The sea of clear, cold air between him and death would embrace him, trying to hold him up and win the battle with the pull of the wilderness below. Only his parachute could ease the tug between the opposing forces of nature and gravity to lower him safely and softly enough to save his life.

He sat back in the webbed seat of the big transport, leaning his head against the fuselage. He closed his eyes and tried to visualize the checklist he'd made when he'd ordered the supplies, now getting ready for their fall to earth.

Had he requested everything he needed? Had he forgotten anything? Had there been enough time to do it right? Medical supplies, clothes, boots, socks, long johns, sleeping bags, tents, tarps, rope, water bottles, camp stoves and fuel, water purification tablets, flashlights and batteries, GPS units, lanterns, candles, toilet paper, soap, towels, even extra bootlaces and food, both ready-too-eat meals and dehydrated backpacker meals. Enough food for five people, three meals a day for three months. Just add boiling water and WHAM! Instant gourmet.

Cooking utensils, scouring pads, plates, eating utensils. Everything had to be included. In his mind, he strolled the aisles of Cabela's, Bass Pro, and the Gander Mountain Store, his favorite supply points for hikes and hunting trips in the Great Smoky Mountains of North Carolina. And the L.L. Bean store in Maine, where he would shop before entering Baxter State Park, his favorite eastern mountain wilderness location. If he had covered everything he needed to survive in these two areas, he would be okay.

Satisfied, he reviewed the next category of items on his long-term survival list. Pump-action twelve-gauge shotgun with 12 boxes of shells, 30.06 Springfield rifle with another twelve boxes of ballistic-tipped ammunition, a fifty-pound compound hunting bow with three dozen razor-tipped arrows and replacement blades, two Buck-brand skinning knives, two universal camping tools, and, finally, two bright red Swiss Army knives with all the blades, as well as a toothpick and tweezers.

He was satisfied. He liked to say to his friends who sometimes hiked with him, "If you ain't got it, you don't need it." He had no idea how long he would need to be supplied or how many people he would need to keep alive, fed, and sheltered. Over two thousand pounds of supplies occupied each of the two skids, ready to sustain life for months if necessary and to enable him to return in one piece and in good health, if he found them...or if he didn't.

If he found them alive, they would need medical attention and food. He knew that he would have to either transport them to the supplies or the supplies to them, depending on their condition, distance, and the weather. He would have to find them, evaluate their condition, and make decisions that would be a matter of life and death for the president, his daughter, and the two agents. He would have to take command of the situation, take command away from the man who headed the armies of the free world.

Maybe he'd get real lucky. Maybe his Wild Ass Guess, his W.A.G., was so good that he'd drop these two skids right next to the entire party and find them sitting around a nice big fire, warm and dry, all in one piece, snacking on Cracker Jack and sucking on Diet Cokes. Then all he'd have to do was signal the aircraft he was now riding in, and they'd all be back home by Sunday afternoon, just in time for him to watch the Giants play Dallas. Yep! Just maybe! Fat chance.

Dan felt the C-130 dip. They had been flying at about eight thousand feet, below the altitude that would require oxygen and pressurizing the cabin. The dip meant the pilot was descending to parachute level about twelve hundred and fifty feet above ground level.

His mind jumped forward to the search. He would set the skid location on his handheld GPS as his number one go-to location. His plan was to use the spot where the supplies landed as the center of an expanding circle, using every available hilltop, rock outcropping, and tall tree to enhance his search pattern and line of sight.

Using this method, the distance back to the supply skids would only be the radius of the circle, no matter how far he might walk in his search. He would investigate every crevice and thicket that could possibly conceal a small aircraft. This mission would require a lot of walking, climbing, looking into dark, shadowy tree-covered hillsides, a lot of looking, and one hell of a lot of luck.

"Five minutes, Sarge. Five minutes to the drop zone," the crew chief shouted over the din of four powerful engines grasping at the thin mountain air to pull the plane forward. The crew chief's words snapped him abruptly back to the present from his review of the jam-packed hours since he had first walked into the Oval Office to deliver some weather reports and photos. Simple job for a man, a soldier of his experience. Now here he was. What the fuck had he gotten himself into?

He slipped into his parachute harness. Without any discussion, in a totally automatic way resulting from uncountable hours of training, one of the flight crew went through an equipment check with Dan to be sure everything was right, all straps and buckles in the right place and secured properly. Dan then waddled toward the rear of the big plane, grasping webbing and handholds to maintain his balance. All the jump school training at Fort Bragg, North Carolina, surfaced to prove its worth.

The crew had already hooked themselves to the aircraft with safety lines and were now ready to push the two skids down the rollers and out the rear door. The skids would go in one direction, straight down! The heavy loads would not fly very well at this low altitude and airspeed. Dan, on the other hand, all one hundred sixty-five pounds of him, could be flipped around quite a bit if he exited the aircraft with a weak body position, or if the ground winds were higher than expected. A windy landing in a heavily-treed area unfamiliar to the jumper could be extremely dangerous. It could be a killer. He hoped the meteorologists and their forecasts were right.

He expected to exit the aircraft close behind the two skids. Close enough to see them land. He wanted to know where they were so he could locate them quickly once he was on the ground. He also hoped he would be able to watch them land so he could see what their condition would be. He needed to know if they landed in one piece or were destroyed on impact. Supply airdrops were not perfect. Many skids and their loads never survived the trip.

Normally, there are many stages in a parachute jump. The first stage begins the night before, lying in bed in anticipation. Many men never sleep. Some cry. Others sleep to hide. Some lie to themselves, saying they have no fear of the coming event. Others will jump only if fear is with them, their number one companion. Without it, mistakes are too often made. Only one thing is certain: all who jump love it! Otherwise, as the cliché goes, "Why jump out of a perfectly good airplane?"

Dressing and eating breakfast the morning of a jump is purely mechanical, especially for the new guys, the cherry jumpers, the sixers, their first jump following the five jumps required for graduation from Basic Airborne Training school. You have to do these tasks. Eat. Dress. Act normal. But your mind is somewhere else.

The nervous chatter during the ride to the airfield in the back end of a deuce and a half truck, filing through the storage sheds to pick up your main and reserve chutes: these actions quiet all but the youngest and dumbest jumpers. The least experienced. The most afraid. Boarding the aircraft begins to quiet the running bullshit. The takeoff separates the young from the experienced. The flight to the drop zone, designed to calm nerves, begins with the... puking.

The command, "Stand up!" shouted by the jumpmaster, finally settles all emotions by shifting all consciousness to reflex actions instilled during training. No time to think! React or die! Brain and body follow the verbal commands without thought, albeit with a pounding heart.

"Stand in the door! Step out!" Against every instinct of brain and body, against all logic, against all sensible reason, you step out into the void, into nothing, knowing damn good and well that you are about to fall to your death,

unless everything goes perfectly. Step out into the crisp, clear, cool blue sky, falling to your death until you look up and see a white bloom above your head. The canopy fluffs open above you, reaches out and gobbles up a dome of invisible air, lowering you slowly, safely, to the earth below, just like it was planned. Just like all the training instructors told you. Just like you knew it would. Shit! Nothing to it!

The crew chief watched the two small lights mounted on the inside fuselage of the C-130. One was lit. The red one. The other one would light up green. But right now it was a lifeless black, waiting to be electrified into life by a "Go!" command.

Dan hooked his static line into a cargo ring on the floor of the flight deck and waited with the crew. Moments later, the green light flickered, then fully snapped to life. The crew pushed the first skid. The drag chute was released to catch the air to pull the skid over the edge of the ramp. Gone! The second skid followed immediately.

Even before the second skid cleared the ramp, Dan had stepped into the gaping hole in the rear of the aircraft. He turned toward the crew chief. The chief saluted him and pointed to the open doors. Dan returned the salute and stepped out. He was now alone.

For Sergeant Dan Travis, what he loved the most was the silence following the opening of his chute. The quiet lasted only as long as the soft ride down. How myste- riously the roar of the airplane engines vanished from this world he had voluntarily entered. The quiet soothed him. It sucked him in. Enveloped him. Penetrated him. Cleansed him. In the brief time it took him to land, each jump engulfed him. It was the quiet that made him come back for the next jump. That was the reason, his reason for loving this experience.

Today's jump was not normal, however. The normal night-before didn't exist, never got around to existing. The events leading to this jump were unprecedented, events he'd never anticipated in his wildest imagination. Yet here he was, and it was time to go to work. Time to stop all the day dreaming. Time to switch gears and put all his years of training into effect. Right now on the ground. Time to think.

Chapter Three

Adding up all the jumps Dan Travis had made as a skydiver and his military jumps, this one was number 286, and it was going well. He could see the two cargo skids floating to the ground slightly below him. The lower one was now just above the tops of the tallest trees and about to land in an area of small growth of what looked to be young trees and scrub brush. From what he could see, the entire area looked about the same: small, young, soft trees no more than ten to twelve feet high.

It was a good area for an easy landing. The first skid touched down, then the second. Both landed upright and fully intact. He would have double supplies. Far more than he would ever need, he hoped. Dan judged that he would land about two hundred yards to the northeast of the skids and would have no problem finding them.

He took advantage of the last few seconds of his elevated position to scan the surrounding area. Around him, he saw a valley he guessed to be three to four miles wide and ten to twelve miles long. It looked to be the exact location he'd chosen before taking off from the airfield. The pilot had done his job well.

Dan and his cargo would land in the southwestern third of the valley. He saw that the entire area immedi- ately below him, and for at least a mile in every direction, was composed of the same young trees and scrub brush. He also saw black, traces of black on tree stumps, downed trees, and up the sides of the few older trees still standing in the area.

Fire. There had to have been a fire five to ten years ago, if the height of the new trees told a true story. The fire must have been either rained on or blown out by the same forces of nature that started it. Or it might have just burned itself out of fuel. There didn't seem to be any signs of humans being present. No roads, no dug-up ground, no cut trees, or anything else to indicate human firefighting activities.

His feet were at treetop level, then almost instantly he was on the ground. He didn't want to risk any broken bones or other stupid injuries, not out here, so he executed a classic textbook landing. Feet, calves, thighs, butt, hip, and shoulder, roll over on your back and spring back up on your feet into a standing position to gather in lines and collapse your main parachute.

Reserve chute unclipped, he twisted the breastplate on the main chute, hit the quick release, and his harness fell away. He gathered in the Model T-10 parachute and stuffed it into a cavity next to a dead log, threw a few rocks on top of it, and headed off toward his supplies.

It took fifteen minutes to locate the first skid. He climbed on top of it to retrieve the handheld radio he needed to contact the aircraft and confirm his safe landing.

He waited until he heard the plane's engines approaching as it circled back over the valley to receive his signal. Travis flipped on the radio and waited until it came to life.

"Taxi to stowaway, over."

He was to wait for the second call.

"Taxi to stowaway, over."

"Taxi, this is your customer, over."

"How is the DZ? Over."

"Everything's in one piece, me and both suitcases. Put your flag up, cut off the meter, and go on back to the garage, over."

"Roger, the one piece plus two. The flag is flipped. Meter's off. Going to the garage. Good luck on your campin' trip. And keep your head down. Over and out."

"Thanks, driver! And thanks for the ride. Don't forget to get paid for the trip. Dispatchers' got the big bucks. Over and out."

The big aircraft made a final lazy, lumbering turn toward the south. Travis could see the tail doors beginning to close. Mission completed. He watched it climb until it disappeared, and he could no longer hear its engines. He was surrounded by silence once again. Not the same silence he enjoyed just a short while ago. No! This was a different silence. This silence was... big. And if he wasn't careful, it could be dangerous, even deadly!

Chapter Four

Sergeant Dan Travis was on his own. What he did from this moment on would decide if he lived or died and, if he was correct, determine the fates of two Secret Service agents, a young woman he'd never met, and the president of the United States. The first thing he had to remember was to care for himself. If he went down, they all went down.

The first thing was to choose one of the skids to use as his primary resource. He would use only one skid and keep the second in reserve. In his mind, he named the skids after the two grocery stores he always went to when he lived in North Carolina. The first was Harris Teeter, and the second was Piggly Wiggly.

He removed the tarp covering Harris Teeter to reveal his very precious storehouse of supplies. He would be going out on a long cross-country hike to start his search pattern, so he had to think in terms of supplying himself for this effort.

His shopping list began with the frameless, form-fitting backpack. Next was food, enough to last at least a week. Water bottle and purification tablets. Tent. Sleeping bag and ground pad. Medical kit. One complete change of clothes with three extra pairs of socks. Cook stove. Uten- sils.

Once he had all the essentials packed, he began to select other items. One 30.06 rifle with a box of ammo containing twenty rounds, and a 9mm pistol with two full clips of ammo. One hunting knife with a six-inch blade sharpened to a bright, shiny edge, able to shave hair off his arm. He mounted this on his belt. One Swiss Army knife, into his pocket. Last, but not least, a compass and maps. Mental check: he was ready.

He set the supplies against a tree and found his way back to the parachute. He cut off a piece of bright white cloth and returned to the supply cache. He found a skinny, straight dead tree and tied the white cloth to one end. He then stuck the other end of the stick into the webbing that held the supply fast to the Harris Teeter skid. There was now a bright white flag sticking up twenty feet above the supply dump and fluttering in the soft breeze. Dan knew he would have to be able to find it again to survive. Time to go.

The valley he had chosen as the center of his search area had been easy to scan from his vantage point when he was dangling beneath his parachute. There would be no need to spend time searching the southern half. Had a plane of any size, big or small, crash-landed in young growth he had seen, it would have stuck out like a sore thumb.

Besides that, the C-130 had flown over the entire length of the valley at low altitude as it approached his jump point and again at a higher altitude when it circled back to make final radio contact to check on his landing status. Had there been signs of anything unusual, the crew would have seen it and notified him to investigate that area immediately.

Dan's plan was to hike southwest toward the nearest range of hills, then climb to the ridgeline and hike in a northerly direction, hoping that the ridge would provide a vantage point to scan the valley on either side of the hills, east and west.

He checked his watch. It was almost noon on Tuesday, just over twenty-four hours since he had entered the Oval Office. The Oval Office. Inside the White House. Inside Washington, D.C. Inside the Beltway. Inside the massive confusion of activity that surrounds power. Now he was here. What a contrast.

So little time had elapsed since the frantic level of activity that had brought him to this point. People are scurrying about, yelling for no reason, and acting with no role to play. Washington, D.C. to here. This is where God lived. Here, and every other spot like it on earth. He lived here, not under some golden dome.

Dan hadn't gotten much sleep in the last two days. Now, out here in the wilderness that he loved, peaceful and quiet, unspoiled by human greed and ego, he began to feel the effects of the long hours. He knew he couldn't give in to it right now. He had to get the search started. So, he modified his plan. He would hike across the valley floor, climb to the ridge, and find a good place to camp for the night. A good, hot meal and a sound night's sleep in these surroundings would recharge him. The search would begin in earnest at daybreak.

He lifted the heavy backpack and slid it onto the shoulder straps. He adjusted the waist belt, hitched up the load, pulled down on the shoulder straps until he had a snug, comfortable fit, and turned southwest. A thought flashed through his mind. This was a real-life example of every journey beginning with the first step. How long would his journey be? And where would it take him?

An hour later, he came upon a small stream trickling down from the hills ahead of him. It was his first break. He unbuckled his backpack, lowered it to the ground, took out his two water bottles, and filled them with the crystal clear icy mountain water. After a long cooling drink and a trail snack, he rested for ten minutes and was on his way again. Bushwhacking, hiking cross-country without a trail, was slow and exhausting work. He would have to be patient.

Once he hiked through the area that had been burned, the going was more difficult. The underbrush was thicker. The bare, stiff lower limbs of the white birch trees slapped and scraped his hands and face. The evergreen stands cedar, pine, and firs—were so thick they had to be circled. They were far too dense to penetrate for a man carrying a backpack.

Nature's maintenance crew, fire, had not been at work in this area. But it would come. Someday, it would come. A lightning strike somewhere nearby, and the cycle would begin. The natural cleansing of Mother's works of marvel would begin. She knew what was necessary to perfect her magic.

As the incline began to steepen, the trees and underbrush thinned out and were replaced by rocky outcroppings. The load on his back, the branches grabbing at him, at his clothes, had a message: "No, you cannot go forward,

you cannot invade me, go back." Dan guessed he was carrying a little over sixty pounds on his back. The weight, the hill, the lack of sleep, and four months of sitting behind a desk on his fat ass in an office in the lower levels of the White House, all hit him at once. His muscles were telling him that there would be a price for this, and that he would have to pay up real soon.

Breathing heavily, with his calf and thigh muscles protesting loudly, Dan continued to climb. He had to. He had to climb through the pain. He had to push through the stretching of those lazy, fat, shrunken muscles and lungs. He had to push through to the forgotten skills. He had to keep climbing.

The terrain became increasingly rocky as he climbed. Huge spires of rock jutted out of the ribs of the hillside, stabbing upward and outward from the darkening forest floor. Four times he dropped his pack to climb to a vantage point and search the valley below, scanning the panorama below, looking for any sign of an airplane or a crash site. Four times he saw nothing—nothing except the breathtaking landscape, the mountains holding up the sky, the painted valley floor.

And the water: streams, creeks, brooks, all slowly, patiently sculpting and crafting, guided by the hand of the One who could see it all from high above the cottony white clouds. The architect of the master plan.

It was late afternoon when Dan reached the spine of the ridge. He flopped to the ground, soaked in sweat. It had been a difficult climb. His body had protested, but it had met the physical challenge he placed upon himself. He played mind games all the way. Each step its own test toward the final exam. Each exam had to be met, then immediately set aside, replaced by the next only an instant later.

A step. A tree. A rock. Another step. Another test aced. The body was screaming louder and louder. And the only reward was the accomplishment itself. He knew that once he got past this test, his body would respond as it always had. It would harden, get stronger, respond to his demands, to the demands that lay ahead. He slipped out of his backpack and leaned back against a tree to rest, dozing off a couple of times in the next fifteen minutes.

He had to force himself to get back on his feet and make camp. It would be easy, too damned easy, to simply curl up next to that tree and let the peace of his surroundings penetrate him, body and soul, to sleep for hours. He had to concentrate, force himself to keep the real task clearly in his mind. It would be so easy to let it slip away and evaporate into the miles and miles of vast wilderness around him.

He had to find the discipline of a soldier, the regimen- tation of his training, to keep his mission clear. He was Travis, Daniel J., Master Sergeant, U.S. Army. He couldn't allow himself to forget that, not for a moment.

He challenged himself aloud. "Get up, fat ass. You need to eat. You need to put up a tent. Get going. Get up!" In the past, during long hikes and hunting trips into the backwoods of the Adirondacks and the Smoky Mountains, he often talked to himself for motivation, but sometimes just to hear his own voice, keep his own company.

Dan explored the area immediately around the spot where he had flopped to the ground. It was a lot easier moving around without the pack. Near the point where he had first reached the spine, he found an outcropping of rock from which he could again view the valley below. From this perch, he could see clearly for miles to the east, from where he had begun his hike. He could see the burned-out area in the valley to the south, and for the first time, to the west, he into a new valley visible only from this vantage point.

He removed a pair of compact binoculars from his pack and began to search the vast territory now exposed to him. Magnificent! But no sign of any disturbance man's presence would have brought to this holy scene. No human. No aircraft. No wreckage. No fire. Nothing. He could see all the way to the rim of the hills that enclosed the end of the valley. If there was anything to be seen, it would be easy to at least spot enough to know there was something to investigate. He was convinced that the valley to the south and east held no promise for the president and his daughter.

The new valley to the west was slightly higher with thicker, unburned tree growth. A possibility. He needed to check it out.

Further to the east, beyond the valley he had just hiked across, who knows? It was big, and anything was possible! Add it to the list.

To the northwest was a high, broad saddle, first sloping downward from the ridge he was on, then flaring out to either side and rising up to link two very high mountains. He judged them to be twenty to twenty-five miles away. He scanned each through his binoculars, but they were way too far away to reveal anything. It would take time, a great deal of time, to search the entire area.

Time! How much time did he have? Forever, if they were all dead, but if they weren't, how long could they last?

Injured, hungry, cold, thirsty, without shelter, and scared shitless in this strange, alien environment. Being all alone in these mountains could scare the crap out of anybody, certainly those who had never been in them before and were now fighting for their lives.

There was plenty of water, if they could get to it, and if they weren't hurt too badly. Maybe they could find shelter inside the cabin of the plane, if it was in one piece, if it hadn't burned in the crash. Even if they found shelter, mountain nights were cold. No fire, or they would have been seen by one of the scout planes or the satellite. No blankets. No heavy clothing.

And would they panic? Panic could kill them faster than just about anything else. Lose your senses, and all else goes down the tube. Panic destroys all knowledge, all training, all intelligent thought. Panic leads to stupidity and foolish, deadly behavior. Panic kills!

Suddenly, the urgency of the task he had accepted hit him, taking on a wholly new meaning. The romance of being the center of attraction, being in the company of the vice president and the Governor of Maine, having airplanes scheduled for you, having generals making things happen for you, all paled as the importance of this mission slammed into him.

There were people out there, people who, if he was right, would live or die because of him. This was no camping trip, no backpacking hike in the woods on a sunny day. This was much more than his spinning mind had accepted before now. Four people if alive, four souls if dead. Either way, they were out there waiting for him to find them, to rescue them, to put them to rest...or bring them home.

North! Something said north. Why? His gut... intuition... instinct? Something on one of the maps? Something tugged at him. Tugged and pulled and urged him north. So much territory. So big. All around him, in every direction. He couldn't possibly search it all in time. He had to commit, to risk all by choosing the direction that would give him the best chance of succeeding.

He had learned long ago, in these mountains, in the Smoky Mountains of North Carolina, in the Adirondacks of New York, and in war; he had learned to listen to that inner voice. It had saved his life in the past. Maybe it would save the lives of others now.

He returned to his gear, lifted and strapped it on, and began hiking north along the spine of the ridge. He hadn't planned to hike any further today. He was physically drained. Now, he was running on adrenaline and emotion. The sudden renewed urgency drove him, overcoming his body's call to stop.

For three more hours, he hiked north across the rough, rocky terrain, the thick underbrush and low tree limbs slapping at his face and body. Cross-country hiking, blazing a trail as you went, was the most demanding, most physically punishing way to hike.

The sun was getting low. Once the sun dipped behind the mountains, the forest could change from daylight to dusk to dark very quickly. It would be foolish and very dangerous to continue any further. He would drop down below the ridgeline to make camp, using the ridge to protect him from any storms that might blow up during the night.

But first, one more look. One more sweep of everything within sight, one more look for the so far unseen.

He found a high spot, placed the binoculars to his eyes, and searched the vista below. The majesty of all that was before him again absorbed him. The sheer vastness. The colors! The soothing sounds that when combined, had the same effect on him as silence. His mind and body were equally and peacefully quieted and re-energized.

He could see nothing that would aid his search. But he knew it was there. Somewhere it was out there. They were out there. He could feel it. He had to continue. He had to keep going north.

Dan replaced the glasses in his backpack and walked only a few more yards before he found a place where he could see down the eastern hillside to a fairly clear and level area about a hundred yards down the hill. He made his way to a spot large enough to pitch his two-man Eureka backpacking tent and still have enough room to set up a one-night camp.

It would not be necessary for him to find a stream today. He was carrying enough water to cook supper, brush his teeth in the morning, and splash a few drops on his face before starting north again. Besides, Dan knew it was very unlikely that he would find water this close to the top of the ridge.

It didn't take long to set up the ultralight tent. Tension poles extended and slipped over corner pins. Canopy loops clipped over the poles within minutes, instant shelter against wind, rain and cold. Next, Dan unrolled his insulated ground pad inside the tent. This time of year, it would add a tiny bit of comfort more than it would serve its real purpose of creating a barrier between the camper and cold ground. Atop the pad, he spread a goose down sleeping bag rated to keep the occupant warm to temperatures as low as twenty degrees below zero, but remarkably comfortable at much more moderate temperatures.

Cook stove, pots, and utensils were easy to find in his pack, leaving only one decision left: what to eat. Besides its low weight, one thing about dehydrated camping food was that it pretty much all tasted the same. But, somehow, for mysterious non-scientific reasons known only to the camping gods, after a long day of hiking in the woods... it tastes great!

He chose stew. A packet for two to make up for the meals he had missed during the past couple of days, and also as a reward for getting refocused on his mission and realizing the confidence to carry it out. Besides, stew was easy. One pot. A spoon. Some boiling water. Done. Very little cleanup and a full belly.

Dan lit the miniaturized lightweight stove, poured the prescribed amount of water into a pot, and placed it on the stove. He slit the food packet with a knife and waited until the water came to a boil. He didn't want to consider any further effort. He knew that once the meal was done, he would be too. He could feel it in his bones. His body had had enough for one day.

As the water heated, he leaned back against a tree, thinking about all the times he had done this. How many campsites found, how many tents pitched, meals cooked, miles hiked, nights spent under the stars? The real question in his mind was how many more were ahead of him on this mission. How many miles? Would they be alive?

He also felt a sense of guilt. Here he was, about to stuff his face with a hot meal and crawl into a warm sleeping bag protected by a tent. Yet, those he sought, if alive, were out there somewhere, exposed and probably very hungry, cold, and scared. However, he knew none of that was his fault. He was there to help, not hurt, and he had to keep a positive attitude toward the task at hand.

If he really tried, he could probably recall most, if not all, of his past experiences in the forests and mountains of the East and the

West. For many years, he had kept a logbook, posting each night when he camped out. Where, with whom, time of year, temperature, how many miles hiked each day, any incidents worth remembering, and people met. It read like a National Geographic adventure. From Maine's Baxter State Park, watching the beginning of a new day atop Mount Katahdin, the first place the sun kisses the United States each morning. To North Carolina's Linville Gorge and Mount Mitchell, at almost seven thousand feet, the highest point east of the Rocky Mountains. To the high mountain valleys of the Cascades in Washington and Oregon. Exploring what was left of Mount Saint Helens. Each different. Each is the same. Each owns its own beauty, different from any other. Each is the same in the respect demanded if you wish to see their beauty and live to remember it. The reward of seeing what God's hand had sculpted, the penalty of death for being careless or stupid.

Peace and violence. Beauty and death. Reward and penalty. He knew them all. Dan Travis knew them all. He had reaped the rewards and seen the beauty. Felt the peace and cheated the penalties. Been nourished by the solitude and the isolation, the quiet and the endless beauty.

He knew how to blend into the wilderness, how to use it, how to become one with it. He knew it as a boy, learned it as a man, and perfected it as a soldier. He existed and survived in war by using his boyhood experiences. He survived by watching and learning from his enemy how they became a part of the land, from swamps to mountains to the desert. They became blended with their surroundings like water in a sponge. No longer separate. A single unit. Often fight the most modern army in the world to a standstill. Fighting it not only with weapons but with their environment. By becoming their environment. Dan could feel himself, his mind, and his body, once again accepting, acclimating, adjusting, and remembering the presence of these mostly unconscious skills and instincts.

The water began to boil. He added the contents of the stew packet to the pot and removed it from the flame. While he waited for it to cook itself, he turned off the stove, buried his trash, and found a comfortable place to sit. Dinner was served.

Ahh! Home cooking had never been any better. Freeze-dried packet of mystery meal, some boiling water, and a bit of cool fresh air as spice. No further special ingredients needed except an appetite.

By the time he had finished eating, darkness had pushed the daylight off to the west; without the warming rays of the sun, the air had begun to cool and seep into the soul of the dying day. Dan got to his feet and quickly cleaned and stowed his equipment, then placed his backpack and rifle inside his tent. Taking advantage of the last moments of the day's mild temperatures, he stood outside of the tent to undress for the night. Boots were placed inside the tent to be sure they were dry and bug-free for the coming day. Pants and shirt were folded and placed flat between the ground pad and the sleeping bag. They would be both dry and warm when he slid back into them in the morning.

All chores completed, he crawled into the tent and zipped it behind him. Next, he unzipped the end flap windows to provide the airflow that would allow the stale air and moisture his body would produce during the night to be removed by the cool mountain air.

Mechanics, mechanics, mechanics. Follow the mechanics and survive. Follow the mechanics and live to tell your story, to live to find others who are lost. Dan knew the mechanics, and he would complete them by the numbers. He would encourage them to go on. If the president and his daughter were out there, it would be the mechanics who would lead him to them and get them home safely and in one piece.

He unzipped his sleeping bag, flipped it open, and lay atop it on his back, hands behind his head. He studied the ceiling of the tent above him, blanking out the exhaustion he felt overtaking him. Dressed only in his underwear, housed only in a seven-foot by five-foot tent, Dan felt as snug as the proverbial bug in the rug. Remarkable how such a thin layer of nylon cloth could satisfy the human need for the security of a safe shelter.

Within minutes, Dan's eyelids were being pulled down by the weight of the day. Darkness rapidly flooded all the spaces between the trees and swallowed the tiny two-man tent that would protect Sergeant Dan Travis while the renewing trance of sleep carried him to the new day's dawn. Each of the last rays of sunlight within his new world of Godly wilderness was sought out and pushed away by the invading darkness.

Dan never heard the night creatures come to life.

Part IV

Discovery

Chapter One

Dan did not wake up at first light as a television script might have had it. He didn't jump out of the tent and do a quick five minutes of exercise with Jane Fonda music playing in the background. No. It was almost 8:00 a.m. when the rustling of leaves high in the trees as they kissed each other in the morning breeze, and a couple of squirrels frantically squealing at each other and the intruder below brought Dan back to consciousness.

"Shit!" he yelled at his wristwatch as he checked the time, and the glowing numbers penetrated the morning fog around his brain. He stared at the eave of his tent for a moment before remembering where he was and collecting his thoughts. He had slept so soundly in the quiet of the mountains that his mind was briefly disoriented.

"Okay, Danny boy! Get your ass in motion. Let's get this show on the road."

He pulled his warm clothes out from under his sleeping bag and quickly dressed in the chilly mountain air. Then he heated some water, made a cup of instant coffee, and two packs of stick-to-the-ribs instant oatmeal. After eating, he used the leftover hot water to wash his utensils, then his face, and lastly to brush his teeth. Once he had taken care of himself, he knocked down and packed his tent, stuffed his sleeping bag into its sack, rolled up his insulated sleeping pad, loaded all gear either into or onto his backpack pack and was ready to go.

He policed the campsite and once satisfied that it was at least as good as when he had arrived, he strapped on his pack, grabbed his rifle, and headed north. Thirty minutes from waking to walking. Not bad for the physical condition he was in, he thought to himself. It would get better in the days ahead. He knew his muscles would condition, and his brain would soon catch up.

For the next two days, he fought his way through, around, over and under every obstacle that the rugged, unspoiled mountains could throw in his path: Fallen trees as big around as a small car, boulders bigger than a pick-up truck, thickets of birch and cedar dense enough to block out the sun, and rockslides as slippery as owl shit.

Dan tried to stay as close to the crest of the ridge as possible to be able to see to either side at every opportunity that nature afforded a clear view. He was often forced down one side or the other by some impassable obstacle, sometimes losing hundreds of feet in altitude before he could regain the ridge.

These descents would block portions his view into either valley, creating a nagging worry of having missed something important, something critical. In other areas the ridge would flatten out for a few hundred feet, some- times for a couple of hundred yards. These areas were much easier hiking, but again, created difficulties in scan- ning the lands below.

He tried to find places no more than an hour apart with a clear view into the valleys. He often had to drop his pack to climb to a perch atop an outcropping of rock, or to climb a tree, or to the top of some other vantage point with a clear view of the territory below, to both the east and the west. The majestic landscape around him was breathtaking, one startling panorama competing with another to capture his soul. Dan's eyes were challenged to absorb what lay before him. But there was no sign of human life...or death. Had he been wrong?

Each night, he repeated his campsite routine. Dan knew it was important to take care of himself, to maintain his personal condition at the highest level. Anything less could cost him his life or the success of his mission or both. He could help no one else if he himself were in need of help; he knew he was the only one out here experienced and equipped to do the job of saving himself and others. He could not allow himself to become the second subject of the search.

Midafternoon of the third day, he heard thunder rumbling through the valley to his west. He dropped his pack and found his way to a place where he could see the sky more clearly. Massive, dark storm clouds were moving rapidly in his direction ahead of a Canadian cold front.

He continued to push north for another half hour. It was 3:30 in the afternoon, and the thunder was now all around him. Lightning flashes were lighting up the sky. The violent cracks ripping the air were almost on top of him. This could quickly turn into a very dangerous situation. The wind picked up, grasping the branches at the tops of the conifer trees overhead, tugging and bending them to the east. The thought flashed through his mind that they were pointing the way for him.

He would have to move down the lee side of the slope and quickly find an unexposed area to pitch his tent before the bottom fell out of the clouds above him. Walking would be next to impossible, and attempting to go on would be careless of him once it began to rain. He knew the soil would become like grease under his feet, once it became soaked, to say nothing of the danger of lightning strikes. Even without the lightning, one slip of his foot and he could fall, straining a muscle, breaking a bone, or sending him sliding down a mountain slope, ending everything, including himself.

He managed to find a small opening that would do. He quickly pitched his tent, tossed in his backpack and rifle, and crawled in just in time to avoid the first wave of water that came smashing down through the treetops. It rained so hard it sounded like his tent had a tin roof, and he had pitched it under a bathtub faucet. This was no passing rain shower; this was a major storm. His tent bent under the weight of the water. The drops hit the thin, waterproof cloth so hard that a fine mist penetrated through to his sweaty face.

His day was over. Dan lay back on his gear to wait out the storm and relaxed, happy to have found a spot level enough to pitch his tent before he got soaked to the skin. It would be a long night, and a hungry one. Cooking inside a tent is not a very smart idea. He would have to make do with some trail mix and water. No television here. No ball game to pass the time. No feature movie. Just time.

Listening to the rain beating on his paper-thin roof. He'd just have to wait it out. He... his eyes closed.

The quiet woke him. Graveyard quiet. He brought his left wrist up in front of his face. The glowing numbers told him it was after midnight. The rain had stopped. The air outside sat heavily and silently all around him. It was too late to get up and cook a meal. He rolled over and mentally reset his biological clock for 6:00 a.m.

When he awoke, his appetite was pushed aside by the urgency of having lost precious hours of searching the day before because of the storm. He heated a pot of water and downed two hefty cups of coffee. He then packed his soaking-wet tent. The vision of the day ahead did not sit well with him when he thought of the extra water weight he would be carrying around all day. He would have to stop later on when the sun came out and dry the tent, or it would take a heavy toll on him before dark. And he didn't want to pitch a wet tent for the night ahead.

By 10:30, the sun was high, bright, and unseasonably hot. The mountains were giving back last night's rainfall, releasing it back to the heavens. The land was sweating. He could feel the steam rising up on his face.

He found some rocks jutting out from the hillside, naked to the sun's rays, and spread the tent to dry. He could see the valley below, and for the first time, he could see where the ridge he had been following for so long began to slope downward, giving way to another valley beyond the one he had parachuted into four days earlier. He would soon have to make another decision on the direction in which to search next.

By noon, the tent dried and repacked, he resumed his hike. Suddenly, he realized he was hungry. Very hungry. The descent down the slope of the ridge was much steeper than he had expected and had taken extreme effort to safely negotiate the wet, slippery mountain soil.

He could hear rushing water in the distance and figured there was a large stream pouring out of the next valley and rushing down through the one he had landed in. It sounded inviting. He was hungry, hot, and he smelled bad. A cold bath in a mountain stream, followed by a hot meal, would revitalize him for the charge ahead into the high valley to the north.

Dan found another perch where he could get one last view of the valley below before he left behind the vantage point of the higher altitude along the ridge. He pulled the monocular from his breast pocket, thinking of the cool bath that awaited him down below. He studied the terrain to the north, trying to get the lay of the land ahead of him. He could plainly see the entrance to the next valley. The ridge he had been following continued to fall off sharply, but did not descend to the level of the valley floor. The valley ahead was clearly higher in altitude than the one directly to his right.

From what he could see, its western boundary was formed by a very steep slope up the side of a peak. It would require a very difficult climb if he decided to go that way. To the east, it was bounded by a more gently rolling ridge much like the one he had been following for the last four days. The plan forming in his head was to descend to the stream below, cross it to the east side, and then hike up the gentler slope to search both sides of the new ridge.

He picked a distant point high on the ridgeline to the north and began tracing a path in his mind. He would be able to follow this mental route over the coming days. He adjusted the focus as he continued to trace the route as it got closer to his current position. He searched, and "What the hell is that?" he exclaimed to the trees around him. He dropped the glass from his eye, blinked three or four times to regain his natural focus, hoping to erase any false reading his mind might have registered, then lifted the glass back up to his eye for another look.

"Holy shit!

What he had seen snapped Dan to his feet, as if he had been hit by a surge of electricity. With pack and rifle strapped in place, he began running, plunging forward down the final stretch of the hillside, crashing through the underbrush, small trees, and low-hanging branches, each one trying to stick its thorny fingers into him to rip his skin off. He ignored the stings that punished his hands and face and tore his clothes.

Leaning back, practically sitting on his ass, he somehow managed to maintain his balance as he lunged forward, nearly out of control, narrowly avoiding a headlong tumble down the hill and into the creek and coming to an abrupt stop just short of the bank of the stream. He studied the obstacle now in front of him. It was fifty to sixty feet across, its banks struggling to contain the heavy rain-swollen flow of water cascading down from the valley above. The water boiled violently over the rocky, narrow waterway filled with rocks and boulders of all sizes.

Dan quickly plotted a crossing and, without further thought, he dashed ahead, jumping from rock to rock. One slip and he would be swept away, tossed like a toy in the torrent, and drowned by the weight of the pack on his back. He negotiated the crossing quickly, but not easily. Twice, his feet almost lost their purchase on the wet, mossy rocks.

Had it not been for the deep tread on his boots, he would surely have plunged into the icy water. Luckily, all that happened was two belly landings on the rocks. Both times, he bounced to his feet, avoiding the downstream death ride.

Once across, he crawled up the muddy bank to higher and drier ground. Above him was a prehistoric rockslide of weathered gray granite. The slide ran up the hill for about two hundred yards before giving way to an area of scrub brush. Above that, the brush blended into a thick forest.

He set his rifle down against a large rock and unsnapped the waist belt of his backpack. He lowered the pack to the ground and began to climb up the slide area, trusting his instinct to direct him to the spot he was looking for. Every time he attempted a foothold or pushed forward with one foot, a small avalanche of loose rocks and gravel gave way under the pressure of his boot, making the climb slow-going and very difficult.

And finally, there it was. There, ahead of him...fifty yards... forty yards... thirty... now ten... He stopped. He had found it. He had reached what he thought, what he knew, he had seen from high on the ridge above. A dead man!

Lying on his back, head toward the creek, feet to the mountain. Toes and eyes to the sky! Dressed in a dark blue business suit, a light tan trench coat, and black dress shoes.

His mouth was wide open, gasping for the next breath that would never come. He stared skyward, not seeing the soft, white, puffy clouds lazily passing over him.

Dan knelt on one knee next to the body, visually examining it from head to toe while he tried to catch his breath. It was easy to see from the twisted angle of the man's head and shoulders that he had died from a broken neck. Dan reached down to close the mouth and eyes in an attempt to return some dignity to the man lying before him.

He began a search of the body. He flipped the trench coat back to reveal the suit jacket underneath. A nine-millimeter semi-automatic pistol was holstered at the waist. Inside the jacket's breast pocket, he found a small leather folder. Inside was a government I.D. and gold badge. The man before him was Secret Service Special Agent Thomas J. Black, assigned to the President of the United States.

Chapter Two

After removing Special Agent Black's personal effects, including his I.D. card, gold badge, pistol, wallet, wristwatch, and wedding band, Dan wrapped the body in the trench coat and buried it beneath rocks he gathered from the slide area. He marked the grave by tying an aluminum food packet and a white sock to a stick with orange plastic tape and planting the stick firmly among the rocks in plain view of anyone who might come looking for it. Agent Black's body had not begun to decompose, nor even discolor. It showed no signs of being fed upon by animals, birds, or insects. This pointed to a very recent death. Dan was no doctor, but he guessed that the man had died only hours before, certainly no earlier than yesterday.

He climbed back down to his pack and rifle. Loaded and ready to continue, he started to climb back up the slide and past the grave. Sergeant Daniel Travis, United States Army, saluted Secret Service Agent Thomas J. Black in a final tribute to a fellow warrior who had given his life for his country.

He would try to find Agent Black's trail and backtrack along it. He was confident now that there was a president and a young woman at the other end. His wild-ass guess had been stepped up a notch.

Climbing up the rockslide was slow, now that he was loaded down with all his gear. It wasn't easy to find firm footing. Once he reached the treeline at the top, it was easy to see what had happened to Agent Black. He found a skid mark he believed was made by the man's body sliding out of control down the side of the mountain.

Black had lost his footing in the slick, wet soil and begun to tumble down the hill. He must have hit a tree or a rock when he reached the slide, or maybe just, falling head over heels, his neck snapped, turning the slide into a death ride that ended his young life. His slick-soled street shoes had betrayed him.

For the first two hours, following Black's trail was extremely easy. It had obviously been made since the previous night's rainfall. The freshness of the footprints confirmed two things. First, Black's prints showed signs of slipping and sliding in almost every stride. It had been difficult for him to get any kind of a grip in the slick soil with his dress shoes.

Second, it confirmed that Black had been dead only a few hours. He had died sometime this morning after the rain had stopped, or most of his trail would have been washed away. But, more importantly, it confirmed that Dan's W.A.G. about which way to search had been correct. Somewhere ahead of him was what he was searching for. Every ounce of him moved forward with a renewed sense of urgency.

The easy part of backtracking ended at a dry spot under an overhanging rock formation. He found a circle about a foot and a half in diameter. Black must have found this spot and sat here during the storm, hunkering down, trying to keep dry and warm under the rock's shelter. It was the only protection he had besides the flimsy trench coat he had on when Dan found him.

From that point on, it was a bit more difficult, but still fairly easy to follow Black's path. A man as ill-equipped as he was, one wearing smooth-soled shoes, was out of his element here. He hadn't hiked through the woods; he had sort of blasted his way through.

Following his trail up to the spot where Black had stopped before the storm was almost as easy as tracking a bulldozer across a soft grass meadow. After that, it was more like trying to follow a kitten across a newly-waxed kitchen floor. The signs were there, but only if you knew where to look for them.

Black's kitten-track trail led to the top of the east ridge that Dan had targeted as his new route. After only a few hundred yards, it turned back toward the stream and the west ridge. When Dan reached the stream, Black's trail turned again, this time to the northwest, following the water's route from the valley higher up.

The upward slope was fairly gentle, but it was dramatic. The water roared through the trees and over the boulders within its ancient banks. The stream tumbled, boiling and foaming down the hillside, trying to push everything out of its way. Brilliant white water glistening in the rays of sunlight, it caught from above and threw it out to light up the forest. Sparkling like tinsel on a Christmas tree, the stream led the way up the mountain, finally cresting at the southern end of the high valley.

Black's slide to death down the rocks would have taken only seconds. It must have taken him days to hike the same distance Dan had now travelled in only hours. Just like a carpenter trying to build a house with the wrong tools, Black's job was not only much more difficult, but it became impossible. It became deadly.

The trees and undergrowth thinned almost as soon as Dan reached the floor of the valley. The hillside gave way to a flat, marshy area. Black's trail turned slightly to the south for a short distance and then again back to the west, bending around the perimeter of the marsh. Finally, it crossed the stream to the opposite side of the valley. Dan had to enter the water to cross to the other side.

The crossing was narrow, and the water was cold, coming to just above his waist. The flow was heavy, but not rapid. It pushed against him with constant pressure, but he managed to keep his footing without too much difficulty. Had the water been much deeper, it could easily have swept him and his heavy load away and over the edge to join Agent Black far below.

Back on dry land, the trail turned again to the northwest. Dan stopped only long enough to empty his boots and change his socks. Sitting there re-lacing his boots, he realized he was awfully hungry. But the new infusion of urgency had silently crept into him. Something had crawled into his gut and under his skin. Food would have to wait. He would wait until he camped for the night before he took the time to answer the call of hunger.

There was another call he had to answer right now. One, he knew he had the answer to, but couldn't quite hear it inside his head. An itch he couldn't quite scratch. He could see that there was a broad area with no trees that stretched out beyond the marsh. Probably a high mountain meadow, he thought.

The trail Agent Black had carved out in stumbling through the forest seemed to be tracing the western boundary of this area. He continued retracing Black's footsteps for almost another hour before he decided to stop for a short rest. He unbuckled his backpack and lowered his gear to take a look around. He climbed to the top of a large boulder to get a better look and saw that he had been wrong.

It wasn't a high mountain meadow. Dan found himself looking out over a beautiful, crystal clear, silver blue mountain lake. It filled the southern end of the valley. He unbuttoned the breast pocket of his fatigue jacket and took out his monocular. He put the glass to his right eye, focused it, and began to scan the shoreline of the lake, beginning right in front of his location and then looking further into the distance. He could easily see both the east and the west shorelines, gauging the lake's width to be about a mile and a half.

He could barely see the north end from where he stood. It was four, maybe five, miles away. The lake was almost a perfect oval with a small island closer to the western side, about halfway up toward the north end. From where he stood, Dan realized that the stream he had followed up from Black's grave must have been the spillway for the lake, the main source of the water feeding the stream running through the valley below. He examined the island and then continued to scan the shoreline to the north again, left to right.

His head was snapped back to his left by some instinctive impulse. There! Just beyond the island, just before it blocked his view of the northern shore, a mile, maybe a mile and a half from where he was standing. There...

"Son of a bitch!" he shouted to the mountain spirits. "Wild assed guess, my ass!"

Dan Travis spun on his heels, jumped down off the boulder, and bolted into a run. After a few yards, he stopped short, digging his heels into the wet soil. He turned back to his gear, picked up his pack and rifle, and started off again, strapping himself in as he ran. He hurried forward as fast as he could under the now very familiar weight of house, home, and grocery store riding on his back.

He jogged as close to the shoreline as he could, trying to keep his objective in sight. Trees to his left, water to his right. Within minutes, he could see it clearly. A single-engine aircraft! Its white tail fin barely sticking out of the tree line. Its right wing was busted off and lying on the ground among the trees just yards away from the main section of the fuselage. No sign of fire. No sign of life.

Dan slowed his pace to catch his breath as he neared the plane. That feeling in his stomach grew much more intense. About a hundred yards from the aircraft, he released his pack and lowered it to the ground, leaving it there to retrieve later. He slowly moved forward, rifle at the ready. There was an eerie, uncomfortable sense around the aircraft. Death was near. He held onto his 30.06 as a cold, fearless companion of wood and steel, providing courage and support.

He reached the fuselage. He looked into the cabin, not wanting to see what he knew would be there. Again, he was wrong. Both front seats were empty. Both yokes thrust fully forward. Seat belts lay slack and draped on the floor. The left side of the rear seat was also empty. But the right side was not. It held the body of a man, one dressed almost exactly like Agent Black.

Dan circled around to the right side of the aircraft. The door was closed. That was curious. He saw immediately what had killed the agent in the right rear seat. A tree limb had smashed through the side window just to the rear of where the wing had once been. It struck the man dead center in his chest about four inches below his throat and penetrated his upper rib cage, impaling him to the rear seat. Hopefully, it had killed him instantly. He had survived the crash... but not the landing.

A small creek fed into the lake about ten yards to the right of the airplane. Dan went over to it, knelt down, and splashed handfuls of the icy water onto his face. He didn't handle death very well. Especially this kind. Even after two tours in the Middle East, or maybe it was because of those two tours. He wasn't sure, and right now, it didn't matter.

He looked around the immediate area. Either the rain had erased all signs of human presence, or there weren't any.

"What would I do?" he asked himself. "Just what the hell would I do if I had been in that plane and lived?"

"Mr. President!" he shouted as loud as he could. Cupping his hands around his mouth, he faced the woods and shouted again. "Mr. President! Miss Richardson!"

"Yes! Over here." The faint reply struck him like a sonic boom, damned near knocking him back on his butt, like a voice from a cemetery would on Halloween night.

"We're here," repeated a weak female voice. The presence of a living voice where he hoped, but really didn't expect, to hear one, surprised the hell out of him. He regained his composure and rushed toward the voice. I'll be a son of a bitch, I found them. They're alive!"

"Mr. President. Miss Richardson."

"Over here," the female voice called again, slightly stronger or perhaps only slightly closer than the first reply.

He found them huddled beneath a large fir tree, covered up with limbs that had been broken off the low-hanging conifers around them. The limbs and their needles were all the protection they had from the elements. It was a miracle they were still alive.

They were damned near invisible under the green limbs. No wonder he hadn't seen them from the plane. The president's daughter was struggling to sit up. Dan could see a large, ugly bruise over her left eye. She looked disoriented, disheveled, dirty, and soaking wet, her stringy hair hanging in her face. Her clothes were wet and torn, the front of her dress practically ripped away. He saw a long cut running from her left shoulder down to the middle of her right breast. It was still oozing watery blood. Something, a tree branch, something broken inside the plane's cabin, had ripped her clothes away and cut her badly in the process.

Her face was a picture of exhaustion. Fear and resignation to death were painted in her eyes. She was almost too weak to care. She made only a feeble attempt to cover herself with the rags that hung from her body.

The president, her father, lay next to her, flat on his back, his Ivy League-styled steel gray hair caked with mud. Nearly a week's worth of beard masked the handsome face that had helped him win his second term in office almost two years ago. Dan removed the branches covering him. His clothes were wet and muddy, but still intact, covering him completely.

Dan knelt beside his Commander and Chief. "Mr. President," he called softly.

"He can't move. I... I think his legs are broken," his daughter strained to explain. "He's very weak."

The president tried to lift himself. Dan placed his hand on his shoulder to stop him.

"Don't move, sir. What else?" Dan asked the young woman, looking up at him in wonderment.

"I don't know."

"Mr. President, can you hear me okay? Do you understand me?"

"Yes," a weak and sleepy voice whispered. "Good. Do you have pain anywhere?" "Yes...my legs and my hips."

"Your legs and hips. Okay, anywhere else, sir? On your back? In your head or neck?"

"No."

"How about your chest, sir?"

"No."

"Good. That's good."

"Just my ass!"

"Wh... what?"

"I said just my ass."

"Your ass, sir?"

"Yeah! My hemorrhoids are giving me a fit from being on this wet, cold ground for so long."

He had a boyish little grin on his face. Even hidden behind the growth of beard and mud, it was clear to see that his famous sense of humor hadn't left him, even under these conditions. Incredible! Absolutely incredible!

Dan couldn't restrain his own grin in response to the president. "Yes, sir. Your ass. I'll get to it real soon."

He turned his attention to Sydney Richardson. He reached out to examine her forehead. He lifted the matted hair from over a bruise the size of a silver dollar. It had turned a greenish purple color. There was still a slight lump under it. She blanched and drew back when he pressed on it.

"How bad does that hurt?"

"Not too bad. Only when I touch it."

"Do you have a headache? A constant headache?"

"Not since the second day."

"Good. How about your neck and back?"

"A little stiff, but nothing really hurting."

"Good, good!"

He dropped his hands and eyes down to examine the cut on her chest. Again, he gently lifted the dirty, matted hair and what little was left of her dress. The full extent of the injury was now revealed. She did not resist his touch, but submitted as a good patient would to a doctor.

The cut was still oozing blood, and he could see some surface-level infection. Dan pressed all around the area with his fingertips, particularly along the collarbone. No sign it was broken. The infection would clean up easily. The cut could have used some stitches when it happened, but it was too old now. Dan was glad of that. He wasn't sure he wanted to render his level of medical skills, stitching up the body of the daughter of the President of the United States. Best to just clean it up and leave it open to drain and dry up on its own. He knew she would have a scar to remind her of this adventure for the rest of her life.

"Anything else?" he asked, trying to sound very businesslike, even to himself as he tried to concentrate on the injury and not be distracted by the beautiful woman he was touching.

"Legs, neck, back, ribs, or chest?"

"No, just scratches on my legs from walking through the bushes."

"You're sure?"

"Yes."

"You've been mobile? You've been walking around?"

"Yes."

"Good. That's real good. I'll take care of that cut in a little bit. Try to relax now. Everything's going to be okay. Try to relax. You're safe now."

Dan turned his attention back to the president. "Mr. President, where do you feel pain in your legs? Above the knee or below?"

"Above."

Dan pushed the branches further away so he could get a closer look. There was no sign of blood anywhere near his boss. That was also very good.

"Mr. President, I'm going to start at your knees and run my hands up your legs. Okay? One leg at a time. If I hit a spot that hurts real bad, let me know. Ready?"

"Okay, go ahead," the president replied as he braced himself for the pain that lay ahead.

Dan began on the left leg. He gently but firmly felt every inch of the president's leg. He could feel no lumps, no bumps, no protrusions. The president did not moan or yell out. Dan went higher. The president groaned. Dan continued upward until the president cried out in pain.

"Sorry, sir."

"It's okay...it's okay," the president replied, blowing and sucking air to help his tension find a place to rest. "I'm okay. Go on. I'm okay."

Dan moved to the right leg, repeating the examination process until he got the same painful reaction. He sat upright between his two patients, looking into the president's face to get a sense of the man's pain level.

"Well, do you want the good news first, or the bad?" Dan asked, trying to remember that both his patients were alive beyond anyone's highest hopes, and that this was a man with a keen wit and a sense of humor.

The grimace slid from the president's face, and the devilish grin returned.

"I'm not pregnant, am I?"

That got a tense chuckle from all three of them.

"No, sir. I'd have to give you an internal exam to determine that, and with all due respect, sir, I don't think either one of us is ready for that."

"But your legs aren't broken either. Your hips are dislocated. Both of them. You must have pushed hard and jammed them when the plane impacted. That may not sound too good to you, but it's a helluva lot better than busted bones. I'll be right back." Dan got to his feet.

"Where are you going?" Sydney Richardson asked in a fearful voice.

Dan placed his hand on her shoulder to reassure her. "Just down by the plane. I left my backpack down there. Don't worry. I'm not going anywhere. I'll be back in two minutes." He had a strong feeling that if it took him three minutes, she would panic and come running after him.

When he returned to the marooned pair, he unzipped his pack and removed the medical supplies, taking a quick visual inventory to be sure that everything he needed was there.

"Miss Richardson," he addressed the president's daughter formally, "I'm going to clean and dress that cut and check out the bump on your head before I tend to your father. I'll need your help with him, okay?"

"Yes," she replied softly.

Dan popped open a sterile gauze pad and soaked it with disinfectant.

"This is going to hurt some and sting. I've got to scrub out the infection before it gets any worse. Scream if you want to. There's nobody around these parts to hear you except me and your dad, so let it rip if you need to. If you don't mind, I've got to open the front of your dress." She offered no resistance. "Ready?" She nodded as Dan slipped on a pair of surgical gloves. "Okay! Here we go."

Dan began lowering the remains of her dress. He tried not to lower it too far. He didn't want to fully expose her breast and embarrass her, her father, or himself. He began to pat the wound at first to help build her up for what was coming. He pressed harder and began to scrub the skin surface around the wound, moving slowly to the cut itself.

Next, he spread the cut open to expose the muscle and flesh below the surface and scrubbed deeper into the heart of the wound. He felt the young woman's body tighten and pull away a fraction of an inch. He stopped to change to a new gauze pad and to give her a short break without asking her if she needed one. He could sense the same strength and pride in her as in her father, and he knew she wouldn't ask for relief.

He began again. When he was satisfied that the wound was clean and clear of all pus, he took a wad of cotton and soaked it with disinfectant. He again spread the cut and squeezed the cotton, allowing the iridescent red-orange liquid to drip onto the red raw flesh.

Sydney Richardson sucked air through clenched teeth. She squeezed her eyes closed hard enough to fuse the lids together. Every vein, every muscle, and tendon in her neck and chest tried to pop through her skin. But she did not scream.

Dan patted the surrounding area with more disinfectant, blew on it to dry it and to help cool the stinging burn he knew she was feeling, and finished by placing a protective dressing over the entire area. She had broken a visible sweat on her forehead. The relief from the pain was replaced by a weakened expression on her face, even more so than when he had first arrived. But she did not, would not scream.

"All done, Miss Richardson. Sorry, I had to hurt you like that. It's all done now. Are you okay?" Her head bobbed silently up and down, fighting back the tears trying to flood from her eyes.

"Okay. Now let's take a look at that bump on your head."

There wasn't much he could do for this nasty bruise. The skin wasn't broken. He cleaned the area with disinfectant. If he'd had some ice, he would have used it to get the swelling down. But there was no ice, and there were other concerns with a hit on the head hard enough to cause this.

"Does it hurt when you look up? Ya know, when you lift your eyes without moving your head?"

"Yes, but not as bad as it was a couple of days ago. More like a mild headache now."

"Thought so. You've got a concussion, is my guess. Being still and quiet for the past few days took care of most of it. Here, take two aspirin every two hours and call me in the morning," he kidded. Then he reached into his pack and handed her some dry clothes.

"Here, go find a private place and get out of those wet clothes. And I mean all of them. Sorry, my size isn't exactly right, and the color doesn't match your eyes, but it's the best I can do at the moment. Oh! Here's a pair of my boots and some dry socks. Pitch those pantyhose, too. When you're dressed, I'll need you back here. We'll get started on some hot food. Hold it! Hold it! One more thing— Here's some soap and a towel, if you'd like to wash up a little. If you want hot water, it will take a while before I can get it for you."

She sheepishly accepted all the items Dan handed her and complied with his instructions. She took her first step toward the lake to wash up. Suddenly, she stopped. The plane, her plane, was directly in front of her. It still contained the dead body of a Secret Service agent. She turned slightly to the left toward a clump of fir trees fifty or sixty feet away near the water, where she could wash and dress in privacy.

Dan turned his attention to the president, who had been watching as Dan attended to his daughter.

"Now, Mr. President, let's talk about those hips of yours."

"Hold on, son! Before you start on me, would you mind answering just a question or two?"

"No, sir, not at all. I don't mind."

"Good. Would you mind telling me who the hell you are?"

"Oh! Wow! Yeah, I guess I forgot to identify myself. It would be nice if you knew my name. Well, Mr. President, I'm Staff— I mean, Master Sergeant Daniel J. Travis, U. S. Army."

"Special Forces?"

"No, sir."

"Delta Force?"

"No, sir."

"Ranger?"

"No, sir."

"Well, what are you then? What special group do you train with to be out here?"

"None, sir. But I've had a lot of different types of training in my career."

"None?"

"Yes, sir. I mean no, sir."

"How many men do you have with you?"

"None, sir."

"None."

"No, sir."

"You're alone? You're out here all alone." It was a statement, not a question, tinged with as much sarcasm as the injured President could muster at the moment.

"Yes, sir."

"Well, Master Sergeant Daniel J. Travis, just who do you work for?"

"You, sir."

"Yeah! Yeah. I know, I'm the Commander and Chief. But who sent you out here?"

"The vice president, sir."

"The vice president? No, no, I mean…"

"Yes, sir. I know what you mean. That's what I'm trying to tell you. I work for you. I work in the White House!"

"The White House!"

"Yes, sir."

"My God! Well, son. Please tell me how in the world you got out here."

Master Sergeant Travis related the entire story to the president, from the moment he first encountered the vice president to the flight, to the meeting with Governor Mel Adams, to his parachute jump into the wilderness at the coordinates he had chosen, finishing with his search for them. Sydney Richardson had quietly returned in time to hear most of Dan's story.

"Early today, I found Agent Black."

"Oh my God! Where is he?" Sydney jumped in.

"He's dead." Dan watched and waited for the impact of his words. "He either slid or fell down a rock slide. I buried him there." He didn't provide any details about the broken neck.

Both the president and his daughter were visibly upset. Black had died for them. He had survived a plane wreck in the mountains only to die because he was wearing the wrong damned shoes.

Dan's tale and the news of Black's death were a lot to absorb and hard to get past. But he had to get past it and attend to his two living charges. "One more thing, Mr. President. Vice President Carson told me to be sure to tell you if I found you... alive, that is... that I was to tell you that your office was waiting for you. That he would not take the oath of office until or unless you were found dead.

"Gruesome message, but he meant it as an indication of his loyalty to you. On top of that, I told him I wouldn't come back until I found you. So, let's get on with it. Let's take a look at those hips of yours. We've got a long way to go to get you back to Washington and into that Oval Office. Besides, I'm getting hungry. We could all use some good hot stuff in our bellies, and you need to get dry and warm."

Dan pulled an eight-inch-bladed knife from its sheath on his hip and began to cut away the president's suit pants until they lay beneath him like a tablecloth under a Sunday roast waiting to be carved up. Next, he slit the president's boxer shorts up to the waistband and pushed the cloth aside to examine each hip. Just as he expected, he could see the bulge of bone beneath the skin and muscle.

"Miss Richardson, please sit on your father's chest facing him. Full weight. And I want you to look into each other's eyes. With help from both of you, this won't take long."

She hesitated. "Come on. Let's go!" Dan ordered.

"Okay," she said, her voice loaded with doubt and embarrassment.

Travis gently put one hand on the president's right ankle and the other under his knee as he watched Miss Richardson move into position atop her father's chest.

"Full weight," he repeated.

"Okay."

The instant Dan saw her weight settle on her father's chest, he lifted the knee and pushed the ankle back toward the president's buttocks. The hip joint popped back into its socket with a thud, felt only by Dan's hands and in the pit of the president's stomach.

The president let out a gasping scream, more of surprise than of pain. "Shit!" was the only word he uttered. Dan paused to allow his patient to catch his breath. Peeking around Sydney, he asked, "You okay, sir?"

"Yeah!" he replied, grimacing through the pain painted across his face.

"Why didn't you warn me?"

"Didn't want to. You would've tightened up on me, like pullin' a Band-Aid off a hairy arm. Just gotta do it. Expectation is worse than the real deal."

"Gotcha. By the way... Ahh! Shit!" Dan had just repeated the process on the second leg and hip, again without warning. Once again, he felt the joint pop back into its proper place. Beads of sweat were strung across the president's forehead, pearls of pain glistening in the fading sunlight.

Sydney Richardson's head snapped around. Her eyes locked on Dan's with a look of hatred directed at the stranger behind her. Her gaze stabbed the man who had just hurt her father. Her protective instincts overruled the trust that this same man was here to save her father, not to do him harm or cause him pain. She grabbed Dan by the arm. "You hurt him again, and I'll kill you." She spat the words in Dan's face.

Dan immediately reacted to the challenge to his mission. His hand snapped out and grabbed her firmly by the throat. "You get in the way of me getting him out of here alive, and I'll kill you. I'll bury you right next to that guy in your plane and not lose a minute of sleep."

Dan held his grip and her stare until he felt her whole body loosen. He knew that she knew he meant what he said, and he knew it too. He had found his president, and nothing, nobody, would stop him, short of his own death, from completing his mission. Not the mountains. Not weather. Not injury. Nothing. Certainly not this woman.

Chapter Three

"Hold on, you two!" the president shot in to break up the confrontation between his two protectors. "Sydney, that wasn't called for. Sergeant Travis did what had to be done. It was necessary. He wasn't trying to hurt me. The pain was inevitable. Unavoidable. Sydney! Do you hear me?"

"Y... ye... yes... Daddy. I hear you." She began to calm down. Her hand was shaking. Her eyes dropped away from Dan's. Her attention returned to her father, but not before something else happened. Something unsaid. Unspoken. Something between her and Dan Travis.

Never in her life had a man stood his ground with her. Everyone before this had been intimidated by her presence or by the presence in her life of the most powerful man in the world. She could push men around. Threaten them without even trying. But not this one. This one just threatened to kill her, and she knew he meant it.

Travis stood without another word, walked over to his backpack, and removed the lightweight nylon tarp that was the ground cloth for his tent. He spread it out next to the almost naked president. Without any indication of emotion carried over from the encounter just seconds ago, he asked Sydney to help him move her father onto the tarp. Once they had worked together gently to achieve the task, Dan wrapped the tarp around the president.

"Do you think you can get yourself out of those wet clothes, sir?"

"I don't know, Sergeant. I might need some help."

"I'll help you, Daddy," Sydney volunteered, without any challenge in her tone of voice. She was being her father's daughter and nothing more.

Dan continued, "This tarp will keep you warm until I can get you dressed in something else. You were about to ask me something just before I popped your second hip."

"Oh yeah! I was about to ask if you had ever done that before. You know. Fixed a hip."

"Well, sir, I can answer that question honestly now. I've done it twice. Both times within the last five minutes."

They both laughed, not from the humor of the moment, but from the release of the tension. It had been a difficult time for all of them. Sydney laughed, too.

"Mr. President, I'm going to heat some water, wash you down, and get you into something warm and dry. I've got some more clothes in my pack, but not everything you'll need. We'll have to make do with what I've got for a day or two. Then I'm going to cook some supper, feed the two of you and me, and put you two to bed. Tomorrow we've got some talking and deciding to do."

Two hours later, it was done. Hot supper was topped off with hot chocolate. The tent was pitched along beside a roaring campfire. The president was bathed and dressed in Dan's underwear and warm socks and was lying atop his sleeping bag inside the tent with his head peeking out of the open end. Dan had strung up the tarp and stretched it among four trees so that it provided an additional ten-foot-square area of protection from above. The campsite was taking on a decidedly settled look.

While Dan was rearranging his backpack and storing all his supplies, Sydney decided to go back down to the lake and take a bath. She had cleaned herself up earlier, but had not completely immersed herself in the water. Her new sense of security allowed her to wash herself from the top of her beautiful auburn-crowned head to her once brightly polished toes.

When she returned, she was wearing Dan's warm, dry clothes, a hot meal in her stomach, and enjoying a skin that for the first time in days did not itch. She began to relax and accept that she and her father had been found by this stranger, this man who came out of nowhere and assured her that he was going to bring her and her father back to the world they knew and understood, and commanded. She began to accept him in a way strange to her. In a way she couldn't put her finger on. What was it about him?

Dan plopped down in front of the tent, leaned back against a tree, and let out a deep sigh. It had been a long day for him, too. A very long day. He had found the president and his daughter. He couldn't quite believe it. Holy shit.

He had been right. He actually had found the President of the United States and his beautify... lovely... gorgeous... "Hold on, Dan," a little voice in his head told him. "Don't forget who you are, and don't forget who she is, or the guy lying in your tent. Slow down. Get a grip!"

It was almost dark. It wouldn't be long before total blackness took over their little world. Had he completed all his chores for the night? For a moment, the three of them seemed to be listening to the silence falling around them. A sense of peace and safety settled into Don and Sydney Richardson. Without speaking, they both seemed to know they were in the hands of a man who could bring them out of this... adventure... safely and alive.

The president broke the silence. "Well, Sergeant Daniel

J. Travis, what now?" "Well, Mr. President... "

"Hold it, son. Your finding us has, at the very least, prolonged my life, and certainly saved my daughter's. Hopefully, mine too. On top of which, I have a very strong feeling we're going to be out here together for quite a long time before you manage to get us back to Washington. So let's drop the formal bullshit, okay? 'Don' will do fine. And this is my daughter, Sydney. Okay... Dan?"

"Yes, sir. But it might take me a while to get used to it."

"Fair enough. Now, please go on. What were you going to say?"

"Well, Mr. President... '

"Unh-uh," the president corrected.

"Okay," Dan began again. "Well, umm... Don. The first thing is for you two to get some sleep. You need rest and a few solid meals in you to build up your strength."

Hugging her knees, Sydney leaned forward to hear every word. She looked into the eyes of this man seated before her. His face. She examined him as he spoke. Every word. Every sound. Unaware, she was absorbing him and being absorbed by him.

Dan was speaking. "You're not going to be able to walk with those hips for a while. Not more than a few steps at a time at first. You're going to be stiff as a board. We'll start down that road tomorrow. Problem is, I've got enough food in my pack for only a couple more days, and I've got no more clean clothes or sleeping bags with me. My supplies are strapped on the supply skid back where I jumped in.

I figure we're out here for at least a couple of weeks, maybe a month. Totally depends on how you heal up and rebuild your strength. We've got to tough it out until you're ready. If you weren't injured, it would take us less than a week to get out. But,

"Once you're ready, I figure we've got at least fifty to sixty miles to hike and climb to get out to the nearest timber company road of any kind, and there's no telling if there will be any people around when we do. This is a big country out here and pretty damned rough going.

We'll be hiking cross-country the whole way. No trails. No roads. That makes for slow going. If we're lucky enough to find a road, there's no telling how far it will be to a timber camp or a cabin or a town. Even if you're a fast healer and are in really good shape when we finally get started, I figure the best we can expect to do is five to seven miles a day, and that's tough in this country.

"Trouble is that at this latitude, this time of year, it won't be long before it begins to get cold. Real cold. Snow can hit us at any time now. Then we're in trouble. Not as far as making it out or not. It will just take us a lot longer and be a lot tougher."

He hesitated, looking into the two faces studying him. "Go on, Dan. What's your plan?"

"Well, sir, when the Air National Guard dropped me in, they also dropped a couple of thousand pounds of supplies. Everything we need to last as long as we need to. All winter if we have to. I figure I landed twenty, twenty-five miles south of here four days ago."

"Then it was you!" Sydney blurted out. "It had to be your airplane. Why didn't I figure that out earlier? The other Secret Service Agent, Agent Black, he said he saw an airplane. Said he was sure of it. He also thought he saw a parachute. It had to be you. We thought he was seeing things, but he insisted. Said he was sure it was someone coming to help us. To find us and get us out of here. He left two days ago to try and find whoever was coming. It was you."

"Yeah! And it cost him his life. Like I told you, I buried him this morning and tomorrow morning I get to do it again. The agent in the plane needs burying."

"Oh, God!" Sydney sighed, remembering.

"Dear God," the president echoed. Both men had given their lives for their president. They gave their maximum to their duty. The enormity of their dedication hit both father and daughter. Two men had died for them because it was their job.

Dan remained silent while it all sank in. "Sir?" "Yes, Dan."

"Like I was saying..."

"Yes, Dan, go on. Please go on."

"Well, the way I see it, we've got two choices. We stay here, and I ferry supplies from the drop sight, or we move down to the supplies."

"My father can't move," Sydney snapped. "That's out of the question."

"I know that, Miss Richardson. Not now he can't. But we can figure a way to move him in a few days when he's feeling up to it.

"Here's the problem. If I ferry supplies, I've got to go back and forth on a regular schedule. It'll take me at least two days to get to the supply skids. That's if I'm carrying nothing but a rifle. No supplies for myself. Then, once I load up, it will take me at least two, more like three days to get back. And that's if nothing happens, like bad weather moving in.

"That's a four to five-day round trip during which you two will be here on your own. All alone! I should be able to carry enough food and supplies to last us about a week, maybe a day or two more. So that means I'll have to leave again within a couple of days after I get back here. That's what I estimate, assuming good weather. If it rains or snows, it's going to take me longer. And if it snows real hard, I might not make it back in time, if at all.

"We've also got to think about shelter. That tent you're lying in isn't big enough for the three of us, doesn't offer your daughter any privacy, and just isn't going to do the trick if the weather turns real bad. On top of that, we're going to need a waterproof shelter to store supplies in. Weather and animals will take their toll in a hurry if we don't protect them."

"Hold it, Dan," the president interrupted. "You're not a pack mule, and Sydney won't be able to handle everything that might come up while you're gone."

"Dad!"

"Now hang on, Sydney! You're a great gal and very capable, in your world. But face it, sweetheart, this is not your world. You wouldn't have a clue how to handle half the things that might come up out here. Suppose it snowed? Suppose our tent blew down in the middle of the night? Suppose a bear came marching through here looking for a free meal?"

Sydney did not protest. Dan could see the reality of the president's words and the situations they might find themselves in, sink into her mind. "Yeah, I guess you're right, Daddy. Okay, what do you want me to do, Sergeant? Oops! I mean Dan."

"Well, I'll have to make at least one trip back to the supplies no matter what. We don't have enough food or supplies to last long enough to wait for even the earliest possible attempt to move your dad. Even if we tried starting tomorrow, we don't have enough to last us to get there. So I'll leave early tomorrow morning. The sooner the better right now.

"I'll try to blaze the easiest trail I can. Just before I saw Agent Black's body, I had a view of the valley where I landed, and I'm pretty sure I can cut the distance back to the supplies by following a different route. Like I said earlier, I judge that I hiked over twenty miles to get here. If I'm right about a new route back, I should be able to cut that at least in half.

"I'll bring back as much food, dry clothes, and other supplies as I can carry. What I bring back should last us long enough to figure out how and when we'll be able to take the next step. I can also hunt in this area for fresh meat to extend that time. There's more to eat in these woods than you would ever imagine. Hope neither of you has a weak stomach.

"You'll have to work with your dad... Sydney. Get him up and moving. Work out the stiffness. But watch the swelling in his hips. Take it slow and easy, but don't let him lie around or sit too much. That will only prolong the healing process. We'll figure out a schedule to move based on how he feels when I get back. When he's ready, we'll head south to the supplies, find or build better shelter that will give us more protection than a tent. And then we'll just have to wait out the healing process.

"If I have to make additional trips, so be it. We won't be able to tackle the hike out of here until you're able to walk and carry some supplies, Mr. President. The two of us, Sydney and I, won't be able to carry enough for three people. So you've got to work on healing and getting your mobility back. Don't push it too hard. If you hurt yourself, we could be spending Christmas together."

"And then?" Sydney asked, hoping the answer to her question was what her emotions demanded. She needed to hear the words spoken by the man whom she had begun to accept as one who held her life in his hands, one who had the knowledge and skill to survive in the wilderness, this man who was having an effect on her that was completely different from anything she had previously experienced.

"Then we go home," Dan answered. "I promise you it won't be easy, even in the best of circumstances. This ain't gonna be a Sunday walk in the park with your boyfriend. You're going to be cold. You're going to get wet. You're going to do without things you never believed you could do without, and you're going to hate me in the process because I'm going to push you, order you to limits that hurt.

"And if I don't, you'll die out here. But I'll promise you something else. If you do what I ask you to do, don't challenge me every time I ask you to do something, or second-guess me every step of the way; if you'll be real careful and help me as much as you can, I'll get you home, no matter how long it takes us. I'll get you home! I've got to."

"I don't have a boyfriend!" Sydney blurted out for no reason. Her father glanced at her with a puzzled look, wondering why she had erupted with that statement, even though he knew it was true. Then he turned to Dan.

"Why's that, Dan? I understand that you want to get back, but why did you put it that way?"

"I've got to, Mr. President. I made someone else that same promise I just made you."

"Who?" Sydney asked immediately, embarrassed as soon as the words were out of her mouth. "That is, if you don't mind my asking," she added, trying to cover her minor blunder.

Dan hesitated and then spoke thoughtfully. "My daughter, Lucy. Lucy Rose. She lives with her mother, my ex-girlfriend, in Virginia. I had time to talk with her before I left. Just told her I was going on a long trip. She's only six and wouldn't understand what was really going on even if I could tell her. I just promised her I would be back, and nothing will keep me from fulfilling that promise. Nothing. Nobody."

"Sounds good to me, Dan. I'll do my best in the healing department. Just be patient with an old guy like me, okay?"

"And I'll do whatever you think I can to help," Sydney chimed in. "I want to meet this little woman of yours. Anybody who can light up your face the way you just looked? She's got to be a very special little girl."

"Good. And thank you," Dan replied. "Now we'd better get ready to sack out for the night. It'll be black as the inside of a coal digger's a, " he caught himself before he added the ss. The president and Sydney grinned at his near slip up. "A good night's sleep will go a long way toward your being ready for tomorrow. You need to be ready to be alone again, Miss Richardson."

"Sydney," she corrected him.

"Yeah. Okay, Sydney, you sleep in the tent with your dad. There's enough room for the two of you, and it will be warmer. You should be okay with just the one sleeping bag. I'll make do out here. In the morning, we'll get things a bit more organized around here to make it easier for you while I'm gone. I'll try to leave by midmorning. Now, try to get some rest. You both need it."

They followed Dan's instructions without any question. Sydney began to bounce around like a twelve-year-old on a sugar high her first day at summer camp. She seemed to be making a dramatic transition from only a few hours earlier. Trust had been found and accepted in the form of Dan Travis. Food and dry clothes didn't hurt either.

She carefully slid into the tent next to her father, careful not to bump into his newly reset hips. The president spread the sleeping bag in an attempt to share it with his daughter. Within a couple of minutes, they were settled.

Dan policed the campsite for the last time, making sure everything was cleaned and stored in its proper place. He didn't want any tidbits of food left lying around to tempt any unwanted nighttime visitors. It wasn't long before he heard the steady, deep breathing of his two wards, now sound asleep with the assurance of being alive in the morning.

Once he was satisfied with the campsite, Dan walked down to the crashed aircraft. He found the stiff, smelly body of the dead Secret Service Agent and removed it from the plane. He thought it best to take care of this chore now instead of in the morning. The less seen by Don and Sydney Richardson, the better.

He removed all the agent's personal effects and identification, then dragged the body seventy-five yards north, away from the campsite and the lake. He found a good supply of rocks and piled them atop the remains. When the stack was about two feet high, he was satisfied that the temporary grave would keep the body safe from animals, at least for a while. It would be retrieved later.

By the time he was done, it was dark. He made his way back to the campsite, stumbling over rocks and roots the whole way.

His last chore was to find himself a place to sleep. He gathered up some of the tree branches that the president had been lying on when he first found him, sat down next to one of the trees that held up the tarp, leaned back, and pulled the branches over himself. He drew up his knees, dropped his head down, and slept.

Chapter Four

In the mountains, morning comes very early. No artificial environment to drug the senses. No walls of plaster and glass to filter out the sounds of the morning chorus of birds. No forced hot air filled with dust to flood and clog our noses, blocking the sweet, natural aromas of the earth. No cooking fumes or stale cigarette smoke to foul the brain's sensors. Nothing to block our God-given senses from reaching out to touch and be touched by all the living things with whom we share our existence.

The trees live. The birds and animals, the rocks, the water, the air. All those who lived and those still alive. All help each other to continue. To wake up a part of this, to be accepted into the embrace of nature created by His touch, by the mere tip of His finger, can be the most humbling, most exciting experience our minds can encompass. The most rewarding and comforting of all feelings. This is real. This is the way it was in the beginning. Not the four-bedroom, all-brick ranch home with two cars housed at one end.

Sergeant Dan Travis had slept well and rested even better in this, his preferred home. His body and mind were both very tired when he gave in to sleep last night. During his sleep, sometime in the darkness of his mind's resting hours, he had come to accept that he had reached his objective, at least the first part, at least the next to impossible part. With this objective in hand, his mind and body joined in peaceful satisfaction and slept together in perfect unity. He knew survival was the easy part. He knew getting home was going to be work. But he knew he would get them there. He knew his stuff, and this was where he felt most confident.

He woke with a slightly stiff back and a slightly wet rear end. He had slept the entire night in a sitting position, leaning against a tree, a position and skill learned from the Cherokee father of one of his childhood friends, who had taught him much about the mountains. As boys, they would go on overnight hunting trips into the hills with nothing more than some dried fruit and a blanket. When night fell, they would find a tree and sleep as he had done last night. In the morning, they would eat some fruit, drink some fresh, clear mountain stream water, and return to the hunt.

Dan remembered the first time he tried to copy this sleeping position. They were on a hillside in the mountains of North Carolina. When he awoke in the morning, no one was in sight. Panic grabbed his heart and stomach. He jumped to his feet, looking all around him for the others. Had they left him out there all by himself? At last, he saw a path plowed in the leaves. He followed it up the hill to find the others waiting with broad grins embroidered across their faces.

His first attempt to be a Cherokee warrior had fallen short. Never was a word said about the incident until his friend's dad was on his deathbed. Dan was at his side in the moments before he passed away. They shared their own recollection of the event and laughed at each other's version. The sick man laughed as hard as any healthy man might, and died that night with a smile of pride on his face. He was proud of the effect he'd had on Dan's life and proud of the man Dan had become.

Dan began to make breakfast for three without waking the two who so sorely needed the sleep that still cradled them. Being alone gave him the time to enjoy the feeling of self-satisfaction of having succeeded in his mission, and to appreciate the noisy quiet of the morning slowly and softly blooming all around him.

He walked down to the lake with his first canteen cup of coffee, sat down on a big flat rock at the water's edge, and leaned back against a large boulder. The low angle of the early morning sun made the light twinkle and sparkle across the water. It looked like wildly flickering Christmas lights and tinsel. Each breath of fresh mountain air changed the pattern of celebration, welcoming the new morning to earth.

A cup of coffee to warm his insides, the warming morning sunshine wrapping its arms around him to light up his soul... what more could he ask for? He leaned his head back and closed his eyes. He could sleep and be at peace in this embrace, this total peace and beauty. If only...

"Good morning!"

He about came out of his skin, jolting all the way to his feet in one automatic reaction. He whirled around to find the source of the slap his brain had just received. His momentum carried him to the edge of the water, where his feet locked onto an unseen slippery rock that immediately rejected him. He fell backwards, landing on the flat of his ass, feet, arms, and hands now grasping air that would not hold him up. He landed with a splash, coming to rest chest-deep in ice-cold mountain lake water that would not wash away the embarrassment of his flight.

Sydney Richardson stood motionless, except for her jaw dropping, watching the action unfolding in front of her, a startled look on her face, until Dan came to a very wet stop in the middle of a big splash.

Then, uncontrollably, she burst into a laugh. No, not just a laugh, but a total body-shaking, muscle-convulsing, belly-aching, laugh strong enough to knock her legs out from under her.

She fell to her knees on Dan's flat rock, the one still holding his canteen cup filled with hot coffee. She wrapped her arms around her chest and stomach to keep her insides from bursting out onto the rock where they, too, would have burst out laughing. Looking at Dan sitting in the water with an expression of shock, surprise, and embarrassment on his face added more energy to her spasmodic contortions.

The picture of himself finally reflected off her eyes and back into his own, creating an infectious reaction. He began to laugh almost as hard as she, each reaction feeding back to the other until neither one could hardly breathe.

"Hey! What's going on down there?" called a voice from the tent. "You two all right?"

Sydney struggled to reply through her laughter. "Nothing, Daddy. We're okay. Dan just decided to take a quick early morning bath... with his clothes on."

Dan finally got control of himself enough to stand and walk out of the lake. He was slipping out of his wet clothes when he realized he was doing it in front of the daughter of the president, a complete stranger. He stopped and blushed... all over.

"Wait here, I'll get you something," Sydney laughed. "There's a poncho in my pack," Dan said.

Sydney returned with the poncho and a towel. He wrapped himself in the poncho and continued to strip. She turned her back and walked... laughed... her way back to the campsite. Dan arrived a few minutes later to find the president lying partially out of the tent, laughing at his daughter's description of the events at the lakeshore. The event was therapeutic for all of them. At Dan's expense, walking barefoot in the dirt, wrapped only in an army poncho off one shoulder like an evening dress, the tensions of yesterday and events prior to it evaporated. Bonds were forming. Friendship exchanged.

They sat in front of the tent drinking coffee and talking about the days ahead. Dan told them that he had buried the Secret Service Agent last night while they slept. Sydney's gratitude showed clearly on her face. She would not have to witness or be any part of the gruesome necessity.

It was agreed that Dan would leave as soon as his clothes dried. Over the objections of the president and Sydney, Dan told them that he would leave everything behind with them and live off the land for the two days and one night he expected it would take him to reach supplies. He would carry only his poncho, a hunting knife, and a pistol he had taken from the body of one of the agents.

"At the south end of the lake, there's a large stream. I'm certain it's the lake's outlet. When I jumped into the lower valley, I landed less than a hundred yards from a stream about the same size. All the while I hiked along the ridge, I didn't see or cross any other stream like it anywhere. I'm betting they're one and the same. If I'm right, it will be real easy to find my way to the supplies and back. Traveling light will make it easier and faster. So, everything stays here with you two."

"What if you're wrong?" asked the president.

"Then it will take me a bit longer, and I'll be a bit hungrier. But there's plenty to eat out there. The Army sent me to jungle warfare school a few years back and taught me how to survive off the land. Remember the three timelines of survival: Three minutes with no air, three days with no water, three weeks with no food. I think I'll be just fine. I'll have all the water I could possibly need with the stream keeping me company. That's the most critical, as long as I'm still breathing."

"You two have just got to take care of yourselves. Stay dry and warm. If it rains, the tent will give you all the protection you need, and eat. Both of you have to build yourself back up. We're going to have a long way to go once we get going. I'll need you both to be as fit and strong as you can possibly be. So rest... and eat. That's the order of the day."

He showed Sydney how to use the small backpacker cooking stove, how to connect the fuel bottle, and safely light it. He stressed the importance of being careful. These little stoves were an unbelievable piece of engineering, but treated carelessly, they could explode like a bomb. He told her to be sure that the campsite was cleaned up every night before they went to sleep. The smell of any food, just the tiniest bit, would invite unwanted guests, while the smell of humans would ward them off. "I don't want any black bears paying you a visit."

Next, he gathered the extra handguns he had collected from the agents, along with his service 9mm. He wrapped them in a foil food bag emptied from breakfast, and when the president was nodding off and Sydney was busy, he pretended he had to relieve himself and walked off into the woods. Forty or fifty yards from the tent, he stuffed the guns under a large rock.

They would stay dry and out of the way until he got back. And they would stay out of the hands of two people unfamiliar with handguns and their use. Not only were they the most dangerous type of gun, they gave the holder a false sense of security because of their inherent limitations. He didn't want to think of the possibility of having wards trying to hold off a hungry bear with one of these.

By this time, his clothes had dried in the sunshine. He brought them back to the campsite and lightened his load even more by emptying the pockets of everything except a waterproof match case. He would need those to build a fire for warmth tonight. Without a tent or a blanket or a sleeping bag, he would need a fire. Everything else would stay behind. Wallet. Pocket knife. Even the hand warmer that Governor Adams had given him only a few days ago. Gosh, it seemed like a year had gone by already.

"I'll carry my bow with me," Dan said. A last-minute change. "I might need it to eat. And I'll take an empty water bottle so I can scoop up some water when I need it. Everything else stays here. Don't forget, eat good, but don't waste what food you have. Stretch it as far as you can, but don't go hungry. You've got enough food for at least four, maybe five days. I should be back before then. And Sydney, be damned sure you don't throw any leftover scraps anywhere near the camp. Bury them if you don't eat everything. The same goes for dirty dishes and posts. Wash them real good. Don't send out an invitation to a skunk or a bear to come for a treat.

"And by the way, if a bear should come wandering in for some reason, don't get brave. Out here, brave is pronounced stupid. That's S.T.U.P.I.D., and stupid means dead, or badly hurt, which can mean the same thing, only in slow motion." Dan handed over his rifle to the president. "Here, you keep this. But if a bear comes visiting, don't try to shoot it. One shot is not likely to bring it down unless you hit the heart or the brain. If you don't hit either spot, you'll just piss it off and get it real mad.

"Shoot into the air if you have to. Let the noise do the work. If it doesn't leave, just make sure you're not between it and where it wants to go. Don't be brave, just be still. Sit still, stand still, lie still. Whatever it takes. They react to smell and movement, anything that seems to be a threat. Don't forget they're not interested in you. All they want is food. Let it have it. It's okay to be hungry when I get back. It ain't okay to be dead. I found you alive once. I don't want to come back and find you dead. Okay? Lecture over."

It was time to get moving. He got back into his cold clothes. They weren't quite as dry as he thought they would be. He shook hands with the president and attempted to do the same with his daughter. She didn't take his hand. Instead, she wrapped her arms around his neck and kissed him on the cheek. "Good luck, Dan. Hurry back."

Speechless, he turned and started hiking south toward the supply skids, following the lakeshore to the spillway at the south end. But, instead of crossing the stream, he stayed on the west side. He had crossed it twice, once when he had found Agent Black's body, and then again here, at the base of the lake.

He had not crossed the stream during the hike to the ridge west of the valley. So, the supply skids had to be on the west side of the stream. He would follow it down to the valley floor and continue until he felt he was close to where he had landed. Then he would search in a grid pattern until he found the skids.

Or he would find a perch high enough to help him find his target. The concealing underbrush had been burned away by a forest fire, witnessed long ago only by the forest itself. And, he hoped, the flag he had placed in the webbing was still flying bright and high enough to make his search easier.

Once he was past the stream's headwater, the terrain sloped down toward the valley. Without carrying a backpack loaded with gear and supplies, Dan found the hike relatively easy going. The downhill grade wasn't too severe, and he was able to move rapidly without the degree of care necessary when he had a heavy pack on his back.

He was able to find a way that he knew would be reasonably easy for his return trip. He managed to either avoid or plan alternate ways around all major obstacles, marking his trail by breaking small limbs and by placing small rocks in little piles and placing white squares of toilet tissue in just the right places.

He could hear the voice of his Cherokee friend. "Toilet paper, the tool of many uses. Never leave home without it."

He reached the valley floor shortly before dark. Finding a flat area sheltered from the wind, he settled in for the night. By his best estimate, he was only about half a mile away from where he had buried Agent Black.

He carried no food. He had set his mind on not eating until he reached the supply cache. The power of the mind amazed him. Overcoming, even ignoring, the most basic responses to hunger and pain was a fairly easy trick to learn. But he had never quite understood how it worked. He remembered well, too well, how he'd had to control pain in order to survive when he was in the Near East, at times fighting for days without a proper meal.

Not eating was only a mild annoyance. No cooking, no eating, no cleanup meant no time consumed by standard camping chores. The lack of duties stretched the time between dark and sleep.

He walked to the stream that had become his traveling companion and bent to fill his water bottle with the crisp mountain water. He drank half of it to satisfy his thirst and to help fill his empty stomach. Cold, fresh, and sweet, the water satisfied his taste buds and settled him.

Finding a tree to sleep with, Dan draped his poncho around his shoulders to protect himself. It would keep him warm through the high-altitude night and dry from the early morning dew. Knees drawn up, head down, he waited for sleep to join him for the night and to help speed the arrival of morning.

Sleep found him slowly, almost purposefully waiting as sunset and twilight crept slowly over the mountains from east to west, dragging the blanket of darkness behind. This bridge of time in the mountains between day and night is unmatched by any other time in any other place. The constantly changing light and colors can't be captured by any mortal artist. No painting, no photo, no work penned by man or woman, can ever describe the majestic slow-motion artistry of color as the sun kisses its canvas farewell for one more night, only to caress it again with the return of dawn.

When night wrapped its ebony cloak around Dan's shoulders, the subtle shades of twilight were replaced by dense darkness and the mysterious sounds of the night. Countless stars, close enough to touch, attempted to replace the sun, but only etched black shadows on the forest floor. The ridges, trees, and rocks that had reflected colorful beauty moments earlier now gave birth to the sounds of a thousand ghostly night creatures. For each living thing entering the darkness to hunt and to feed, a dozen imagined creatures came to haunt the alien human mind, seeking temporary shelter in their world.

The images of the night, created in the mind of the human alien, came to torment their source. Attackers floated from a tree dressed as leaves. A black wind cuts through garments to bite and wrinkle the alien's skin. The thunderous roar of a killer avalanche emanates from the fall of a pine cone. Footfalls of prehistoric man-eaters disguised as chipmunks crash across the forest floor.

Only in the darkened world are these monsters born in the mind of the civilized intruder. He, who carries an ax and a gun, and a match. Each night, these two would meet. Mountain and man. Darkness and demons. It took this transitional eternity of time between dusk and dark for sleep to arrive, darkness winning out in the end, lecturing the tiny speck resting against a tree.

"You have seen enough for now. I will reveal no more to you this day. I have found you hiding in my bosom of beauty. My magic will put an end to this for now. Rest invader, close your eyes, so you can see me again when I choose to show you more."

With one final blink, the history of another day was written into the land forever. Dawn would tap this man's shoulder only after sleep had finished its work of replenishing his strength.

He woke when first light was announced by the avian chorus. Dan stretched the remains of the night from his muscles, joints, and bones. He stood and stumbled to the creek, where he plunged his hands into the clear, cold water and splashed his face and mind to alertness. Returning to the tree that had supported him through the night, he took up his protective poncho and folded it. Turning south once again, he renewed his trek, aware of, but ignoring, the call of his stomach.

The valley floor was almost flat, making it easy to cross. The burned-out underbrush offered little resistance. The old fire had reached this far and done its damage. Each time he came point with a line of sight to the ridge to the west, Dan looked for a familiar landmark. He had traveled that same ridge only days earlier and hoped he would see something that would orient him to his landing location.

By early afternoon, he found what he thought was the area where he first reached high ground on the first day, but the angle was wrong. He had to go farther. He continued to follow the creek across the valley floor. The creek had flattened and broadened now as it cut its way across the gentle terrain, its voice softened from the roar of yesterday to a soft gurgle and trickle.

Close to four o'clock, he climbed a leafless, burned-out tree to again check the angle to his mark on the ridge. Dammit! It was wrong again, doubly wrong. He had gone too far. He had passed the point that would have lined him up correctly and led him to the skids. He began to back-track, but at a quicker pace. A sense of urgency pushed him. He was afraid that he wouldn't find his objective and waste another night on the trail.

Thirty minutes passed, and again he climbed to check his mark, this time atop a stack of boulders piled nakedly amid the forest green. Bingo, right on the money. It was time for him to head west and play bird dog. He felt sure he was within half a mile of the supplies. All he had to do was sniff them out.

It was almost dark when he stumbled upon one of the skids, actually tripping over one corner of the platform hidden in the darkening shadows. It was as if it had reached out to trip him, saying, "Hold it, stupid. Here I am."

The fear of nearly missing it pumped adrenaline through his body. Regaining control of himself, he flopped down on the ground and let out a very long and very deep sigh of relief. There had been moments in the last hour when he doubted that he would ever find this stuff, both it and he, lost in the wilderness forever. Alien thoughts were closing in with the darkness. It was that time of day again.

He pulled back the protective tarp to find the supplies he needed: lamp, sleeping bag, cook stove, and food. He prepared himself a hot meal, a double portion, stuffing himself to quiet his stomach and washing it down with water from his bottle. After he cleaned up, he found a clear area of soft grass, spreading the poncho and the new sleeping bag on top of it. The night was cool and clear; the moon was almost full. He wouldn't need a tent tonight. No rain would foul his rest. He would sleep under the stars.

The black wind once again surrounded him, but sleep was kinder this night. It found him quickly and closed the book on this day more swiftly than it had on the one before.

Morning didn't come quite as early. The warmth of his new sleeping bag, the tonic of sleeping under the stars, and the drug of a full belly delayed day's return. He prepared another double-portion breakfast meal. It would be his last meal until he camped for the night. While he ate, he made a mental list of the supplies he would need to bring back to the president and Sydney.

Food was the primary item. All he could possibly carry. Clothes. Boots. Medical supplies. Another tent. Two more sleeping bags. A second rifle with a supply of ammunition, an ax, and a hand saw would also be good additions, helpful in gathering firewood or building a shelter. Another bar of soap and a couple of towels wouldn't hurt either. An additional supply of arrows for his bow. He felt that he would need to do some hunting when he got back to the camp and preferred a bow over a rifle.

After breakfast and the mandatory cleanup, he began to assemble the supplies for the return trip. It didn't take long for him to realize that the pile of items he'd pulled from the skid would be impossible to carry. He could justify the need for everything he gathered, but the pile was getting bigger and bigger.

Pulling from the skid. Skid. His mind worked. The skid... a skid... that's it. A skid. An old Indian-style A-frame skid, a travois. That made sense. He could fill a new backpack with as much lightweight freeze-dried food as it would hold, tie a sleeping bag on top and another on the bottom, load the remaining heavier supplies on a skid, and pull and drag it back to the camp. The trail he had marked on his way down was fairly easy, and he couldn't remember any place too rough to pull a load through. Even the slope of the hill up to the lake was compatible with this plan.

He found nylon rope in the mass of supplies on the skid and, within an hour, had the A-frame built and loaded. He even found some web straps and buckles with which to fabricate a shift harness that he could slip over his shoulders and across his chest to pull the load.

He tied everything down and went through a check of his mental list. Satisfied, he strapped on the backpack and slipped into the harness to test the load. To his surprise, the combined load was easier to deal with than he had expected. He pulled more food out and loaded it on top of the A-frame. This would prolong the time between visits to get supplies.

The last thing he grabbed was a new .300 caliber lever-action rifle and four boxes of ammunition, good for hunting medium-sized game. All this done, he cinched up his load and started off toward the creek, marking a trail as he went. He wanted to be able to find his way back without walking past his target as he had yesterday afternoon. By now, it was almost 10:30 a.m.

For the next two days, Dan pulled, tugged, dragged, lifted, pushed, carried, and swore at his load, determined to get the entire load back to the downed aircraft and the President of the United States, waiting alone in the wilderness with his only child. Late in the morning of the third day, he found himself thrashing through the underbrush at the very top of the slope, giving way to the high valley lake. He felt sure he could reach the campsite well before dark.

Part V

Unwelcome Guests

Chapter One

Dan paused to catch his breath. He'd found out that he wasn't in as good a shape as he thought after two days of hauling supplies. But the pains and aches in every muscle had worked their way through his body early in the second day, and his wind had improved dramatically. He now felt his body hardening again with each yard.

When he stopped to rest, the noise of the leaves and twigs crunching beneath his feet stopped. Quietly leaning back against a tree, his ears perked to a familiar sound, a sound that his mind associated with pain and fear.

The dull, flopping thuds popping in his ears struck a raw nerve in his memory. His body twisted from the pain of the recollection. He automatically stood to defend and hold his ground, controlling his instinct to take shelter and hide. He studied the sound, the sound of war that came rushing at him, flooding his senses. What was it? Had he flushed a covey of quail? No! The beat... the rhythm... so regular... so mechanical.

Mechanical! His fear gave way to a rush of excitement. Mechanical! Helicopter! The blades of a helicopter were slapping the mountain air somewhere overhead and not too far away. But where? From which direction did the sound initiate before it bounced from hillside to hillside? Could those aboard see him? Were they even looking for him and the others? Had help arrived?

A minute later, it was gone. The deafening silence of being alone again returned. The chirping of the birds and the hiss of a light breeze brushing the hanging leaves aside returned. Head down, feeling abandoned, Dan lifted his load and started off again to return to President and Sydney Richardson.

Two hours later, he was less than half a mile from camp. He was tired, but he knew he was almost there and that his day was almost over. He stopped to catch his breath one more time. The disappointment of the disappearing helicopter had sapped his energy.

So close to being found. If only he could have signaled somehow. If only he had had a radio. He decided to drop his pack and harness and dip his head into the cold lake water. One last splash to refresh him, to provide the needed energy for the final push.

Dan walked to the lakeshore, dropped to his knees, and plunged his head into the clear liquid, a lungful of exhaled air boiling the water around his face. Refreshed, he stood up, head hanging to allow the water to drip away. With a whip of his neck, he flipped his hair to the rear. He now stood staring out across the lake. His heart skipped a beat.

"Son of a bitch! It's the chopper!!" he announced to the trees surrounding him.

There it was, floating on the lake on pontoons. It was tied to a tree stump near the tail section of Sydney's downed twin-engine.

He ran back to the supplies he'd left on the ground. He lifted the backpack to strap it on when his mind clicked into gear. Help, rescue, was only a few hundred yards away. He lowered the pack to the ground, picked up his two weapons, the rifle and the bow, and began to jog toward the campsite. Leaving the weapons behind was totally unacceptable to a man with his military training.

He started out at a rapid trot known fondly at Fort Bragg, North Carolina, and Fort Campbell, Kentucky, as the "airborne shuffle." In a few short minutes, he reached a point where it would be faster for him to go over a small hill that would bring him in from the wooded side of the camp instead of from the lake side. He would have followed the flatter path along the lake had he still been carrying the heavy load of food and supplies.

He reached the crest of the hill and started down the other side. About seventy-five yards from the tent, he came to a spot where he had a clear view of the camp through an alley among the trees. He stopped to catch his breath. He could now see the president and his daughter, circled by six men. Their rescuers.

Two of the six were wearing jumpsuits. Must be the pilot and co-pilot of the helicopter. The other four were wearing black pants and black windbreakers. All were carrying sidearms. One was carrying a rifle and looking back toward the south end of the lake, as if standing guard or protecting something.

The president was lying on the ground at the front of the tent with Sydney on her knees, bent over him. Three of the men dressed in black stood over them.

Dan placed his rifle and bow against a rock, cupped his hands around his mouth to direct his voice toward them. He was about to yell an announcement of his return to those who had come to help. The words formed in his mind, but never escaped his throat.

He choked on them as he saw a second man from the rescue team lean forward and slap Sydney Richardson, first forehanded, then quickly retuning the stroke, he swung and hit her a second time backhanded, knocking her face-down to the ground. He grabbed her by the shoulder, lifted her, and slapped her again, knocking her backward until she landed on her butt.

"What the fuck!" The words slid quietly through his lips. His first instinct was to yell out for the man to stop hitting her. Instead, his methodical combat training took over. The training and survival skills of war snatched the sound from his throat. Silence is best. Sound kills. He slithered to the ground, taking up his rifle and bow, and crawling on his belly until he was behind a large fallen tree where he had a clear view of the scene below.

Sergeant Travis peeked over the top of the tree trunk to see the same man slap Sydney again as he screamed into her face. Dan could not understand the words, but it was obvious that he was threatening her with harm.

She was crying. The president said something. The man turned, drew his pistol, and aimed at the president's head, again screaming words that Dan could not quite make out, but whose meaning was very clear.

He would have to get closer. He looked from side to side, searching for a route that would keep him concealed, hidden from this newfound, unknown enemy. The two men in flight uniforms had moved about twenty yards away from the slapping scene. They were now closer to the shoreline, where their aircraft was tied up.

With the man guarding the trail, there were now three men by the lake and three hovering over the president and his daughter. Dan could not see any others. Six. The total was six.

"They're expecting me to walk right in through the front door!" Dan thought. He instantly moved to his left, away from the lake-approach to the camp, toward the back door. He would find it, open it, and kick some ass.

Sergeant Travis now moved closer to his target, keeping as flat to the ground as possible. Creeping from tree to tree, rock to rock. He reached the stream that ran alongside the campsite. The soft, soggy ground on its banks helped him move in almost complete silence until he could see the entire area clearly and could hear the words of the men nearby.

"Where is he?" the man shouted.

"We told you. He went for help," the president answered. "He said he'd be back in a week with a doctor and men to help carry me out to a road or a plane."

"Bullshit!" the apparent leader yelled. "He got dropped in with over a ton of supplies. He wouldn't leave you here like this, without food and water to last at least a month. He's a Boy Scout. Too stupid to stay home. Now! I'll ask you one more time. How long has he been gone? When's he due back?"

"We don't know," Sydney sobbed.

There was a large, thick fir tree with low-hanging branches only a few feet from where Dan now lay.

"Bullshit, lady! He's a soldier. The true-blue, salute-the-flag kind of shithead. He's not gone. He's on a mission. He wouldn't leave his Commander-in-Chief lying here in the woods now, would he?"

A rocky outcrop a few feet beyond the fir tree.

"Now, when is he coming back? Today? Tomorrow?

Can't be beyond the next day."

A thicket of small cedar trees beyond the rocks.

"He's dead. If you tell me now or wait till he comes prancing down the trail. Either way, he's dead."

The camp lay just beyond that. "And so are you, Miss rich bitch!" He crawled to the rocks.

"And so's your fuckin' old man..."

Dan stood.

"... The mighty Mr. President."

He nocked an arrow to the bowstring.

"He'll never see either of you again..."

Drew it back slowly until the string touched his lips. "It's over for,"

It was the last sound his foul mouth would utter for all of time. Dan's arrow cut through windbreaker, shirt, skin, ribs, heart, and backbone without even slowing down. The impact surprised the target. He couldn't talk. The shock and surprise halted everything, including his life. His eyes went dead before the forest floor caught his body.

The two men standing near the dead man reached for their sidearms. Shock and fear dressed their faces with a new mask. They couldn't tell from which direction the arrow had come. Arrows are silent. Arrows don't leave a puff of smoke to reveal the archer's hiding place. But arrows scare the shit out of a man. A primeval fear right down to the gut.

Modern men at war in the jungles or in the streets are taught to duck and dodge the crack of a rifle or a pistol, or a machine gun. But an arrow, a primitive, slashing shaft of razor-sharp steel slung so silently, so secretively, through the air. An arrow, with no loud clap or bang to warn you of its coming. It doesn't hit you with the impact of a bullet, doesn't lift you off your feet, doesn't knock you backwards like a punch hitting you: it just cuts. Without warning, it's there, slicing the meat you call your body, sticking in you, violating you, and mincing your innards.

The two men twisted in every direction, trying to locate the source of the silent killer. But fear anchored their feet. Dan remained still, almost invisible in his camo fatigues. Only if he moved would they see him. He picked an instant when both were looking away from him. He stood, nocked another arrow, and took aim. The two targets had not yet uttered a warning to the men down by the lake. Stunned and confused, saving their own lives was their sole focus.

Dan let loose the bowstring, and the second arrow flew to its mark. Striking the man standing closest to the president, it pierced his chest with a thud.

"He's back!" the third man yelled to his comrades by the lake. "The fucker's back. He just killed Owens and Green." His cry was filled with panic. But the damned fool hadn't moved from his spot near his dead companions. The man guarding the trail and the two pilots came running toward the campsite, weapons in hand.

Dan let loose a third arrow, and it too struck home. Three men lay dead around Donald and Sydney Richardson. He was on his knees near the cedar trees. The three remaining men had not yet seen him. All they saw was three dead bodies, each with a hole gushing blood in his chest and the grin of death on his face.

"What the hell?" the fourth man wearing a windbreaker said to the corpses staring sightlessly at the puffy white clouds overhead or with mouths agape, trying to suck up the mossy forest floor. His head swung from side to side, his eye seeking to find a sign of the killer who stalked him.

"Where are you!" he shouted in his spinning search for any movement that would reveal the killer of his comrades, the spoiler of their mission of treason. "Where the fuck are you, you son of a bitch? Show yourself!"

Frustrated and tense, he started firing his weapon at every bush and tree within range. To his right, to his left, behind him, and in front. Then silence. He was out of ammunition. The only sound was Sydney lying on the ground, curled up in a ball of fear next to her father, sobbing as she tried to absorb the chaos around her.

"Get the chopper going," the man in black barked at the confused crew. "Get the fuckin' thing started." The puzzled men began to back slowly away toward the lake. A couple of stumbles, and they turned and ran to fire up the floating transport. The scene that had unfolded before them was not what they had either expected or signed on for this mission for. They were pilots, not killers, not soldiers.

The windbreaker put the muzzle of his reloaded weapon to Don Richardson's head. "Come out! Show yourself, you bastard, or I'll blow his fuckin' head off right now." His eyes darted from tree to bush, bush to rock, rock to tree. His very own personal forest monster was hidden somewhere in front of him, close enough to smell. "Now, you bastard. Now or he's dead, and the bitch goes next!"

Dan Travis held fast. He froze himself. Not a muscle could be allowed to move. Not an eyelash. He watched the man's eyes. The eyes would tell him what he wanted to know. The eyes would tell him when to act. Less than fifty yards away, yet a million miles. He knew that if he showed himself, he, the president, and Sydney Richardson would all be dead.

He heard the whine of the helicopter motor being turned by its powerful starter batteries. He used the noise to cover his next move. He laid his bow down and picked up his rifle. He slowly raised it to his shoulder and aimed. He had to get a clear shot. A kill shot. An instant kill. Anything else, anything allowing another second of life to the traitor, would sentence the president to a bullet in the brain.

The chopper engines fired. The man blinked, reacting to the noise. Dan saw the eyes move. Dan's finger moved with them. The bullet entered the man's brain slightly above and behind his left ear. The entire right side of his head exploded in a red mist, falling to the ground like lumpy oatmeal. The body stiffened, every muscle contracting, and fell slowly, landing on top of the brain matter it had just lost, trying to gather it up to live another fraction of a minute.

The helicopter pilot saw the last man go down. He revved his engines to lift the aircraft off the lake. Travis jumped out from among the cedar trees and ran to the president.

"Are you all right?" "Yeah, Dan, we're okay."

Travis looked down at Sydney. She was as white as snow. He jumped over the dead bodies and ran toward the lake, coming to a sliding stop at the waterline in under three seconds. The helicopter had just cleared the surface, water pouring off the pontoons. The pilot glanced toward Dan. Their eyes locked for an instant that felt more like a lifetime. Travis raised his rifle, took aim, and fired, rapidly squeezing off four rounds. The pilot's face went blank, and his eyes rolled back. With the last shot, his head erupted like a smashed cream puff slapped with the flat of a hand on a hard tabletop.

The cockpit filled with a bright pink haze. The chopper yawed violently to the right, showing its soft underbelly. It slipped along the lake's width, but it did not climb, pitched over further and further until the clear lake water reached up and grabbed the main rotor blade. It continued to fly under the surface until a bright flash burst it into little pieces. Bits of metal and flame flew into the air until each was sucked down into the lake and slid hissing beneath the surface.

Within minutes, the lake's face was smooth again, hiding all traces of the helicopter and crew. Only a slight wisp of smoke drifting off to the east testified to the prior existence of man and machine.

Sergeant Dan Travis stood by the lake as the chaos around him, and in him, subsided, until the mountains absorbed the unnatural noise. When the sound and smoke had been sucked up and peace had returned, he realized he was trembling.

From the first arrow to the last shot to the peace and quiet of the mountain valley had taken less than five minutes. Six earthly lives gone. Ended for all time. They would haunt the mountains, here alongside this quiet lake, forever.

His shoulders suddenly sagged under the emotional and physical load. His head dropped, his chin on his chest. His rifle was suddenly too heavy to lift above his waist. He turned and slowly and dragged his feet back to the two lives he had extended at the cost of six others. President Richardson was trying to calm his daughter, just for the moment, again, his little girl, curled up next to him with her head buried in his lap, searching for safety.

She was crying, sobbing uncontrollably. Killing sucks, Dan thought. It sucks the life from the living as well as from the dead, only tomorrow is different.

"You all right?" the president asked. "Yeah."

"What happened?"

"I fired at the front of the chopper, at the cockpit. Must have hit the pilot. The chopper pitched over; he flew it right into the lake. It exploded right after it hit. Nothing left of it. Neither of them could have gotten out alive."

There was a long pause. Both men were exhausted. Each for his own reasons. Each from his own participation in the events of the past few minutes, each knowing that he had been a blink away from death. Neither knowing why.

The only sound was Sydney's sobs. The little girl in her grasping for the protection of her father's embrace, his arms the only comfort she needed. His tender touch calmed his frightened, trembling child.

"What now, Dan?"

Dan was jerked back to the present by the question. His lungs expelled all their air in a deep sigh, as if to blow away the past half hour like the candles on a birthday cake. Dan looked into the blue sky, searching for an answer to what had just happened, and wondering what to do next.

"Just, Sydney, calm down. I've got a lot to do. I'll get rid of these bodies, try to find some I.D. on 'em. Clean up this mess. Try to figure it out.

"I've got supplies down the trail a short way. I've got to get them up here before dark. Got to get a handle on what the hell is going on here."

Don Richardson could hear the stress in Dan's voice. He knew this young man had the weight of the world on his back, that he'd found himself in a situation beyond anything he could ever have imagined.

"Okay. I'll take care of Sydney. Dan, I'm sorry I can't help you with... with... "

"Yeah, I know. Not to worry. It's okay. I'll take care of it. Ain't exactly what either one of us planned, is it? Thanks anyway, Mr. President."

"Dan?"

"Yes sir."

"What the hell happened here?"

"I don't know. I sure wish I did. This didn't just happen. This was planned. These ain't no hunters who just happened to bump into us while out in the woods looking for deer. This ain't no dueling banjos movie. No, sir, this was planned."

"But why? Who's behind it?"

"Mr. President, I'm just a lowlife G.I. I don't play in the same circles as you. I'm afraid the answer to your question is with you, not me. I don't get paid enough to have answers to that question. But I'll bet you one thing. I don't think these guys came out here to do my ass in. Not unless GMAC Finance is a lot more pissed off about a late car payment than I ever thought they'd be. No, sir, they ain't here after me."

"You're right, Dan. Well, we'll have to figure it out. I'll need your help. Be careful, Dan."

"Yes, sir. You'd better keep her eyes covered until I can get this cleared out," he said, pointing to the bodies on the ground.

One by one, Dan dragged the dead men, the men he had killed, away from the default home of the president. One by one, out of sight, and, he hoped, out of the mind of this sobbing young woman. He found a depression once occupied by the roots of a fallen tree. The uprooted stump had left a hole large and deep enough for him to pile the bodies in.

He searched each man's clothing: every pocket, waistband, and even inside their boots. Nothing. These guys came here sterile. No I.D. Ready for something to happen. Ready to deny their own existence.

Once he had finished, he covered the bodies the best he could with loose dirt, rocks, limbs, and leaves, marking the grave so he was satisfied that he could find it again. Finished, he returned to the campsite and found Sydney calmed and resting, beautiful, even though her eyes were still puffy from crying. She looked up at him, the veneer of the hard-headed modern woman erased by the day's events, the tender, soft, scared little girl within fully exposed. Even in her vulnerability, the directness of her gaze unsettled him.

"You two okay?" Dan asked sheepishly. The president nodded his head.

"Dan?"

"Yes sir?"

"Who did this? Who's responsible for this?"

"I don't know, sir. Like I said before, I'm just a grunt. I'm not in the pay grade to play in this league. I guess we'll have to figure it out when we get back to D.C."

"If we get back."

"No, sir. When we get back, I'll get you back, come hell or high water. I promised you that. Besides, I just wasted half a dozen guys, and I don't even know why. I buried six guys in the past week, and there are two more strapped into that helicopter. That's not something that makes me happy."

"But they wanted to kill you too," the president said, trying to relieve Dan of any guilt for his actions.

"Yes, they did. And that flat pisses me off. I'm okay with what I did. I've had to do it before. But I knew why. I knew who the enemy was. But I don't know who these guys were, and that pisses me off, too.

"And somebody owes me. This started out as a rescue mission. I found you, just as I knew I could. Now I find myself in the middle of another war right here in my own country. Right here where I camped and hunted as a kid. Not halfway around the world in some stinking desert. Some son of a bitch is trying to take my head off right here. Believe me, I'll get you back home, Mr. President. Yes, sir, I'll get you home, you can count on it."

Chapter Two

Sergeant Travis hiked back to where he had dropped the supplies he'd carried from the drop zone back up to the crash site. He returned within an hour to find Sydney sitting next to her father, holding his hand and talking to him softly. Her composure had returned.

Hungry and exhausted, Dan went about preparing a hot meal. There was little conversation while they ate. By the time he was finished cleaning up, it was dark. Sydney had fallen asleep with her head in her father's lap.

The president had leaned back against a tree and also fallen asleep, his hand on his Sydney's shoulder, protecting his child from the events of the day. The long hours had ordered sleep to overtake these children of the forest, sleep to allow for the healing of their minds.

Dan took a sleeping bag from the new supplies, unzipped it, and spread it over Sydney and her father. Next, he covered them with a poncho to keep the early morning moisture away. And before giving in to the

aches in his own mind and body, he found a sleeping bag and poncho for himself.

By the time the beautiful young woman and her powerful father awoke, Dan had a hot pot of coffee ready. They were both stiff and sore from having slept in an unconventional position, but they were well rested. Sydney bounced around the campsite with the spark and sparkle of new determination.

They were starved. The mountain air had done its magic, soothing their minds, calming their emotions, sharpening their senses. Dan and Sydney prepared a hearty meal of freeze-dried coffee with freeze-dried eggs topped off with freeze-dried bacon, and canned bread. Damn, it was great! Tasted as if it had been delivered by messenger from a gourmet restaurant on Pennsylvania Avenue. They stuffed themselves until they couldn't move.

Another cup of coffee, and Dan and Sydney cleaned up the entire campsite to erase all traces of human presence. Sydney picked up the water bottles and headed to the lake to fill them. Dan took the opportunity to address the president.

"Mr. President, we've got to talk."

"I know, Dan. Wait until Sydney gets back. And would you please call me Don now?"

"Yes, Don. Listen, I don't think Sydney should be part of this just yet."

The president hesitated. "Okay, Dan. But she's not going to be excluded easily. Not for long. She's a strong-minded woman, and she obviously knows something's up."

"Yes, sir, I know. But after what she went through yesterday, and the way I saw her break down, I'm afraid of how she might react to, "

"Bullshit!"

Both men jerked in reaction to the loud voice coming from the nearby trees.

"What are you doing?" asked the president.

"I forgot one of the water bottles. As I was saying, Sergeant, bullshit!"

"Sydney!" her father protested her language. "Miss Richardson..."

"Oh! So we're back to that, are we? Look, you two, what happened yesterday shook me up." She looked from one face to the other. "Who wouldn't have been shaken up? But if you think you're going to keep me in the dark and out of whatever comes next, you're both out of your fucking heads."

"Sydney!"

Dan saw the president struggling to hide a grin that was fighting its way to his face. He was hoping for some direction from the president. Finally, it came.

"Dan, I may be your Commander and Chief, but I'm not in a very good position to be either. Looks to me like

you're going to need some help, all you can get, no matter what we come up with. And as for my daughter, the one with the foul mouth... well, I think that what you see is what you get. You'll have to deal with it."

Searching for the words to deal with the beginning of a dangerous passage in their lives, Dan stood and turned toward the lake to buy himself more time. Deep in thought, he did not see two sets of eyes following every step he took, watching and waiting for him to decide their next move. He knew that if they were to survive, it would be up to him. He would have to come up with a plan and carry it out.

He turned back toward his primary task. Looking at both of them, he slowly walked back to the coffee pot and poured himself another cup.

"All right. I guess I don't really have much of a choice." He turned toward Sydney. "How old are you?"

"What?"

"How old are you?"

"Why?" she asked guardedly. "Just tell me. How old are you?"
"Twenty-eight."

"And you, Mr. President?" Fifty-nine Dan. Why?"

Dan looked Sydney Richardson straight in the eyes. He moved within inches of her face and put his finger in front of her nose.

"He's the only one here who's got to get to his next birthday. He's why I'm here. He's my mission. You just happened to be flying that plane. I don't give a shit if you see thirty or not. You get in the way of me getting him home alive and in one piece, and I'll bury you with those clowns back there in the trees. You and I are expendable; he's not. So don't get in my way. Don't get sick. Don't get hurt. Don't even break a fuckin' finger nail."

He held his stare to deepen the impact of his words. His speech was measured and firm; he meant every word of it. She returned his stare with growing determination and resolve. She searched for the right words. Her brain gave her mouth three false starts. Finally, it came. "Sergeant Travis."

"Yeah!"

"Fuck you!"

She staggered to her feet and walked off toward the lake, water bottles in hand. Dan and her father watched until she was out of sight.

"Do you think you scared her enough, Dan?"

"Don't know, Mr. President, but it sure scared the shit out of me. But I got exactly what I was looking for: her determination," he said, a broad grin breaking across his face.

"Had to say it to her, sir. She's got to know this is serious and that there's tough going ahead. It's going to be real rough going before we get out of here... and, I'm afraid, even after that."

"You're right, Dan. But I think after yesterday, she's got a pretty good idea of what's ahead."

"Maybe. But I don't think so. We may see the same damned thing thrown at us again. I wish I knew. She was in a sort of shock after what happened yesterday. Seeing men killed and die right in front of you for the first time plays tricks with your head. A kind of fog moves in, trying to protect you, block your view of what's happening.

"When you realize how close you were to dying, how easy it would have been to die, your mind tries to hide behind that fog. No, sir, she wasn't ready for that, and I'm not sure she's ready yet, or ever will be. I hope she never has to become ready. However, I can't tell you what's ahead. But I can tell you one thing for sure, there's more of something ahead."

"She'll do okay, Dan. She's never let me down."

Dan studied the president's face for a few seconds. "Then tell me when was the last time was that she watched her father being pistol-whipped! Tell me the last time she saw a half dozen men die in front of her. Tell me the last time she had dead bodies bouncing on the ground all around her. Tell me the last time she saw all of that within a few minutes. Tell me that, and then I'll tell you she's ready."

Sydney was walking back up the incline from the lake just as Dan ended his lecture. The water bottles were dripping cool, clear mountain lake water down the sides of her legs. Dan couldn't help being taken, even now, even under these circumstances, with her beauty. She was, in his eyes, perfect.

She sat down next to her father, crossed her legs under her, and asked, "Okay, what's next, Sergeant?"

"Dan."

"What?"

"It's Dan."

They looked into each other's eyes as something passed between them: an understanding, a bond, a new status of equality, of interdependence, of closeness. Her father watched and knew exactly what was happening, far more so than did Sydney Richardson and Daniel Travis.

"Okay, Dan," she said, with a new softness to her voice. "What's next? What do we do now?"

"Well, Ms. Sydney," he said mockingly, "we start packing and get our butts out of here. I've got a plan that will get us home all in one piece and alive."

"But Dan," the president protested. "I can't just jump up and walk out of here. Not yet. I just can't. I'm sorry, but I'm not able to do that." He paused, but he wasn't finished.

"Dan, I've been thinking too. I think you should get us set up with supplies. Food and clothes mainly. You've already brought everything else we would need, sleeping bags, a tent, and other stuff. And we've got all the water we could ever need. If you bring up more food, we can be safe and comfortable for quite a while. Then I think you should leave us here and hike out to find help. Bring others back with you and get us out."

"No, sir. No way!"

"Why not?"

"No, sir, can't do it."

"Why not?" Sydney joined in.

"For a number of reasons."

"Like what?" she insisted.

"Well, for one, how much food is enough? I'm not even sure exactly where we are. How far we are from help. How long would it take me to get out, or if I could get back here and find you again? That took some doing the first time. I ain't too sure I want to try it again.

"Two, if anything happened to me while I was hiking out, you're dead. No one else knows you're here, and I don't think you'd make it out on your own.

"Three, winter's coming. And up here in these mountains, at this altitude, it can come at any time, and it can come fast. Snow deep enough in one day to bury you. Canadian air is so cold, sap-filled trees explode.

"And most of all, I don't know who those guys are." He flipped a finger over his shoulder to point at the spot where he buried the men who had obviously come to do all of them harm. "I don't know who they are. I don't know where they came from. I don't know who sent them, and I sure as hell don't know how they found us. I don't know if they have friends. For all I know, there's another chopper full of those guys in the air right now getting ready to land on the lake, or there's a bunch of them trudging up through the woods trying to get here in time for a hot lunch.

"No, sir, I don't go anywhere without you two, and we're leaving soon. The first thing my plan calls for is to get you as far away from this area as I can get you, as fast as I can. So ready or not, like it or not, we're leaving real soon. I want to be out of here in no more than two hours."

All the while he was talking, the pressure and anxiety inside him were building. The enormity of his task, the killings of the day before, the need to get moving away from this site, the whole mess building up to his being here, the days, weeks ahead, the lives of the President of the United States and his only child now in his hands, all of this welled up within him and vented through his spoken words. He was a teapot on a hot fire.

"You're nuts!" Sydney shot at him. "My father can't walk out of here. He can't even stand up."

"I'm not asking him to."

"Then just what the hell are you asking him to do?" "Nothing. I'm going to carry him out."

"You are nuts! Just how the hell do you think you're going to do that? How the hell do you think I'm going to be able to help you with this goofy idea? Or do you think I'm just going to wait here while you play your dumb little game of soldier?" Her voice grew louder with each question. Her face flushed pink, neck veins popping.

"Sydney," her father warned.

"Look, I'm not too damned happy about the situation either. Yesterday didn't do much for me. I don't look forward to killing people; it sort of upsets the hell out of me. But it does tell me that we've got to get out of here. I can feel it in my gut, and my gut has kept me alive more than once. So we leave in two hours. Besides, I'm tired. Real tired. And I won't rest until we get away from here."

"Big fucking deal... two hours... two days... what the hell..."

That was as far as she would go. Dan's left hand snapped out and grabbed her by the throat. His right hand snatched his 9mm automatic from its holster, with his thumb instinctively cocking back the hammer in a move fast enough to make Wyatt Earp smile. The pressure of the muzzle under her chin bulged her eyes out.

"Look, bitch! You got the mouth of a garbage truck and the personality of my last bowel movement. Now, I've told you this once already, so this puts you way over quota. He's the only thing that counts. He gets out or I die trying. And if I die, so do you because this ain't a place you can ring up room service and order up some bellhop to carry your bags.

"It's him, and only him. You get in my way, even slow me down, and that Playboy chest of yours will be the new home for a pine tree, cause I'll plant your ass right here. So like I said before, don't get sick, don't get hurt, don't break a fingernail, don't even sleep late.

"Now! You've got one hour and fifty-eight minutes to get your butt ready to do what I say, when I say it, or die right here, right now and save me from having to put up with your foul mouth and shit personality. Those guys back there died for a reason. Something they believed in. I don't know what it was or why they believed so hard, but they died for it anyway. Unless you're ready when I say to be ready, you're gonna die, because you made a mistake. You thought you were important. You're wrong, little girl. He's important. All you are is a big pain in my ass. A lump of dead weight."

He meant every word he spoke, and she knew it. Her face was ashen. The shock of looking into the eyes of a man who could and would end her life in a blink had drained every ounce of blood from her face. She could hardly breathe. She flinched when Dan lowered the hammer of his pistol back into its seat, and with a flick of his wrist, flipped her head to the side in a casual dismissal, like tossing an empty beer can into the trash. He turned and walked away.

Sydney didn't realize it, but she had just passed through an intersection, a crossroads, in her life from which she would never return. Dan had just slapped her into a new reality. She was not the center of the universe. He would have killed her to save the President of the United States, who just happened to be her father. He would have killed her to save his mission. He could kill her in a blink, and he would.

She slumped to the ground, feeling as if she had been hit by a truck, her knees weak and rubbery. It took her almost an hour to recover. Her father didn't say a word to her. He knew Dan was right, but it was his daughter who had been threatened. He was helplessly caught in the middle of a struggle between two people trying to do the best they could for him, each in their own way, and, in this situation, Dan was, had to be in charge.

Besides, there wasn't a thing he could do. Unable to walk, having been at the door of death, saved by this man who had been thrust into his life and in whose hands he now found not only his life, but that of his beloved daughter, he could do nothing. President of the United States, Commander and Chief of the mightiest military force in the world, leader of the free world, and all the other bullshit lines used to describe him and his office are meaningless. He was entirely dependent on a man he didn't know. One dedicated to his mission. One who had just threatened to kill his daughter! And whom he had begun to respect more and more with each passing hour.

Two hours later, they were on their way. Dan had built a second A-frame. The one he had dragged up from the valley was now loaded with supplies and rigged for Sydney to pull. The second one, longer and built with heavier wood to support a heavier load, now held the president and the remaining supplies. At least the first part of the trail would be downhill, making the job possible and easier for both of them.

Dan policed the campsite. There was little sign of humans having been there. Only the graves gave away the violation. His plan was simple: drag the president as far in one day as daylight and his energy would permit. He would continue day by day until they reached the main supplies.

Once they reached the supplies, they would rest for a day or two. Then they would start off again, re-supplied with food and other items he thought they would need.

He would then drag the president two days beyond the supplies, stop, set up camp, and leave the president and Sydney there to rest while he returned to the supplies to reload once again. Using this shuttle plan, he would ensure that they were always in possession of enough food, supplies, and equipment to deal with whatever might come along.

Simple. Sounded good. He knew it would be neither, and it wasn't. The hills he had climbed only a day or two earlier suddenly got much steeper, more rocks had grown out of the forest floor, and more trees appeared in the middle of this trail. Dragging nearly two hundred pounds, most of it a human being, was much harder and required much more care than did just a load of supplies.

With each step forward, it felt as if I took one sideways to avoid some obstacle. He tugged and pulled and stumbled hour after hour. He could not gauge their rate of travel or the distance they had covered. All he knew was that his instinct was telling him to get away from the wreckage of the plane and the turmoil they had left behind.

Please God! Don't let it rain. Not now. Not until we reach the supply cache. His prayers were answered. No rain!

It took six days.

Six days. Each meal is a delay, each night a black barrier with no way to avoid it, no bridge over it, and no detour around it. Each stop to rest meant the agony of muscles trying to find a moment of comfort, each night's sleep restless with the dreams of the next day, and the fear of what they had left behind.

Sydney Richardson rose to the occasion. As if a different person, she hiked and carried her pack and dragged her load the entire way without complaining. She helped Dan wherever and however she could. She seemed to recognize his burden, realized the seriousness of what was happening, and came to grips with the life and death aspect of what was taking place, and the fact that she and her father were at risk and dependent on this man who was fighting so hard to save them.

She tried to share his burden by helping pitch camp, cook meals, clean up their campsites, and re-pack supplies and gear each morning. They had become a team. She was his partner. She talked with him. Asked him to show her how to do the things that were necessary for them to keep going. She even laughed with him when they rested and sat around a fire each night.

The president was exhausted at the end of each day. The pain, the bouncing, and the effort to hold onto the frame that Dan had built sapped his energy. He wanted to walk and carry his own load of supplies. His pride was hurt from needing to be dragged and carried like a load of meat. He tried not to complain, knowing how hard it was for Dan.

He was awed by this man of endless energy, Sergeant Daniel Travis. His determination was staggering. Dan was not a big man, owning a storehouse of muscular strength. It was his inner strength, his will, his conviction that set him apart. It was this that impressed the president beyond anything he had ever observed in any other men.

He was deeply impressed with this young soldier, and he liked and respected him more each day. He watched Dan, trying to learn from him, to see what he was made of. He saw his daughter accepting him in a way she had never accepted anyone, including her own father. She drew closer to Dan each day. He saw it develop, and he like what he was seeing.

They reached the supply skids around noon on the sixth day. Dan immediately set about pitching new tents. His request to the heavens had been answered. The rains had held for the six days, but there were heavy black clouds moving in from the southwest, and he could hear the rumbling of distant thunder bouncing its way through the mountains and rolling toward them.

The clouds held their heavy load of water long enough for Dan and Sydney to prepare a hot meal. The three of them were able to duck into their tents just in time to avoid the downpour. They ate in their tents, trying to talk or yell to each other over the din and roar of water drumming on tight nylon roofs and thumping on the bottoms of the upended pots and pans.

The attempts to talk ended; the drumming continued. It didn't let up until well after dark. By that time, with full bellies and dry sleeping bags, the three of them were sound asleep.

It continued to rain all night and all the next day. The weather provided the excuse to take the time to rest their bodies. And it gave Dan a vacation from the anxiety of expecting to see a group of men come out from behind every tree or hear the flapping of helicopter blades. No one could move in this weather. Nothing could fly. A veil of safety had engulfed them, wrapped its gray cloak around them, and would hide and protect them for a brief time. Time to relax. To think and to talk. And to

make plans for the next leg of their journey. The leg that Dan hoped would successfully end at 1600 Pennsylvania Avenue, Washington, D.C.

"Dan, how far do you think we have to go to get to a town? How long do you think it will take us?"

"I don't know, Don. Miles don't matter anymore. Time is the only thing we've got to think about now. This storm has got to be the leading edge of a big cold front moving down from Canada. I'm afraid of the weather. It's going to be getting colder, a lot colder. If we don't get out of these mountains soon, we may never get out of them.

"There's no way I want to spend the winter up here. We could. We have enough supplies to make it. But no way would I want to face that. It's a killer up here in the winter. We'd be damned lucky if we made it through to spring."

"Then you'll have to get me on my feet. If you try to drag me all the way out, you'll kill yourself in the process, and we'll die with you."

"Mr. President," Dan began. "Don," the president interrupted.

"Yeah, okay, Don. You can't get on your feet. Not yet... "

"Yes, I can. You can make me a pair of crutches. Give me a couple of days to rest up, to work out some of the stiffness and practice walking."

"Mr. President, "

"Don, damn it. Don't make me order you to use it."

"Dan," said Sydney. "You've got to help him. You can't keep up the pace you set to get us out of here. You can't carry Daddy and then shuttle supplies. You'll kill yourself, and it will take us forever. Do you want all your efforts to go to waste? All I've heard from you is 'mission, mission, mission,' to the point where you put a gun to my head. Well, damn it. Think about your mission. Help my father heal, and then help him walk."

Dan dropped his chin down onto his chest. Thinking. Absorbing her words. Projecting forward into the journey ahead. "Okay. Three days. We'll rest here for three days. I'll make a pair of crutches for you, and then we'll try. But if you can't do it by then, in three days, it's my way. Agreed?"

"Agreed," the Richardsons responded in harmony.

"But," Dan continued, "we've got to move away from these supply skids. They're too much of an attraction. If anyone is looking for us, these things stick out like a red light at Walmart."

"Tomorrow," the president began again, "I'd like you to help me get into that stream. If I sit in that cold water for as long as I can stand it, it will be as close to ice therapy as we can get. It should help with the swelling and get rid of the stiffness."

"Good idea. Might work."

The next morning, Dan successfully moved them downstream about a half mile. He shuttled everything, making a half-dozen trips back and forth to a new site he located. He found a spot where a thick grove of fir trees was backed up to a rocky cliff that rose up from a flat area next to the stream. He pitched the tents under the trees for protection and got everything settled out of sight from the air, as well as the surrounding area. A team of men would have to walk right into the campsite before they would find the three of them.

For the next three days, they ate and rested. Dan and Sydney made frequent round trips to the supply skids, retrieving any items he thought they might need along the next leg of his mission. Each round trip took about two hours and was well worth the effort. At the end of the three days, they would be fully supplied and ready to go.

To fashion the president's crutches, Dan had cut two small trees with Y-shaped branches and lined the forks with foam that had been used as packing material on the skid. He had taped additional foam around the shafts where the president's hands would grip the sticks, making for a more secure and comfortable handhold.

Three times a day, Dan helped the president to the stream on his makeshift crutches. The cold mountain water was deep enough to reach up to his injured hips. He was able to tolerate the temperature for only fifteen to twenty minutes at a time, but he could feel the effects after the very first session in the water.

On the third day, the president did a solo trip around camp on the crutches. Within an hour, he was actually moving about on his own quite well. By nightfall, he had convinced Dan that he was making such good progress that extending the rest period for another day might do the trick.

Dan had been using the time to instruct Sydney in the use and preparation of the equipment they would have with them on the rest of the journey. Together, they planned the meals and tried to anticipate other needs that might pop up. To Dan, all of this was second nature, but he tolerated and actually enjoyed the process of teaching Sydney. Plus, it gave him lots of reasons to be close to her. He wanted to be near her more and more as the days passed. They had become more than friends.

That night, they were sitting near the fire, soaking up the warmth, dazed by the flickering flames and twinkling stars. The president was asleep in his tent, worn out from the exertion of trying to learn to walk again.

Dan had three tents pitched to form a triangle around the campfire, one for each of them, to allow for maximum comfort and privacy. Once they began the hike again, there would be only one tent. It would cut down on the weight, and the three of them would just have to figure out a way to make do.

Sydney broke the silence. "Dan?"

"Yeah?"

"Tell me about yourself."

"There's not much to tell. I grew up on an apple farm in the middle of the Hudson Valley in New York. Went to college for a year or two. I was lost there, so I quit and joined the Army.

They helped me finish college, so I decided to stay in and make a career of it." He stopped.

She waited. "That's it?"

"Told you there's not much to tell."

"How come I find that so hard to believe? "Married?"

"Nope."

"But you have a daughter?"

"Yep."

"Where is she?"

"Richmond."

"...Is there a future Mrs. Travis?"

"Nope."

"How...?

This is like pulling teeth from a rock. "Dan, I've spent days with you, and I know you can put together a sentence with more than one word. You sure did when you chewed me out back at the crash site. By the way, would you really shoot me in order to get my father back alive?"

"Yes!"

The calm expression on his face and the conviction in his voice scared the hell out of her. "I thought so! Tell me about your daughter."

"She lives with her mother. She's nine years old. She's my little Pooh. She's an angel, or at least she's my angel."

"Your Pooh Bear?"

"Yeah. She had a Winnie the Pooh bear when she was a baby. Wouldn't go anywhere without it. Slept with it, ate with it, so I started calling her Pooh. It kinda stuck."

Sydney didn't ask any more questions. She could see the joy in his face and wanted to give him time to enjoy his memory. She saw a different side of him at this moment. A soft side, loving, and tender side. Not just the tough soldier. She waited. It didn't take long. After a few seconds and without any prompting, he went on.

"Her mom was a one-nighter. We met in a bar in Fayetteville, North Carolina, and spent the night together in a motel room. Next thing I know, I'm off to the Middle East, and when I got back, I was a dad.

"Barely got to say goodbye to her. I call her every other day to talk about school. She hates it when I don't call. I know she's got to be worried and wondering why I haven't called. The vice president said he would call for me, but I'm not sure about that. Not much he could tell her anyway.

"If I told her what was really going on, God knows what her mother would say to anyone who would listen. A woman would tell the Russians where to attack us if she thought she would look good doing it. I sure hope somebody can tell Pooh not to be scared."

"Would she worry about your being out here in the mountains all by yourself?"

"Nah! She knows her old dad could survive out here forever if he had to. I just hope somebody told her that I was on a camping trip or something that was close to the truth, so she doesn't worry. Last time I was deployed to a combat area, she had a very hard time with it. She's a bright little girl. If she thinks someone is lying to her, or trying to hide something from her, she'll know it, and then she'll really get scared and worry. She thinks she has to take care of me because I'm alone. I'll bet you five bucks to a flat tire she'll be there when we get back, ready to lecture me, and then give me a big hug."

"You don't have any doubt that we'll get out of this, do you?"

He didn't respond right away. She could feel the power of his self-confidence. She could almost see the thread of love sailing off into the darkness and connecting him to his little girl so many miles away, almost feel the pulse of strength and love being transmitted in both directions along that thread. She was envious. "Nope," he finally answered softly.

"None."

After a long pause, he took his turn. "Well, what about you?"

"What do you mean?"

"It's your turn. Tell me about yourself."

"Don't you read the newspapers? My life's an open book. Every rag sheet in the country has something to say about my life."

He slowly turned toward her. They were sitting on the ground near the fire, warmed and feeling secure. He reached out and took her hands into his. He held them gently. He couldn't believe that he was actually doing it. He didn't know where the courage came from for him to actually touch her. But here he was holding her hands in his. He held them gently.

"Sydney... you're a jerk."

"What?"

"Not for acting like a jerk. Yeah, I read the papers, but that's just your act that they're reporting. You're a jerk for believing that everybody buys your act. You come from a wealthy family, so you act like a spoiled little rich bitch. Your dad is president, so you act like the ego-tripping little brat that everyone wants you to be. You may be selling that act, but I ain't buying it. So, while I've got some time on my hands, and I can't get a ball game on the TV I'm toting around in my back pocket, and I haven't got a six pack to suck on, all of which I'm sure is your image of a dumb G.I., and you can't get very far away from me, how about telling me about yourself."

She melted, tears welling up in her eyes. They talked for hours. Neither looked at a wristwatch. None existed. Time didn't exist, didn't matter. It wasn't necessary, and would only be the third wheel in this developing relationship.

Chapter Three

They awoke to silence. The rain had stopped, replaced by a thick, gray fog. At this altitude, the fog was more likely clouds that were part of the weather front moving through.

Dan and Sydney emerged from their tents simultaneously, their eyes meeting in a moment of embarrassment when there was nothing to be embarrassed about, their minds on a rewind of last night, searching to be sure the closeness they each felt was equal and not turned off by either of them at this new moment, their first of the day and the first dawn of their new awareness of each other.

Dan finally formed the words in his throat. "Good morning," he said.

Her answer came in a soft velvet wrapper. "Good morning."

They couldn't see more than thirty yards in any direction. It was eerie. Not a sound. No birds singing. No wind stirring the leaves and needles overhead. Not even

the drumming of the rain that had lulled them to sleep a few hours earlier. Even their voices were muffled by the pasty, heavy, wet air.

It was the fourth day of the president's rest and healing time. There would be no traveling today. Not in this stuff. Not as long as the fog covered and surrounded them. There was no way for them to sight ahead for bearings. No way to see mountaintops or valleys, nothing to direct their line of travel. Dan would use his compass to guide their way, but he still needed to be able to see off into the distance.

He decided to turn the rest day to good use by helping Don Richardson get more practice on his new crutches. As soon as breakfast was over, he picked up the crutches and headed toward the president.

"Okay, boss man. Up and at 'em," Dan said, as he stood behind his patient and lifted him to his feet. Still holding him up, Dan placed one of the crutches under each arm and backed away slightly until the president's weight was fully on the sticks, and he was maintaining his balance.

As she had the day before, Sydney looked on nervously, ready to catch her father should he fall forward. But he held his own, balancing himself and very slowly testing his hips by lowering his weight onto his feet, putting pressure on his hips and legs.

"How ya doing this time?" Dan asked. "Okay, so far. A bit lightheaded." "Any pain, Daddy?"

"Not yet, baby."

Dan and Sydney backed away a little to give him some room.

"Head clearing yet?" Dan asked. "Yeah."

"Okay. Take your time. There's no rush." "We're here to catch you, Daddy."

"I'm okay, baby. I've got to learn to do this myself, even the getting-up part." He shifted his full weight to his legs and pushed the crutches out in front of him to take the first stride of the day, testing himself carefully. "Feels good," he smiled. His first venture of the day into the world of self-mobility took him completely around the campsite. He was slightly winded by the time he got back to the spot where he had started.

Sydney glanced at Dan a number of times during the circuit, looking for reassurance that her father was okay. Dan's eyes gave it to her.

"How do you feel, Daddy?" "Great."

"Pain?" Dan asked.

"Stiff and sore, but no real pain. Feels like I'm trying to work out a bad cramp. You know, just stiff like a Charlie horse. "

"Yeah, I know. That's good. Want to sit down?"

"No, Dan. Let me get my breath for a minute. I want to do some more. I think I'm going to be okay. Need to stretch these old bones and muscles. Trust me, I feel fine."

"Okay. Just don't overdo it. I don't want you to hurt yourself and be worse than when you started."

By noon, the patient had made a dozen laps around the tent area, each one a little faster. As his confidence increased, he put more weight on his legs and less on the crutches. Finishing the last lap, he headed off in a new direction.

"Where are you going, Daddy?"

"To the creek. I'm going to sit in it for a while."

He kept up this routine for the rest of the day. He would walk for half an hour, then plop himself into the ice-cold creek. He barely took time out for lunch. The thrill of renewed mobility kept him smiling all day. The cold water sucked the soreness from his body and kept the swelling from interfering with his success. By late afternoon, he was barely putting any weight on the crutches, using them more to steady himself than for support.

Sergeant Travis decided to take control around four o'clock. "I think you've done more than enough for one day. You're pushing it. Tomorrow we hit the real trail. I need you to be able to walk out of here. Too much today and you might set yourself back a week. We can't afford for that to happen. Let's call it a day."

"Okay, you're right," Dan. I'm starved. How about some supper?"

Dan and Sydney cooked up a hot meal, including quantities of soup, the ultimate comfort food. Soup warms the innards of a man living in the wild. Something about soup feeds the brain; its wholesomeness is soothing.

The president was asleep early again. Dan and Sydney again found themselves alone, sitting by the fire. Conversation was awkward; the magnetism, strong, two young people wanting to surrender to their feelings and fighting not to, each unsure of the reception they would get from the other.

Dan tried unsuccessfully to avoid looking at her, not wanting to be caught in the act. Sydney nervously flitted from one unnecessary chore to another, trying to burn up emotional energy. Dan tightened the anchor ropes on his tent. Sydney placed another log on the fire.

Both stood and turned at the same time, colliding head-on. Face to face. Nose to nose. Lips to lips. Their kiss lasted only seconds. Neither planned it. Neither avoided it. Neither wanted it to end.

But it did end. Dan backed away. If it had been daylight, his face would have shown red as a fire truck. It almost glowed in the dark.

She stepped back and drew a long, slow breath.

"I, I'm so, I'm sorry. I, I didn't mean to get in your way."

"No, it was my fault. It was all my fault, Sydney. I'm sorry."

"No, It was... uh... I, I think I'm going to bed now.

Good night, Dan."

"Okay. Good night, Sydney."

She turned and crawled into her tent, and he into his. Neither slept for a long time. Neither was aware that her father had awakened and watched the whole scene. He fell back asleep with a big smile on his face.

Part VI

The Visitors Return

Chapter One

Morning brought skies the color of wet clay, but the rain had finally stopped. The air was still thick with fat beads of water weighing down every limb, every leaf, every pine needle.

Dan was discouraged. He had hoped to get things together today and get on the trail. But there would be no hiking today. Lack of visibility and wet ground conditions made it far too risky to even think about beginning the trek out, particularly with a man on half-assed homemade crutches.

Every rock, every log, and the slimy mud between each one was a trap waiting to slip up anyone stupid enough to try and gain traction. This mountain, solid when dry, was slick as owl shit on a flat rock when wet. Dan knew that today was a lost day.

And he didn't like it. Something was itching at him, telling him to get moving, that something was up, and he needed to get this show on the road.

"Mornin', Dan," the president said as he came out of his tent, scooting along on his butt atop a poncho.

"Good morning, sir."

"You look kind of glum, young man. What's wrong?"

"Well, sir, I had hoped to get started today, but this weather has sort of screwed up my plans."

"You really wanted to get started today?" the president asked, sounding surprised.

Sydney crawled out of her tent to join them around the fire pit Dan had made the evening before.

"Yes, sir. I figured we would take it slow and easy, giving you a chance to get used to your walking sticks without pushing too hard. Just get started with no real plan as to how far we would go."

"Well, Dan, I'm not sure how I will do, but when you're ready, I'll give it a try. But since it doesn't look like it's going to be today, I'll use the time around camp to try to limber up my stiff joints. And I'll also sit in the cold water again to keep the swelling down."

"I'll help you, Daddy. I'd like to see us get started, too. Maybe with another day of exercise and cold water, you'll be feeling up to short stints on the trail."

Dan brightened as soon as Sydney joined them with her positive contribution to the conversation. He said, "That sounds great. I'll start to segregate the supplies we'll need and get all that stuff organized so we're ready as soon as you're up to it."

After a hot breakfast, Sydney and her father worked together, walking in big circles about the camp area. He spent twenty minutes of every hour sitting in the icy water with his rear end and hips submerged in a little pool area about a foot deep, just enough to circulate around his body without the current dragging him downstream.

While he was taking his icy bath, Sydney would join Dan in his work.

Midday approached with the promise of brightening skies. The muddy grey was slowly turning to dull silver, and the ceiling seemed to be increasing by the hour, a hopeful sign of things to come.

The two of them joined forces to prepare lunch. They chatted the whole time as if they had known each other far longer than they actually had, and it was getting easier by the hour. Their relationship, their trust in each other, and their spark of mutual attraction deepened more and more as they shared time and tasks together.

By midafternoon, the sky had cleared dramatically. The sun was breaking through, and a touch of warmth was in the air. The president excused himself to take a nap. He was whipped from his morning of exercise and cold dips in the stream, but the results were obvious. He was moving much better and able to stand and walk with only one crutch.

Sydney decided to do the same and was headed for her tent when Dan told her, "I think I'll wander around in the woods close by. This front moving through should have the wildlife up and moving. They'll hunker down during rain and fog, so after a couple of days, they're hungry and moving. Maybe I'll get lucky and be able to add some fresh meat to our dinner tonight. I'll see you in a couple of hours."

"Okay, just be careful. We need you."

Dan picked up his rifle, loaded with ballistic-tipped bullets, and started walking off into the woods. A short distance from camp, he cut across what appeared to be a game trail crowded with deer prints leading toward the stream. The prints only went in one direction, so he knew that the deer were crossing the stream to a feeding or bedding area.

He had been hunting since he was a little boy and was an expert when it came to stalking and killing deer. To be successful, he knew you had to learn how the animals think and behave: where and when they feed, where and when they drink, and where and when they bed down.

In a short time, he came to an area where the game crossed from one side of the creek to another. He found a rocky knoll overlooking this area, climbed up, and sat down to wait.

Hunting like this could take a few minutes, or it could take all day. As a boy, he had learned to sit like this for hours, all day if necessary. Sometimes, he would bring a paperback and read while waiting for a deer to come his way. He didn't have a book with him on this trip, so he just settled back, leaned up against a tree, and waited. Watched and waited.

It took a little over an hour. He saw movement on the other side of the little clearing, and sure enough, there was a deer coming his way. He couldn't tell if it was a buck or a doe, and he didn't care. He wasn't sure if the hunting season was open or what he was legally allowed to shoot. But, under the circumstances, he really didn't care. He wasn't much concerned with a game warden walking up on him to check his hunting license and ticket him for killing a deer out of season. He could only hope that a warden would show up. He would probably kiss him right on the mouth and tell him, "Oh, by the way, I just happen to have the President of the United States and his daughter camped out a little ways from here; would you mind giving me a hand to get them the hell out of here?"

What would the guy say? "Oops, sorry, can't do that. Gotta go! Little woman is waiting for supper for me. Good luck! See ya around. Oh, and here's your ticket for hunting out of season."

The deer slowly made its way toward him, dropping its head down to feed every couple of steps. It took almost twenty minutes to reach a spot that was open and clear enough for Dan to make a shot. He could smell the meat roasting over an open fire already. He lifted his rifle, took careful aim, and pulled the trigger. The deer leaped straight up in the air, which was a good sign. They often do that when hit squarely. It turned slightly and ran off toward the north. Dan soon saw it stumble and fall, its four legs kicking in the air for a few seconds, and then silence.

As trained in his younger years, he sat and waited. Fifteen minutes later, he quietly and carefully climbed down off his perch and made his way over to the deer. He walked up to the carcass and poked it in the eye with the barrel of his gun to be sure it was dead. It was. He had hit it squarely in a vital area; it was a clean kill. Now it was time to go to work.

He laid his gun and pack down, stripped off his jacket and undershirt, turned the dead deer on its back, and slit the deer's belly from crotch to sternum. Within a few minutes, reaching into the chest cavity and stomach areas with his hands and arms, he had all of the animal's innards cleaned out and was ready to drag the carcass back to camp for supper. He was covered with blood from his elbows to his fingertips, and blood was smeared all over the front of his body.

He retrieved his jacket and shirt and crossed the stream back to the side where the camp was located. He wanted to take a bath and clean up because he didn't want Sydney to get grossed out. He needed her to be okay with this dead deer, and he didn't want anything to get in the way of her being able to eat the meat. He wasn't so worried about the president's reaction, but she was a girl...

Midway across the stream, he tossed the carcass up on a big rock sitting in the middle of a pool a couple of feet deep. He stripped naked and washed his clothes to get as much of the blood off as he could. After scrubbing each piece of clothing in the stream, he tossed it on top of the dead deer, hoping that the still-warm carcass would make donning wet clothes a bit more comfortable. When he'd finished with his clothes, he started on himself.

The water was cold, but refreshing. He had broken a pretty good sweat dragging the deer through the woods, and, along with a week of hiking in the woods, he didn't mind the water temperature so much. A good dip would do his body and soul a lot of good. After washing himself, he lay back in the pool area and floated on his back for a moment, until he heard it.

At first, he thought the sound came from the stream, because his ears were below the waterline. But then it grew stronger: thump-thump, thump-thump. Did he hear it or did he feel it? Or did he imagine it? That constant thumping could come only from one source. A helicopter was coming at him!

Instinctively, he wanted to jump up and start waving his arms to get the pilot's attention. To yell at the top of his lungs to make sure they landed close by. To rescue him and his two companions. But his gut said no. His gut told him to get down, hide, take cover.

Instead of jumping up, he dove into the water and hid behind the rock where his still-warm warm dead deer rested with his clothes draped over it. He watched from behind the rock as the aircraft cleared the treetops to the west of the stream. It was just like the one now at the bottom of the lake, all black with no markings.

There was a camera pod under its nose, and the side door on the starboard side was open. A man dressed in black sat with one leg dangling out of the door and an automatic weapon draped across his lap. Immediately upon clearing the treetops, he opened fire, aiming directly at Dan Travis.

Dan ducked out of sight behind the rock, but the shooting continued. The deer carcass was shredded by dozens of rounds, with flesh splattered in every direction, pink flesh and blood creating a cloud over his head.

The helicopter continued across the stream and disappeared behind the treetops to the east. But it was not going away. Dan knew it would be back very soon. He also knew that he had to get away from this spot. He took the opportunity of the aircrafts being behind the tree tops and out of sight and began to run down the stream bed toward the tent site.

He didn't stop to think that he was bare-ass naked. His only thought was to get to the president and his daughter. He saw them standing on the bank of the stream near the tent, looking up in the direction of the sound of the helicopter and shooting, shocked and puzzled.

"Get down!" Dan yelled. "Get down."

It took a few seconds for them to see him coming and to realize what he was yelling. They stood with their mouths agape as this naked man came running toward them, yelling something they could barely understand and could not yet comprehend.

"Get down," Dan yelled again.

A few yards from them, he jumped onto the bank of the stream as he ran right at them. When he reached them, he wrapped an arm around each and dragged them into the stream, pushing and pulling them to an area of deep water.

The stream was littered with big rocks and deep pools, and this was exactly what he needed. He found a spot where he could get all three of them behind a large boulder where the water was deep enough for them to duck down beneath the surface.

Just then, the helicopter reappeared over the trees about a hundred yards away and slowly made its way along the stream in their direction. As it got close to them, Dan put a hand on each of their heads and pushed them under the surface. Looking up through the water rushing over his head, he could see the belly of the helicopter passing over them.

He pushed Sydney around to the other side of the boulder and dragged her father along, keeping the rock between them and the aircraft.

Slowly, he allowed them all to come to the surface for a breath of air, with just their noses and mouths above the surface of the water.

They waited. Dan could still feel the thumping of the helicopter's blades overhead, but they were fading. He waited longer. Finally, he allowed their heads to surface. They continued to wait.

After what seemed a lifetime, they stood, the president bewildered, and Sydney fighting back tears of fright.

"What the hell was that?" the president asked.

"Looks like our friends had friends after all," Dan replied.

"Do you think we should get out of the stream, Dan?" "Not yet, sir. I want to wait and see if they come back." "But, why here?" Sydney asked.

"Did you see that round black ball at the front end of the helicopter? That was a camera pod. I'm sure they had heat-sensitive equipment looking down for us. They picked up the heat signature of a deer I killed and was bringing back to camp.

"They must have thought it was me. That's what they were shooting at. The cold water covers our body heat, and their equipment won't pick us up. We'll stay here until we're sure they're gone."

"I'm cold, " Sydney said.

"Better than dead," Dan answered. "You're naked," she said.

For the first time, he realized he was standing between them with absolutely nothing on. He quickly lowered himself back into the water to disguise his nakedness. His face glowed bright enough to act as a beacon for the helicopter, but the water quickly cooled him down.

After ten more minutes, Dan gave the signal for them to leave the safety of the cold water.

"Would you please get me something to wrap myself in?" he asked Sydney.

"Nope," she answered playfully. "You're on your own.

You dragged us in there; you get yourself out."

The president was doing his best to hobble out on his own. "Not much I can do for you, Dan."

Sydney crawled out of the water, turned, and looked at Dan from the bank, hands on her hips, daring him to get up and out of the water. He bit his pride and his embarrassment, cupped his hands over his private parts, jutted his chin, stood, and walked toward his tent to find dry clothes.

But this was no time for play. A second attempt had been made on their lives. Clearly, someone did not want the president to return. Someone was out to kill them. That someone might very well try again, and very soon!

Dan's mind was racing as he struggled to get into dry clothes inside his little tent. When he finished, he burst out to find his companions waiting for him, seated near the fire pit, dressed in clean, dry clothes and with expressions of deep concern on their faces.

"We've got to get out of here, away from this area right now."

"I totally agree with you, Dan," said the president. "I'm very concerned, after that last little show of force. We'll help you pack everything... "

"No," Dan barked. "No time for that. We move right now. I don't want to take the time to pack anything. Besides, I want to leave the entire area just as it is. If someone comes back on foot, I want it to look as if we're dead, and not as if we packed up and carried our supplies with us.

"We need to get some distance away from here and then think about what we do next. So, let's go. I'll assist you as much as I can. Do you think you can walk using only one crutch?"

The president stood and picked up a single crutch. "Point the way, young man. I'll be right there with you, and I don't think I'll need a whole lot of assistance."

Without another word, they started the next leg of their journey. Dan led the way using only his compass and that old reliable gut instinct of his to get himself and the two people in his charge away from harm and home safely.

They hiked nonstop for three hours. It was getting dark, and Dan knew he would soon have to stop. He figured they had hiked at least a couple of miles. Now he had to find a suitable place for them to spend the night, exposed to the elements. It didn't take long.

They were hiking through an area that was fairly flat, with a sharp rise to their right. He soon found a rocky overhang that they could crawl under for some protection. It was like a small cave with a wide front door.

Once he got the other two settled, he broke off some pine branches and stood them on end in front of the opening to provide some protection from any wind that might kick up. With their new front door, they could also retain what little body heat they generated, helping to keep them more comfortable in the hours ahead.

The three of them sat on piles of dried leaves shoulder to shoulder with Sydney between them. "How are you doing, Don?" Dan asked.

"I'm sore as hell, but I'm doing okay. Better than I expected."

"And you Ms. Sydney, how are you doing?"

"I'm fine, Dan. Just trying to figure out what the hell is going on and what we're going to do next."

"Don't worry about the 'next' part. I'll take care of that. But I can't help you with the other stuff. Obviously, someone is out to make damned sure your dad doesn't get out of here alive. I don't know why. You two will have to figure all that out. I'm just a plain soldier trying to do my duty. That high-level stuff is way over my head. But, by God, I'm pissed. Whoever is out to get your dad is making my job very difficult, and that plain pisses me off!"

"I'm working on the other stuff, Dan," the president said. "I've been rolling a lot around in my mind ever since the invasion at the lake. I've got some ideas as to who might be behind all of this, but I just can't accept the reality of the whole thing.

"I mean, I've upset some people in my political life, but I never imagined this kind of thing happening. This is third-world politics. It's like a scenario straight out of some Middle Eastern country. This isn't the United States. I'm having a very difficult time wrapping my mind around this whole thing. "

"Well, sir, you work on that, and I'll work on getting us out of here."

"What do you have in mind, Dan?" asked Sydney.

"We'll rest as best we can tonight. I think we're far enough away from the camp that if our friends come back with their heat-sensitive camera, they won't find us out here. This rock overhang will also help if they do.

"In the morning, I'll head back to the camp and see what's going on. If there's no sign of their having come back or having been there today, I'll pack up what I can and come back here. After that, we'll just have to take it as best we can with what we have. Water is the main thing, and there's plenty of that in these mountains.

Chapter Two

Morning met them with warm sunshine caressing their huddled bodies under the rock overhang. The opening faced east, and the rising sun reached them early. Dan stretched his cramped legs and back and stood up to assist the others. Sydney reached up to take his hand for assistance. She took a few stiff steps before the blood completely returned to her lower limbs.

It was the president who had the hardest time. Much of his progress was lost to the miserable night they had just spent, cramped up in their damp, hard-packed dirt shelter. It was difficult for him to stand, and he couldn't walk even a step without help.

Dan was very reluctant to start a fire. They would have to depend on the bright sunshine to warm their bodies and loosen their muscles. Dan's best estimate was that they had gotten at least a mile and a half, maybe two, from the last area of attack, but no more than two and a half miles.

A more accurate estimate was impossible because of the president's slow pace. Dan's concern the previous evening had been just to get the hell away from their last campsite, to concentrate on nothing more than escaping. He didn't pay much attention to factors like time and distance. But this day's plan was forming very clearly in his mind.

"Here's what we'll do today, Don. You and Sydney will stay right here. Sydney, I want you to concentrate on getting your dad's flexibility and mobility back to where it was yesterday, but without pushing him too far. I'm going to hike back to our last campsite."

"Do you think that's a good idea, Dan?" asked the president.

"We don't have much choice. We have to have at least some basic supplies to continue. I'll check out the area before I stick my nose in too close. If everything looks okay, I'll gather up as much as I can carry and drag it back here. At the very least, I'll need a rifle to hunt with.

"If things don't look right, or if I suspect anyone is watching, I'll come back here and we'll have to figure out how we are going to continue with nothing but what we have on our backs. I'm going to leave right away. The sooner I get there, the sooner I'll get back."

"Okay, just be careful. These are very bad and determined people."

"Yes, sir." He had walked only a few paces when he heard Sydney call his name. He turned, and she launched herself into an embrace, wrapping her arms around him very tightly and burying her face in his neck.

"Come back," she whispered, fighting back emotions she didn't know how to control... or want to.

He had been completely caught off guard by her display. "I'll be back. You can count on it."

With that, he strode away, energized in a way he had never imagined. His back straightened, and a smile that he couldn't control broke across his face. He felt like he was walking without touching the ground.

It took him a little over an hour to reach their old site. Not carrying anything, even a rifle, made for rapid travel even in this strange wilderness. As he neared the campsite, he found a high stop atop some boulders. He climbed to the top and stood slowly so as not to be seen should anyone be looking in his direction. He saw no movement below. He waited and listened for a solid fifteen minutes for any human sounds. There was nothing.

He climbed down and began to slowly and quietly circle the campsite. When he reached the area to the north, close to the creek, he crossed over to the other side to gain a clear view from there. No sign of life, no sign of the helicopter having returned.

Crossing back over the stream, he again climbed to the top of the rocks he had used as a perch when he first arrived. From there, he watched and waited another half hour before risking an entry into the campsite. Nothing. He knew that the patience of men on watch was very short. Had anyone been observing the campsite, they would have moved by now, and he would have spotted them. He was satisfied.

He slowly crept into the campsite. Once there, he threw caution to the wind and started to gather everything he thought he could carry into a big pile. When done, he stuffed three backpacks with food, grabbed the sled that he had used to drag supplies to this site, and loaded it. Then he strapped on one of the backpacks, lashed everything else to the skid, and left.

His progress was very slow. The load of supplies he was carrying and dragging was enough for three people to deal with, and he was doing it alone. He struggled over rocks and fallen tree trunks and a million other obstacles that hadn't been there just a short time earlier when he came this way carrying nothing at all.

Slippery rocks, slippery tree trunks, slippery mud, slippery everything! He was quickly out of breath, but he continued. He had to.

It took him almost four hours to reach Don and Sydney Richardson. By the time he got back to them, it was late afternoon and he was exhausted.

He was greeted like a returning hero, with bear hugs from the president and his daughter. The look of relief on their faces lit up the whole area around their little cave. They helped him take the pack off his back and undo the harness attached to the skid. Dan flopped down, trying to catch his breath. After a few minutes of idle chatter, he reported his findings to the Richardsons.

"What did you see, Dan?

"Nothing, sir. No sign of their having returned. I guess they think they finished us off, at least finished me off. Everything was just as we left it."

"What's next?" Sydney asked. "Food!"

An hour later, they had eaten a supper of cold MREs and cleaned up the area. It was getting dark. Dan took an 8' x 10' tarp from the supplies and draped it over the front of their little shelter. It would keep them dry and protected from the wind.

He was still unwilling to build a fire, for fear of being seen from an aircraft. For all he knew, the area was being observed from a satellite in orbit a hundred miles over their heads. They would spend another night here.

Luckily, the president's mobility had improved substantially during the day. Hopefully, he would not regress again from being cooped up in tight quarters. At least tonight, thanks to Dan's efforts, they had sleeping bags to stretch out in and try to get some restful sleep.

Once they got settled, the president asked, "What next? What's the plan?"

"We leave as early tomorrow morning as we can. We'll get the supplies and food packed up and head out. I think we should try to stay within earshot of this stream. It's headed in the right direction, and the downgrade is fairly gentle. Besides, it's a great water supply for us, and hopefully, someone has built a town near it somewhere. We'll just have to take it day by day until we get out of here."

After that explanation and a short conversation, the three of them settled back and fell asleep. They had survived another day.

Chapter Three

The new morning met them with a bite of cold in the air. It had rained during the night, but the tarp had done its job, and they were dry and reasonably comfortable. Dan was glad it had rained. It would wash away the trail he left behind, dragging the pack frame, which could have led a blind man directly to them. At least now, it would be more difficult, and that added a little sense of security.

The weather front seemed to be stalled, or perhaps another had already moved in. The rain last night and a drop in temperature of at least twenty degrees was a warning sign of what might lie ahead. It brought a new and different sense of urgency to bear on his plans.

The president was a little stiff but in remarkably good condition, considering the second night in cramped quarters and limited creature comforts. He walked about the area, testing the progress he had made the day before, and was convinced that he could walk with the support of only one crutch to stabilize him.

He insisted on carrying a backpack of supplies. Dan protested but finally gave in and filled a pack with the lightest items he could find among the supplies he had assembled for the hike out. It was made up primarily of dried food.

He did the same with Sydney's pack. He wanted to keep her light and mobile. He wanted speed now. They needed to cover ground and get some distance behind them. His instinct told him that someone would be back looking for them. Someone would come to verify what was supposed to have been the success of the latest helicopter assault. He didn't know who or when, but the itch in his stomach told him to make distance, and soon.

Whoever returned and found a dead deer instead of a dead soldier was going to be really pissed, and he didn't want to be found and used for target practice again. He needed space and heavy cover between the supply dump and his little band of nomads.

Dehydrated and freeze-dried food, a couple of sleeping bags, and a large tarp would round out their loads. The tarp would be their only shelter from this point on. No more individual tents. They were too heavy and redundant. If they needed additional shelter, he would have to build it for them using the materials that Mother Nature provided.

Travis loaded his own pack with the heavier gear and his own sleeping bag. The A-frame was now loaded with all the other supplies and topped off with every package of food he could lash down, extra warm clothing, socks, and boots.

By the time they were ready to leave, he had applied the golden rules of backpacking: "If you don't need it, don't carry it." And… "If you ain't got it, you don't need it." The lighter the better, without giving up safety. Less weight meant easier hiking. Easier hiking translates into more distance. More distance means safety. More distance means closer to home. More distance means mission accomplished.

It was close to noon by the time they were ready to move out, but Dan didn't think it was a very good idea to prepare a midday meal and further delay their departure. Each of them felt, without saying a word to one another, that they had to begin, that this was the real beginning of their hike home.

They followed the stream as Dan had planned, applying the time-tested logic he'd learned as a boy scout: follow the water, and it will always lead to something.

They were headed generally in a southeasterly direction. He led the way, concentrating on blazing the easiest trail he could, while glancing back over his shoulder every couple of steps to check on the condition of the president. He had put Sydney in the rear to keep an eye on her father.

All things considered, Travis felt that the remainder of the day went well. The president held up better than Dan had expected and was able to keep up the pace with little trouble. Sydney was proving to be a real trooper. She was quickly learning the skills of the woods, which would be good for her and a lot of help to Dan in the days ahead.

By the time darkness approached, Dan estimated that they had put almost five miles between them and their last camp. He could breathe a bit easier now. It was a good first day, but it was getting colder by the hour.

They made camp for the night. Very basic, no fire, no smoke, no odor. Fifty yards away, to the rest of the world, they didn't even exist.

Dan and Sydney threw together a cold meal for supper, stretched the tarp up between four trees, and rolled out their sleeping bags under it. Once everything was cleared and put away, they crawled into their bags and very quickly were asleep, exhausted.

The bite in the breeze brought the morning early to the mountains. Dan was up and packed before either the president or his daughter stirred. He was sitting looking out over the rushing water of the stream when President Richardson sat down next to him.

"Morning, Dan." "Morning, sir."

They sat quietly for a long time. The president broke the silence. "Why did you become a soldier?"

Travis was silent for a moment, then answered, "Because of my dad."

"Was he in the service?"

"Oh, yes, sir. He served in the Army." "What unit was he with?"

"Eighteenth Airborne Corps headquarters. He was stationed on Fort Bragg most of the time he was in the Army."

"Was he a paratrooper?"

"Yes, sir, and damned proud of it."

"So, what made you follow in his footsteps?"

Travis stared off into the distance for a minute or two. The president didn't disturb the young man's thoughts. He knew he was reflecting on something concerning his memories of his father and wanted to leave him to his own thoughts. Dan finally answered.

"He served in Vietnam. He was one of those in the early years of the war when the public really didn't know what was going on. He was wounded a couple of times, and when he came home, nobody even knew that he had been there or even where "there" really was.

"My mom told me that after he was discharged from the service, he watched for years as the war progressed, and he saw all the riots and protests here in the States. She told me he never said much at all. He would just watch in silence and then walk off all by himself.

"She told me that he had lost a lot of friends in the time he was there. On one mission, his team of twelve went out, but only five of them came back. He never talked about it. Never said a word. Then one night, when I was a senior in high school and trying to figure out what I wanted to do with my life, we were all sitting in our den watching the evening news on television.

"Something came on about the remains of an American soldier being found in the jungle of Vietnam and the big deal that was being made of how the current government was turning over what was left to the American representative in the country as a show of goodwill. I glanced over at my dad, and I saw tears in his eyes.

"He never spoke...I don't think he could have at that moment. But there he was, my rock, with tears in his eyes. I moved over and sat next to him, and for the first time since I was a little boy, I held his hand...and he held mine...and then I realized that I had tears in my eyes too. I knew then that there was far more to my dad than I had ever known or would know.

"What I did know was that he was a man. A man that I would be proud to be, and if the Army had made him what he was, then if I were to be like him, I would have to follow him and experience what he had. After high school, I went off to college. But I could never get that evening out of my mind. So, after a year in school, I joined the Army, and here I am.

"Now, every time I see him, every time I look into his eyes, I know who he is, where he came from, and what made him. And I'm proud. Proud of him and proud to be his son. When he's with my daughter, I can see the joy in his face. I can see his soul. And I hope someday, I'll see myself in there."

President Richardson said nothing. There was no need for a reply. He let Dan absorb his own words and let the silence of the wilderness around them help heal him. Sydney Richardson stood leaning against a tree just a few feet behind the only two men currently in her life, and she cried for one of them. The one she had known for only a very short time.

After their second cold meal, they placed all of the gear they had used for the night into their backpacks and, with few words, resumed their journey. The second day was a bit better. The president was growing stronger and stronger. He had some soreness and stiffness, but no real pain, nothing that would stop their progress. Travis was very mindful of the pace he set, to be sure the president could keep up without injury.

He found his mind wandering; it was sometimes hard to concentrate on the real task at hand. He was so taken in by the beauty of the surrounding mountains, all the sights and sounds, and the fresh scents in the air. He lost himself in the majesty of their strength. It helped shorten the miles and speed the passage of the sun across the sky.

The only other time he could remember having this feeling was when he sat on the dunes of the Outer Banks of North Carolina and watched a powerful storm come ashore. Whatever force a person might choose to credit for the power displayed, then and now, was up to the individual. He knew, in his heart, where the credit lay, and it wasn't with any human being.

Late that afternoon, they found themselves on the rim of a ravine overlooking the stream as it fell sharply away, tumbling down the steep face of a hillside. The underbrush was fairly thin, and the hiking equally easy.

However, it was time to call it a day. They needed rest, and they hadn't had a hot meal in almost two days. The overhead canopy was thick enough, and they had hiked far enough away from the area where the helicopter had attacked them that Dan felt it safe to build a fire and cook a proper meal. The moderate breeze would dissipate the smoke quickly. He knew they needed the feel of hot food in their stomachs. It was getting colder by the hour.

Midday on the third day, trouble struck. It began to snow. Travis wanted to keep going, but he knew they had to stop. One slip and the president could pop one or both hips out of joint, and they would be stuck for days.

He went about the business of finding an area where the trees were spaced right for him to put up their tarp for shelter. He had to keep them out of the snow and dry. Wet and cold was a very bad combination out here. He sent Sydney off to collect all the dried, dead wood she could find for a fire before the snow covered it. Once he was satisfied with the makeshift shelter, he too gathered wood. There was no way of knowing how long it would snow or how deep it would get. He wanted to be safe and sure they could have a hot fire for quite a while if need be.

The president refilled all the water bottles and arranged their gear beneath the tarp. He could then sit and rest himself while Dan and Sydney continued gathering wood. The first thing he did was to get the cooking utensils out and ready to prepare that hot meal they were all looking forward to.

The three of them had begun to function as a team. Fewer words...fewer commands...more results. By dark, they were well fed, snug, and dry. The snow was still falling, but had lightened up considerably and with the ground not frozen yet, was disappearing at a steady rate.

Travis decided to take a look around the area. He couldn't get the unsettled feeling out of his bones. He knew logically that they were all alone in this vast wilderness. But he felt uneasy. A little look around would make him feel better.

"I'll be back in a little while," he announced. "I'm just going to take a look around I bit. You two get comfortable. If this weather clears, I want to get an early start in the morning."

"Okay, Dan. But don't be gone too long. You need your rest too, and we can't do with you getting lost out there," the president said.

When he left, Don Richardson, the dad, and Sydney Richardson, the daughter, were alone for the first time in days. She sat staring into the fire without saying a word.

"Sydney, you okay?" the dad asked.

"Yeah, daddy. I'm okay," the daughter replied. "What is it, baby? What's bothering you?" "Nothing."

"Hey, little Pooh. This is your daddy talking. What's up?"

She hesitated. Her father was her best friend, maybe her only real friend. She always shared her problems with him, and they always talked them out.

"Daddy... I, I have feelings for this man. I think I might be falling in love with him."

"Really? Could've fooled me. I thought you two were ready to shoot one another a week ago."

"Daddy, I'm serious. I don't know what to do. I don't even know if I know him well enough to have feelings like this."

"Really, Sydney? I saw you kiss him the other night." "What!"

"Easy, baby. I woke up and was about to say something just as you two stumbled all over each other. Sure seemed to me that you knew who he was then. And to tell you the truth, it was beautiful. You two looked like two thirteen-year-old kids saying good night after your first school dance and couldn't figure out just how to do it."

She didn't respond. They were both quiet for a couple of minutes. Then the daddy talked to his little girl. "Sydney, you're my only daughter. My only child. And since your mother died, my best friend. You're all I've got in this world.

"So, tolerate your old dad for a minute. Trust me. I've met a lot of men in my life. I've had to judge many of them, and I've had to do it in a flash to know how to negotiate successfully with them. My track record isn't perfect, but it's pretty damned good. I've been right far more times than I've been wrong.

"I've watched this man. Every night, I review in my mind the events of the day. I look at what he has been thrust into and how he has dealt with it. Think about all he has faced since he came walking up to us at the crash site. Think about how he got here.

A soldier, an aide, alone in the White House with the vice president, stating his case. Supporting it so well that the Vice President of the United States sends him out here with the full force of his office thrown behind a mere sergeant in the Army.

"The risk was enormous! Yet here he is. How convincing this soldier, this man, must have been. And look at us now. I'm feeling great. I'm in the wilderness, and I feel more comfortable, safe, and at ease than I've felt in most of the world's capitals. Why? Because of this man. This one man, you think you don't know. I'm alive, you're alive, all because of him. He's extraordinary.

"But don't love him for what he has done for us. However, if you can honestly say to yourself that you love him because of who he is, then love him, baby. Love him with everything you've got. Love him as your mother and I loved each other. Be honest with him, and be honest with yourself. If you do that, if you can put all of this aside and still ask yourself 'do I love him or do I love what he has done?', and you still come up with the same answer, that it's him and not everything that has happened out here, that it's the man that you love... Well, what is it you young people say? Go for it."

She didn't speak. Tears were running down her cheeks. She threw her arms around her father's neck and hugged him tight. He returned her hug with all the love a man could possibly have for his child.

Dan came walking into the light of the fire just as she sat upright again. "Everything okay here?"

Before the president could answer, Sydney stood, closed the space between her and Dan with one long stride, and in a continuous motion threw her arms around his neck and kissed him squarely on the lips, holding him tight and close to her body. When she finally released him, she looked into his eyes, hers still wet with tears, his wide open in shock.

"Good night, Dan!" was all she said as she turned and crawled into her sleeping bag without another word to either of them. Dan stood frozen in place. The president was looking up at him with a big grin on his face.

"Good night, son," he said. Then he turned and crawled into his sleeping bag, stretching out an arm to rest his hand on his daughter's shoulder.

Stunned was not quite the right word to describe Dan Travis' emotions. He stood there, not understanding what had just happened or what to do next. He didn't know if he should scratch his watch or wind his butt. Finally, he whispered "Good Night" to his surroundings and went to bed.

Chapter Four

Dan was out of his sleeping bag early. He hadn't really slept. The thoughts of Sydney and the kiss the night before had kept him tossing and turning all night. He was not a young pup. He certainly was not a teenager. Yet he felt as giddy and confused as if this were his first puppy love back in junior high at the Friday night dance, holding sweaty hands with the first girl he knew with breasts.

It would be dark for another hour or so. The snow had stopped falling. There were only a couple of inches on the ground. He knew they would not be able to begin their hike until the sun came up and melted the snow. The ground was still warm, and he felt sure the snow would be gone by midday.

He decided that he would use the time to go hunting. The extra time would provide Sydney and her dad with extra rest, and it would mean that he didn't have to sit around trying to figure out how to avoid eye contact with her all day.

As he was checking out his rifle, preparing to go and try to kill a deer, he heard the president's voice.

"Where are you going, Dan?"

He hadn't expected to hear the president and was slightly startled by the sudden sound. He had hoped he was being quiet enough not to have awakened either Sydney or her dad.

"I'm going hunting."

"You're going to try that again? Last time you went hunting, you came back with a helicopter hovering over your head."

"Yes, sir. I'll try to be a bit more careful this time. We won't be able to hike for a few hours because of the snow, so I thought I'd give it a try. Some fresh meat wouldn't hurt us. I saw some heavy deer sign a short way back in the direction we came from yesterday. You and your...uh...you and...you and your daughter can rest up a bit longer while I'm gone. Should be back in a couple of hours.

"Her name is Sydney." "Yes. Yes sir. I know."

"Dan," the president's voice was soft and consoling. "I know that what happened last night must have thrown you for a loop. Sydney talked to me while you were out looking around the area. She told me how she felt about you. It didn't surprise me. I knew it was coming. I could see it in her eyes...and in yours."

"Mr. President... Don, I didn't... I haven't..."

"I know, son. I know. I'm not accusing you of anything. She's a no-nonsense type, and God knows, she has a mind of her own. Besides, you're both grown people. You both answer to yourselves, not to me. I just want you to know something. She's a wonderful person. She has sacrificed herself to me, to my career, ever since her mother died.

"I've seen her with a lot of men. They all passed right through her life. All were after what she represented, not what or who she is. I've never seen the look, the gleam in her eyes that's there when she looks at you. And, young man, I see the same in your face when you look at her.

"You really don't believe I haven't seen you looking at her, do you?" He hesitated. "I want you to know that it's okay with me. Whatever happens is okay with me. She's strong, Dan, but she's also very soft and very vulnerable. She hides it on the outside. Tries to act tough. But she hurts real easy on the inside.

"And Dan, I love her with all my heart. She's my life. Whatever happens is okay with me because I trust you and think a great deal of you, too. But don't use her and don't hurt her. If you do, I'm still your commander-in-chief, and I'll have your scrawny ass shipped off to Alaska to watch ice melt." Don Richardson had a great big, fatherly, know-it-all grin on his face as he delivered his warning.

"I know, sir. That wouldn't happen. I couldn't do that to her or to you. Please trust me."

"Young man, I'm already trusting you with my life and hers. Now, I'm entrusting you with the future of the only person who means anything to me. Treat her better than you would treat me. She deserves nothing less."

"Yes, sir. I will, sir. You can count on it."

"Good luck hunting. A good venison stew would taste great tonight. Wake me up when you get back."

And with that, the president turned over, pulled the hood of his sleeping bag up over his head, and closed his eyes. No further words were needed.

As Travis slipped off into the woods, the starlit sky was bright enough to show him the way. Had he listened hard enough, he would have heard the soft, tender words, "I love you, Daddy," spoken by a tearful and grateful daughter to her loving father.

He didn't walk for long, only about fifteen minutes. But fifteen minutes in the dark forest could feel like half a lifetime. He had traveled only a few hundred yards when he found a large tree on the side of a gentle slope, where he could hunker down and overlook the area where he had seen deer sign the day before.

He wasn't really interested in hunting. He needed an excuse to get away by himself. He had to get his head screwed on right, and he knew he wouldn't be able to do that if she were anywhere near him. If she should come out of her tent and look at him, he would be dead. His mind would quit functioning right there on the spot.

Once he got himself settled, his mind started racing. What the hell was happening? What the hell was he thinking? She's the daughter of the President of the United States. Me! A grunt sergeant in the Army? Give me a fucking break! Talk about being out of your league! You dumb ass! Sure, she's beautiful. She's everything a man could ask for...and a lot more.

Okay! Okay! So she's not married, not engaged, not dating anyone steady, so she's alone. Maybe lonely. That's it. She kissed me...twice! But maybe she's just lonely. Scared! Maybe she's got things all mixed up because of what's going on out here. But she kissed me! I didn't kiss her! I didn't go after her. She came after me.

Shit! She kissed me, and right in front of her father, for Christ's sake! It's not that I didn't like it! Scared the crap out of me. I almost wet my pants. God! It was good. She's so warm...so soft...so beautiful. What am I doing? What am I thinking.....?

As his mind was racing, the sun came up over the horizon and its warm rays kissed his face. The warmth was the magic elixir it had been ever since he started hunting as a young boy. He closed his eyes, turning his face directly toward the sun, and was asleep in seconds.

He woke with a jolt! Something was coming through the underbrush. It was making far too much noise to be a deer. His first thought was that it was a bear. He waited... watched...listened...

"Sydney?" She stopped dead in her tracks, searching for his voice. "What are you doing here?" he whispered as loudly as he dared. She turned toward him and walked to where he was sitting next to his tree.

"I thought I'd find you and keep you company. And...I just wanted to be with you."

He motioned her to sit down next to him, trying to be as quiet as possible. He wasn't done hunting yet.

"Have you ever been hunting before?" he asked her.

"Never!"

"I've been hunting since I was seven years old. You learn to see these signs, and that's how you learn to hunt."

"Would you like me to explain?"

"I'd love that!"

"Okay, see that?"

"What?"

"That trail. See it? Looks like a very narrow path. Just a line in the forest floor." He pointed to the area in front of where they were sitting.

"I don't see anything. Where are you pointing?"

"Okay, see that birch tree? The white one about thirty yards in front of us?"

"Yeah! I see a couple of white trees; the one on the ground or the one still standing?"

"The one on the ground. See the path that goes up to it about ten feet from the left end, and then see it again on the other side of it?"

"Yeah! Now I see it!"

"That's a deer run. That's a path the deer follow either on their way to or from their bedding areas, and where they feed and drink. Impossible to tell what time they use it. They feed at night and bed down during the day. I'm just hoping one will come this way while I'm sitting here."

"Wow! That's neat! How did you see that?"

Her eyes were wide with wonder as she stared at the barely visible depression in the soft underbrush. "How long do you have to sit here?"

"Depends. If I get lucky, it could be only a short time. Or it could be all day."

"All day?"

"Yep! And the key to success is to sit still and be very quiet."

"Are you telling me to shut up?"

"Only if you're interested in a dinner of fresh meat tonight."

She snuggled up next to him, lacing her arms in his and resting her head on his shoulder. He was suddenly lost in another world. The woman he was falling in love with was already closer to him than any woman had been for a very long time.

She had sucked in every word he had said to her. Her interest in what he was telling her was genuine, even though he knew she had never pictured herself sitting in the wilderness with a man and his rifle, waiting to kill a wild deer.

"Okay, I'll be real still and real quiet. But it's cold. Just keep me warm."

They sat silently, equally enjoying the touch and warmth of the other, the hunt being more of an excuse to be close to each other than to bag any game. Neither dared express their current feelings to the other, and little needed to be said.

Almost half an hour passed. Dan caught a glimpse of movement directly in front of them. He stiffened in anticipation. Sydney sensed the sudden tension in his body and sat up straight. Dan placed a hand on her leg to still her movements and put a finger to his lips.

The movement revealed itself to be a small doe followed by a second doe, somewhat larger. Dan waited patiently. Sydney looked at him, wondering why he hadn't lifted his rifle to shoot one of the deer. His reason was soon clear. About thirty yards behind the two does, a large buck appeared, supporting antlers of eight points.

Dan slowly and silently lifted his rifle from his lap and braced it against his right shoulder, aiming at the buck. He waited. He knew the proper shot would be to aim at a spot just behind the buck's front leg about six inches above its belly.

But he knew that even if he hit it perfectly, the buck would run off into the trees before it would drop and die, and he might not find the carcass. If he took a neck shot, the risk of missing was much higher, but the deer would drop almost immediately if his shot found its mark. He took the risk and squeezed the trigger.

"You hit it! You hit it! Where did it go?"

The buck had jumped straight up into the air in reaction to being struck by Dan's bullet. It then tried to run away from danger before it died only a couple of yards from the point of impact.

"It fell down behind that big log."

"Let's go get it! I want to see!" Sydney shouted.

"Hold on, Sydney. We need to wait a bit to be sure it's down. It needs time to die. Give it a few minutes. It's not going anywhere."

"But, if it's not going anywhere, why can't we go get it?"

"Just give it a few minutes. I need to be sure I'm right and that it's dead. Don't worry, just sit here and relax with me. Don't let your adrenaline run away with you."

After twenty minutes, Dan reluctantly stood up. He could have spent the entire day there with her clinging to him. He took Sydney by the hand. "Okay, let's go see if we have fresh venison for dinner tonight."

He led her to the spot where he first saw the deer jump into the air and immediately found traces of blood. He turned in the direction the buck ran and, within just a few yards, spotted the carcass lying on the ground with its eyes wide open, indicating that it was dead. Dan poked it in the eye to see if there was any reaction, just to be sure the animal wasn't going to spring up and surprise him with an antler in the stomach. Once the stag was confirmed dead, he turned to Sydney and handed her his rifle.

"Here, hold this, please. I'm going to field dress the buck, and we'll take the tenderloins and backstraps with us. Those are the most tender parts. That's all we'll be able to carry. The rest we'll have to leave behind for the coyotes to feast on."

He hesitated for a moment and then said, "This is going to be a bit messy. You might want to go wait over there for me to finish," pointing to an open spot back on the trail to the campsite.

"No, I want to watch! I want to learn."

"Okay," he replied skeptically, as he took his knife and began to gut the buck, starting at its testicular area and running the knife up to the chest. He glanced over at Sydney to see her reaction. The blood had drained from her face, but she stood her ground and continued to watch the process unfold. He rolled the carcass to one side, allowing the intestines to spill out onto the ground, then rolled up his shirtsleeves and plunged his hands into the gory mess to finish the job of dressing the deer. He again glanced over at Sydney, who was now mesmerized by the process.

"Sydney, seriously. Why don't you have a seat over there and wait for me? I'll only be another few minutes."

"No!" she protested emphatically. "I want to watch. I want to see how it's done. I want to learn."

"Okay!" he replied with a big grin on his face, praying to himself that she didn't pass out and embarrass herself. He bowed his head for a moment.

"What are you doing?" Sydney asked. "I said a prayer to the deer's spirit." "What?" she asked in surprise.

"It died for me, Syd, for us. It gave its life so we could gain strength and live another day. I thanked it for its sacrifice. It's an old Indian custom. I believe strongly that all living things have a spirit and that spirit needs to be honored and respected."

She didn't have to wait long. Within fifteen minutes, Dan had the deer dressed out to the point where he could remove the backstraps and tenderloins. He wrapped them in a plastic bag he had placed in his pack before leaving camp. Walking over to Sydney, he took his rifle from her, while she continued to stare at the now very bloody scene before her.

While she was waiting, her mind was racing. Where did this man come from? How much does he know that I don't? How did he get to be so strong, so sure of who he is, so thoughtful? Who is this man saying a prayer to the spirit of an animal? Who is he who came charging into my life and confused my brain and my heart? How do I not love him...who he is...what he is?" She watched him go about his chore, trying to absorb everything she was seeing.

Dan had cleaned the blood from his hands and forearms using the snow that was still lingering on the ground around them. He then took her by the elbow and said, "Okay, Syd, let's go back to camp. We need to get back on the trail before it gets much later."

As he touched her arm, she turned to him, facing him. They gazed at each other in total silence, unaware of anything around them, where they were, or where they had to go. Their arms came up together. They embraced and kissed tenderly. She gave herself up to him in that moment of softness. He gave himself to her with no conditions, no reservations. They broke contact gently, and as their eyes met, their spirits embraced.

Sydney tried to speak. "I, I, lo..."

"Shh," Dan stopped her, gently placing his hand to her mouth. "Not now, Syd. Not out here. I want to say the same thing to you. But I can't. I've got to get you home. You and your father. I've got to. I can't think of anything else right now. I can't be distracted. Do you understand what I'm saying?"

She looked up at him. "Yes, Dan, I understand. I really do understand. I'll help you. I've got a lot to go home to now. Much more than I did a week ago." Her eyes were still fixed on his. She kissed him again. She could feel their hearts joining there in the wild, the spirit of the dead buck coaxing them closer together.

If they could hear that spirit, they would listen to, Thank you. Thank you, both of you. You have lifted my spirit and sanctified my death by the birth of your love. I will watch over you. I will guide you home safely.

Without saying a word, she let herself be led away. Twenty minutes later, they approached the camp, where they were greeted by a father who was seeing an entirely new expression on his daughter's face, one he had never seen before and probably would never see again. He looked over at Dan in wonderment. His questioning expression said it all as Sydney walked past him without a word.

"I heard your shot. Did you get something?" asked the president.

"Yes," Dan replied. "I killed a nice-sized buck. Got some fresh meat for dinner, enough for at least two meals, maybe more."

"Where did you get it?"

"Back about a quarter of a mile. I remembered we'd passed a pine thicket. Figured deer might use that area to bed down and get out of the snow. Got it as it was going to the creek for a drink. Only problem is, I don't have a hunting license for the State of Maine".

The two men laughed. The president noticed that Sydney did not. She was distracted and looking off into the distance. He glanced at Dan and sensed some tension between the two young people.

"Well, don't worry about the lack of a license. I think I can arrange a presidential pardon for you if necessary. The governor is a friend of mine." He paused for a moment and then turned to his daughter. "Sydney, what's wrong, honey? Something upsetting you?"

"She watched me gut the deer and cut out some meat for dinner," Dan jumped in. The president smiled and with an almost invisible nod signaled his understanding of his daughter's current state of mind.

Sydney overheard them. Inwardly, her thoughts were very different from theirs. 'No, Daddy. You're both wrong. It isn't the sight of blood that's affecting me. It isn't the thought of seeing Dan taking meat from the animal. It isn't the idea of killing that beautiful animal. It's him, Daddy! It's him. My world is changing. I'm, I'm wonderfully confused, it's because of him."

Chapter Five

It was noon by the time they were all packed up and ready to move again. The snow from the night before had almost melted away except where the foliage was so thick that the sun could not penetrate to the ground. What was left would not interfere with their progress.

The president had done a lot of the packing while Dan and Sydney were off hunting, but there was still more to do. After a quick, cold lunch, they were off breaking a fresh trail, keeping the sound of the rushing creek just off to their left. It was getting colder.

They hiked non-stop for almost four hours, at one point leaving the creek to climb a large hill. The slope back toward the creek was far too steep for them to traverse it safely. Once over the top of the hill, the slope lessened, and they could hike back within earshot of the water rushing down through the steep gorge they had bypassed. The skies were gray and darkening, and the gray clouds dropped low, wrapping around the higher hilltops.

It started to snow again just before Dan was about to call it a day and find a place to camp. Darkness came to them about 5:00 p.m. It was not safe or smart to be hiking blindly in the dark and they needed enough light to get themselves settled for the night.

Off to their right was a rocky cliff face. Dan had been looking carefully at it for the last few hundred yards. He finally found what he was looking for.

"There's an overhang up ahead, up on the cliff face. You two wait here, I want to go take a look to see if it's deep enough to provide us with some shelter. I think it might be a shallow cave."

He dropped his pack and walked off toward the rock face. Within a few minutes he found exactly what he'd hoped for. It wasn't a cave, but the setback in the rocks was deep enough to provide them with good overhead shelter from the falling snow, and he could stack pine and spruce boughs across the front to keep out the wind and provide some added warmth. Within a few minutes, all three were standing in front of their home for the night.

"Sir, if you could gather up as much firewood as you can, and Syd, if you could help me cut some evergreen branches to stack in front of the opening, we'll have a good place to spend the night. Should be warm and dry."

An hour later, the three of them where sitting beside a roaring campfire, with a supply of firewood that would easily last them through the night. In addition, there were two large hardwood trees that had fallen close by that offered an additional supply. Travis had rigged a couple of branches on the other side of the opening, draped the tarp across them, and then piled evergreen branches on top of that. This would keep the snow out and the heat in.

"How about some venison stew?" Dan asked. Two heads nodded in response. It was dark by the time they finished eating and had cleaned up their meal mess, burning everything they didn't consume. The wall of boughs that Dan had built was doing the job, holding heat in the cave and providing them with a relatively comfortable environment. But, it was getting even colder. He was becoming increasingly concerned as the hours passed.

By the time they were ready to crawl into their sleeping bags for the night, there was already more than three inches of snow on the ground. It was a heavy, wet, early-season snow clinging to everything and piling up on the tree limbs overhead, the kind of snow that snaps limbs and brings down dead trees.

It snowed all night. By daylight, when Dan stuck his head out beyond their wall of evergreen branches, there was well over a foot of snow on the ground and it was still coming down. They would not be able to hike today. Dan slipped back inside their shelter, piled three logs atop the hot coals of last night's campfire and started to get back into his sleeping bag.

"How is it, Dan?" Sydney whispered.

"Doesn't look like we'll be going anywhere today. Try to get some more sleep. It might be a long, boring day."

It didn't stop until early afternoon. By that time, Dan estimated there to be at least sixteen to eighteen inches of snow piled up. Even if he was off by a handful of inches, it was still far too deep for them to even consider hiking farther than their wood pile. The skies were still dark gray, but seemed to be lightening some off to the northwest. A good sign!

The snow had stacked up on their outer wall of branches, keeping the wind out and locking the campfire heat in. Their little cave dwelling was dry, and warm enough for them to sit around the campfire in comfort while waiting out the weather. There was little conversation. Each of them napped once or twice during the afternoon, and when awake seemed to be mesmerized by the flames of the campfire.

"Wish we had a deck of cards," Sydney said wistfully.

"Wish I had a hot cup of coffee and a doughnut," Dan added.

"Wish I had a bottle of single malt Scotch," the president remarked.

That was the full extent of the conversation for the afternoon. There was a lot of nervous fidgeting, little else was said. It was clear they all had the same thing on their minds: getting caught in the snowy wilderness for a long period of time would be a pain in the ass. Only when it came time to prepare an evening meal did they get their muscle and bones moving again.

It didn't snow anymore that night, and the heavy cloud cover was holding the temperature at a steady level. The next morning, the sun came up bright and warm. The sky was clear and a fantastic "Carolina Blue," reminding Dan of his time at the University in Chapel Hill, North Carolina. As the day progressed, the temperatures rose. By late afternoon, there was a noticeable decrease in the snow depth, but not enough to enable them to move on.

It took three more agonizing days for the to snow melt. It was as entertaining as watching paint dry. The air temperature had risen, and with the bright sunshine, the only meaningful snow was tucked up under thick, overhanging evergreens or hiding in the underbrush.

Dan felt confident on the morning of the fifth day that they could safely resume their hike out. The president had made significant progress during their forced rest. He was moving around with much more ease, using only a walking stick the way most recreational backpackers would, for that little added assist in balancing their load. Dan was pleased to see his progress. It would make his job easier by taking one more load off his mind.

The three of them were restless, full of pent-up energy, nervous to begin again. As they prepared, President Don Richardson studied Sergeant Dan Travis. He wanted to know more about this man. What made him tick? Where did his drive and dedication come from?

Dan was moving about nervously. Packing their gear. Checking on the others. His impatience was obvious, but his control of his own behavior was equally obvious. The president knew the man well enough that he could see the tension in him, in his movements.

"What's wrong Dan? What's bothering you?"

"Supplies!" Sydney overheard their conversation and moved closer to listen.

"What do you mean,"asked the president.

"We've been sitting here for more than five days chewing up supplies that we'll need down the trail."

"That couldn't be helped," the president added.

"You killed that deer," Sydney injected. "That helped with our food supply."

"Yeah, it did...but I've been thinking."

"What?" Don Richardson asked.

"Well, I've been thinking maybe I should make a run back to the supply skid and load up with more food to replace what we've used up. I could make a round trip in just a few days."

"I vote no!" exclaimed Sydney.

"So do I," added her father. "Look, Dan, I've stayed away from playing boss. You've saved our lives, and you're worked yourself to death to do it. We need you. We can't get out of here without you. We need to move on. I'm feeling great. We can finally begin to cover some serious distance each day. Besides, if you go back, we will just sit here eating even more of the supplies here, while we're waiting for you to get back. And what if it snows again? Back and forth, back and forth, and never moving another inch closer to getting the fuck out of here."

"Daddy!"

"Sorry, honey, but sometimes I get uptight too! The way I see it, we've got to move forward. We've got to get out of these mountains. I know you want to be sure that Sydney and I are well fed and well taken care of. But this isn't a damned vacation trip to a mountain spa. I vote to keep moving on."

"Dan, let's go!" Sydney added. She reached out with both hands to hold his. Her touch and her voice were as soft and tender as silk.

"If we run low on food, we'll skip a few meals, or you can kill another deer. Please Dan, get us out of here. It's time. Get us home."

Travis listened to their logic and weighed his own. He looked into the warm eyes of the woman in front of him. He wondered if he really wanted to get home. Out here he had her. Back in the real world, her world, he knew he was a misfit. He would lose her to the life she came from. He would be sent off on some assignment, stationed on some remote base to be sure he was kept away from her. The president wouldn't allow his daughter to be involved with some lowlife soldier, some... G.I.

He studied her face, melted into her moist brown eyes, and saw his dreams flash by. "Okay, let's move."

And they did. Day after day for nine more days. Some days hiking only one or two miles, stymied by the terrain. Others days as many as five or six, always staying close to the creek that kept increasing in width and the volume of water it carried, as other streams fed their waters into it.

With no trail to follow, having to blaze every step they took, their progress was difficult and slow. Hills slowed them. Rocks and rain slowed them. Mud slowed them, and one more light snowfall came along to test them and slow them one more time.

Their food supplies held out. They limited their diet to two meals a day. Water was never a problem. So they continued. They slipped and struggled. They climbed and crawled. They slugged it out with the elements until Dan came upon what looked like a fairly well used foot trail. He paused for a moment and the instinctively turned to his left to follow it in the downhill direction. Within a half mile, he came to an abrupt stop so suddenly that President Richardson plowed into him.

"What is it Dan?"

"Look up ahead."

Richardson peered through the trees. "Is that a cabin?"

Sydney had come forward to participate in the conversation.

"Looks like a structure of some kind," Dan said, barely able to contain his excitement.

"You two wait here. This will only take a few minutes."

He lowered his pack to the ground, checked his rifle to see that it had a round in the cylinder, and began to walk toward the building. It started to snow just as he reached what looked like some sort of hunting lodge, not much of one, but a dwelling none the less. He circled it and peered through the only windows, one on each side of the building. The he tried the front door. It opened without any resistance. He entered and inspected the entire building. It was a one-story old wooden structure with a sloped roof.

Toward the back was a kitchen with a propane cook stove, a sink, and what looked like a chest freezer, but there was no sign of there being electricity in the building, so either there was a generator or the freezer was used for storage.

Toward the front of the building, there was a room off to the left that contained two double-bunk beds made out of 2x4s and plywood, obviously homemade. The largest room in the cabin had two old couches, a couple of chairs, and a wood-burning stove that was surely the only source of heat for the entire building. In one corner of the room was a large stack of firewood and a metal five-gallon pail with a small shovel for the removal of ashes from the stove.

On the wall over one of the couches hung a gun rack and a dozen or so pictures of dead deer, with men standing next to each other with big grins on their faces and either a rifle or a bow in one hand. No doubt what this place was. A very primitive hunting camp with minimal furnishings but, from all appearances, snug, warm, dry, and safe.

Dan went back for Sydney and her father. By the time he reached them, new snow had already coated the ground and the skies to the north and west were beginning to darken. It was approaching four o'clock in the afternoon. He could smell the snow, and feel the temperature dropping.

He lifted his pack and led them back to the cabin. They entered cautiously, examining the interior with suspicion.

"You said it was unlocked?"

"Yes sir, but that's not unusual. Lots of hunters will leave the door unlocked and a cabin stocked with firewood so other hunters or hikers who might need a place to shelter for the night can get in. It's sort of a custom in the wilderness.

"If you enter, you are expected to restock the firewood for the next person who might need it, respect the place, and leave it like you found it. I would have been surprised to find it locked up tight. That would only force someone who needed it to break a window to get in."

"What do you think we should do?" Sydney asked.

"That's easy! We'll spend the night here. Build a nice fire in the stove and see what tomorrow looks like. I think we're in for a healthy snowfall, so this place came along just at the right time."

"Sounds good to me," the president said. "I could do with a night of not sleeping on the ground. Those bunk beds look awfully inviting."

"You two grab a bunk each. I'll sleep out here on one of the couches and keep a fire going in the stove," Dan said. "Now, let's get a fire going and cook up some hot supper. Let me look in the kitchen and see if there is anything that we might use to boost our food supplies. Do you two think you can get a fire going in that stove?"

"We'll give it a try," Sydney said.

"Be sure the flue is open," Dan added as he headed for the kitchen. "Don't want to smoke us out before we even get warmed up. I'll look around to see if I can find some candles or a lantern of some kind."

Within a few minutes, Sydney and her father had managed to get a roaring fire going, and Dan had found some cans of vegetables stashed in an insulated box under the sink. He added a can of corn and a can of carrots to a package of freeze-dried beef stew, added the proper amount of water, and placed the pot on the stove.

He then unearthed two kerosene lanterns that he lit and hung on nails in the ceiling crossbeam of the large front room. While dinner was cooking, he went outside and searched the area around the cabin. He found the outhouse about thirty yards down a trail off to the left front of the cabin.

After relieving himself, he returned to the warmth of the cabin, told Sydney and her father about the outhouse, and sat down to soak up the aroma of a hot beef stew dinner. He knew this was not what the president and Sydney were accustomed to, but considering all they'd had to deal with in recent weeks, all he could think was 'there ain't no place like home.'

They ate quietly, enjoying the warmth of the stew and the fire in the stove. Afterwards, it was nearly impossible for any of them to keep their eyes open. The heat, the food, and the relative sense of safety and comfort offered by their new home brought a sense of relaxation they hadn't experienced for weeks.

Dan got up and retrieved the soiled paper plates. He'd found a supply in the kitchen. The used ones were tossed into the stove for disposal. He took the dirty pot into the kitchen, placed it in the sink, and filled it with water. That would do for tonight. He would wash it in the morning after heating up some water. Now, it was time to rest.

When he returned to the big room, Sydney had stretched out on one of the couches, and Don Richardson was leaning forward with his head in his hands.

"Why don't you call it a day and sack out in one of those bunks before you fall on the floor and I have to pick you up," Dan joked.

"I think I'll do just that. It's going to feel good sleeping on a mattress. Sydney needs to crawl into bed herself."

Dan kneeled down on the floor next to her. "Sid! Hey! Time to go to bed." She groaned and rolled over. "Guess I'll just cover her up and let her sleep right here. She's out cold already," Dan said.

"Okay by me, Dan. I'll see you in the morning." And the president ambled off to what served as the cabin's bedroom.

Dan unrolled Sydney's sleeping bag and draped it over her. As he was tucking it in around her shoulders, her hand came up and took him by the arm. "Stay here by me," she whispered, never opening her eyes.

"Okay! Let me load the stove with wood, and I'll be right back." She never heard him. She was sound asleep.

He unrolled his sleeping bag and dropped it on the floor. When he had loaded the stove with logs and closed the flue down to a night setting, he returned to her and sat on the floor next to her shoulder. He took her hand in his, draped his sleeping bag over his legs, lowered his head to rest it next to her torso, closed his eyes, and was sound asleep in a matter of seconds.

Part VII

The Smell of Bacon

Chapter One

When the president awoke, the sun had already started the day without him. He rolled onto his back and stretched his rested body. He'd slept better than he had in years. He listened for the sound of anyone stirring. Hearing nothing, he crept out of bed and, in his stocking feet, walked quietly into the next room.

What he saw softened his heart. There on the floor was his big, rough-and-tough army sergeant leaning against the couch, holding his daughter's hand. She had rolled onto her side, facing him, and her other hand rested on his shoulder. Both were still sound asleep.

He stood watching, unable to move and unable to stop grinning. He finally turned, walked back to his bed, and sat down. His mind was racing, thinking of his daughter and her life with him since her mother had died. She had given so much. Given up so much!

She was a strong, rebellious young woman who had dedicated her life to her father, supporting him in the absence of his wife, her mother. She had sacrificed her own personal relationships to be the "First daughter," where there was no "First lady." Men came after her for all the wrong reasons and evaporated into history once they found out that being next to her was not the path to fame and success.

Yet here in the wilds of northern Maine or wherever the hell they were, here, under the worst of circumstances, she lay there holding onto a man she hardly knew, yet knew so well. A man who had no secret agenda, no ulterior motive, who had only one objective in mind, one mission, to save her father's life. His commander! Not her father, but his commanding officer. That was his only mission. It was as pure and simple and innocent as that. But in the process of completing that mission, they had found each other. Where would it go? Where would it end?

He heard movement and walked back to find Dan stretching his aching muscles.

"Morning, Dan."

"Morning, sir."

Syndey began to stir at the sound of their voices.

"Morning, baby girl," Richardson said to his daughter.

"Morning, Daddy," she replied mid-stretch.

She and Dan looked at each other silently, and then Dan walked over to the nearest window.

"Damn!" he said, under his breath.

"What's wrong, Dan?" asked the president.

"There's a lot of fresh snow, and it's still coming down. I'd better take a look." He opened the door and stepped outside, the president and Sydney only one step behind him. He took a single stride, and the snow reached almost to his knees. "Damn!" he said again. They all knew what this meant. More delay.

The president broke the silence. "At least we have a warm, dry place to wait it out."

"Not good!" Dan said to no one in particular. "Not good!"

The three of them stepped back into the cabin and plopped down on the two couches.

"What now?" Sydney asked, placing a reassuring hand on Dan's shoulder.

"Give me a minute, Sydney... please," he replied, hanging his head down, chin on his chest. "Let me think." He grabbed his jacket, slipped on his boots, and headed outside. Sydney started to follow him, but her father grabbed her by the arm.

"Let him be, Sydney. He needs a few minutes to himself."

"But!"

"No buts. Leave him be."

They waited for almost half an hour, occasionally peeking out the glass insert in the front door to see if Dan was okay. He never left the front porch of the cabin. His head was hanging down with his chin on his chest the first time they looked. The second time, he was looking off into the forest along the path that led to the cabin.

As they were about to peek for the third time, Dan came bursting into the room. His face showed the fruits of his time alone. His excitement lit up the room. "Take a look out there!" he ordered. Sydney and Don Richardson peered through the open doorway. "What do you see?"

They looked out and saw nothing, then looked at each other for help in answering Dan's question.

"I don't see anything but snow and trees," said the president.

"Come on! Look hard. Tell me what you see. Better yet, tell me what you don't see!"

Sydney spoke up, "I see trees... new snow... and the path leading to the cabin."

Exactly! A path leading to the cabin. When guys go hunting, they take all kinds of gear with them: food, water, guns, clothes, coolers full of beer and ice. All kinds of stuff! Heavy stuff. How do you think they get it to their cabin? They drive it! Either in a pickup or on an ATV. One or the other.

"Do you see any vehicle tracks leading up to this cabin? Is that trail wide enough to handle a vehicle? No, no, no! They are carrying everything to this cabin. And if there's one thing I know about guys like this, they don't like to work. They want to drink, eat, sleep, and hunt. They want to spit, fart, cuss, and hunt. But they didn't come up here to work.

"So, what does that tell you?" His two companions looked puzzled. "It tells you that we are close to a road. I'm willing to bet that there is a road within a hundred yards of here. I'll bet you there's a road just beyond where we can see down the path. I'll bet we're damned close to a road of some kind!"

Sydney and her father jumped to their feet and threw their arms around Dan, the three of them bouncing up and down like three kids at the county fair. After a couple of minutes of celebrating, Dan again took control.

"Here's what I'm going to do. I'm going to take a hike down this path to the road and then walk down the road until I find someone. I'll get them to bring a truck back up here, get the two of you and all of our stuff, and head home."

"I'll go with you!" Sydney interjected.

"No, you stay here with your dad until I get back. You'll be warm, dry, and safe here."

"No! I'm going with you!" she shouted, catching Dan and her father by surprise with her volume and insistence. "You are not going alone. My dad will be safe here. He's the one we need to protect until we find out what's going on. But you're not going alone. If anything should happen to you, we'll be sitting ducks out here. So, I'm going with you!"

Dan was speechless when she finished.

"I've got to agree with her, Dan," the president added. "I'll be fine here alone. I'll get everything packed up and ready to go for when you get back. If you're delayed, I'll have all the supplies I'll need until you return."

"Okay," Dan conceded. "Let's get some hot breakfast in our stomachs, and we'll be off."

An hour later, the two of them were on the trail, slogging through the snow, headed toward what they hoped would be the end of a very long ordeal. It turned out that Dan was correct. They walked less than a hundred yards from the front of the cabin to where the path took a bend to the right.

Once around that bend, there was a large parking area twenty yards in front of them, and right next to the parking area, a beautiful, wonderful, glorious road. It was currently covered with almost a foot of new snow, but Dan would bet that under that snow was a well-maintained dirt and gravel road leading to somewhere fairly close by.

"Which way?" Sydney asked. "Wait here. I'll be right back."

Dan went off to their left. He was soon lost to Sydney's sight, fading away behind the falling snow and misty air. He reappeared in only a few minutes, breathing deeply and smiling broadly.

"There's another cabin just up the road, maybe a third of a mile. That's where the road ends. It dead ends into the forest. So, that says we go that way."

He pointed off to their right.

"Let's go!"

They trudged through the snow for almost three hours. Dan found it hard to estimate how far they had walked. His best guess was five or six miles, probably less. The going was very slow because of the difficulty they were having with the depth of the snow and the slipping and sliding. They were nearing exhaustion, and Dan was beginning to fear that he had made a major mistake.

"Hold it!" Dan suddenly shouted.

"What is it, Dan?" Sydney asked, panting for breath.

"Do you smell that?"

"What?" she asked.

"Smell what?"

"Smoke!"

She tilted her head back, pointing her nose skyward and sniffing the air like a bird dog.

"Yes! Yes, I smell it."

"Bacon," Dan added.

"Somebody is cooking bacon."

"Yes! Bacon! I smell it, too," Sydney added, a big grin lighting up her face.

Hugging the side of the road for concealment, they moved off in the direction of the scent. A couple of hundred yards farther down the road, they saw it: a doublewide manufactured home sitting up on cider blocks only yards off the road and anchored to the bank of the stream they had been following for days. It was beautiful! It was a palace! It was the Biltmore mansion all wrapped up in Christmas paper! It was the most beautiful building they had ever seen in their lives. Better than the White House itself!

There was an open expanse between where they sat hidden along the road and the front door of the house, probably the owner's attempt at a front lawn. A dark blue, four-door extended-cab pickup with a cap over its cargo bed was parked near the steps leading up to the front door.

Smoke was coming out of the chimney, and lights were on inside the house. Somebody was home.

"Oh my God! We've made it," Sydney said, sinking to her knees in relief. "Dan, you've done it. You got us out alive. I need a hot bath and a greasy hamburger with some of that bacon, right now!" She started toward the house.

"Hold on, Sydney." Dan grabbed her by the arm as she stood.

"You're forgetting something."

"What?"

"Well, for one thing, your father. Secondly, a few weeks ago, I killed a bunch of people who were trying to stop us from reaching this very spot, and then they tried a second time, shooting up our camp from that helicopter. They were sent to kill your father and anyone else who happened to be nearby. That includes you and me and anyone else who might live to tell the world about this mess we've been through. Before we go barging in, I need to know who's in there. I didn't come this far to rush in for a hamburger and fries."

She thought for a moment. "You're right, Dan. I got a bit too excited. What do you want to do?"

"You stay right here. Let me go in alone and see what's what. If I'm not back in thirty minutes, you head back to the cabin and get your father. Stay in the cabin for the night and then... well, then, if I'm not back by morning, you're on your own."

He tried to stand, but she threw her arms around his neck, holding him next to her. "Dan... I... "

"Shh... not here, not now. Hold that thought until we get out of here. I've got a lot to say to you, too!"

He stood up and walked away without looking back. He knew if he did, he might not go any farther, that he might just take her in his arms and run off, leaving the entire world behind. He walked up to the front door of the house.

He tried to act as casual as possible, to seem as if this was an ordinary day and he was doing a completely normal thing, not posing any kind of threat to whomever came to the door of this remote home. He knocked firmly, while at the same time slipping his right hand under his jacket, placing it on the 9mm pistol that had rested on his hip for weeks.

In a few seconds, the door was opened by a man Dan guessed to be in his early fifties, about five feet ten and a hundred seventy-five pounds, give or take a few.

The man looked Dan over from head to foot with a quizzical eye. For the first time, Dan thought about the way he must look. Weeks of living in the wild, bearded, dirty, and unkempt! But the man stood his ground confidently.

"Hi," Dan finally squeezed out, to be acknowledged by a slight nod of the man's head.

"I need some help. I've got a couple of friends back in the woods. We're lost. Can you tell me how far it is to the nearest town?"

The man looked back over Dan's shoulder in the direction of his footprints in the snow. He then looked back at Dan, examining him once again from head to toe, clearly assessing his trustworthiness. "Come on in, young man," he said, turning his back to Dan with an assured air about himself. "And you can take your hand off that sidearm. There's no danger waiting for you here."

Dan followed cautiously. Once they were both inside, the man turned back to face Dan, stuck out his hand, and introduced himself.

"Mike Stowe," he said, communicating a sense of warmth and welcome that immediately disarmed Dan's concern for safety. Travis accepted his hand with a smile.

"Hi, Mike. Glad to meet you. My name is Dan. Can you tell me how far it is to the nearest town? Do you think you might be able to give my friends and me a ride?"

Stowe stood silently for a moment, looking at Dan before saying, "Tell me what happened, young man."

Travis began to fabricate a story about how he and his two friends went camping and got twisted around in the woods when it began to snow and got lost. Stowe let him talk for four or five minutes. The moment Dan hesitated, Stowe jumped in with a question.

"Do you always go camping in uniform, Sergeant?"

Taken aback, Dan again mentally reviewed how he must look to his host. He stood there staring blankly at Stowe for what seemed a lifetime until Stowe broke eye contact, turned to a small table in the middle of what was his living room, picked up a newspaper, and turned it face up to reveal the headline story.

"It's Sunday, Sarge. Big news day! Seems there's an All-American hero Army Sergeant missing from his job and home for the past few weeks. A rumor that he might have been sent on a secret solo mission by the vice president to find the president and his missing party. That's the soldier's picture there on the front page. Look familiar?"

Dan bent down to pick up the paper. His picture took up a full quarter of the front page. Below was a picture of the president and vice president. He quickly scanned the lead story. It said that the vice president had refused to confirm the rumor. The reporter also pointed out that the vice president had refused to deny the rumor.

He went on to report that the vice president was only holding the position of acting president, refusing to accept being sworn in as president until it was confirmed that the president was, in fact, dead. Without the recovery of a body, his personal loyalty to the president would not allow him to accept the office of his longtime friend.

The reporter indicated that the vice president's position was creating a constitutional crisis of sorts, but that Congress and the nation were in no hurry to force the resolution of the issue while the mourning for the president and his daughter continued at such a high level. It seemed that the public was strongly standing behind the vice president for his stance on honor and loyalty, so Congress wasn't pushing the issue too strongly.

As he read on, he translated the vice president's position to indicate that there was a safe haven within the White House. All he had to do was figure out a way of getting the president there, safe and sound. The vice president was a man of honor, and it seemed to him not a part of the attempt to kill the president and his daughter. He now had a clear destination. The White House!

Dan raised his eyes from the paper to find Mike Stowe looking at him, waiting for him to finish. There was warmth and understanding in the man's face. A respect for the young man now sharing his home.

"Is he alive?" Dan looked into the eyes of Mr. Mike Stowe. He let his gut take over. He let the positive signals he was feeling instinctively lead him.

"Yes, he and his daughter!"

"Is that the woman I saw you leave behind just before you came up to my front door?" Dan weighed his next words.

"Yes, it is. I left the president back in a hunting cabin we came across a few miles back. We've been there for a couple of days watching it snow. The two Secret Service agents who were with the president are both dead. One died when the plane went down, and the other when he was trying to get to me after he saw me parachute in."

"That's too bad. But let's get the young lady in here and get her warm and fed. Then we'll go find the president and get him back here. If you were in a cabin a few miles back up that trail, it's either mine or my son's. Either way, we'll take a couple of snowmobiles and get him back here in no time."

"Hold on, Mike! There's something else I've got to tell you before you jump into this with both feet. Somebody has tried to kill us, twice! They tried to get all of us. There's something going on with this whole situation.

"This isn't over just because we managed to get out of the forest alive. If you don't want to get involved, that's okay, we'll all understand. All I ask is that you lend me your truck and keep this quiet for a couple of days."

"Tried to kill you? Really? Wow! That does add a new wrinkle, doesn't it? Hmm, okay, I understand. But it doesn't change anything as far as I'm concerned. So, let's go get them in here, and we can figure things out where it's nice and warm and dry. You must all be hungry for a good hot meal, and God knows, you need a bath, a shave, and some fresh clothes. Hate to insult you, young fella, but you stink real bad."

"I'll be right back," Dan told Stowe as he walked out the front door. Sydney was sitting on a log just off the side of the road. She knew from the broad grin on Dan's face that he had good news.

"Come on, Syd. You're about to meet a very nice gentleman."

He took her back to Stowe's and introduced her to Mike. In only a few minutes, Stowe had her settled into one of his guest bedrooms with a stack of clean towels and some of his daughter's clothes that he knew would fit the president's daughter just fine. He showed her the bathroom and shower, and made lots of soap and shampoo available for her use.

"Do you know how to operate a snowmobile?" Mike asked.

"Yes, sir, I sure do."

"Okay, then let's go fetch a president!" Dan could hear the shower running as they stepped out the back door of the house. A short distance behind the house was a three-sided shed, and in it were three snowmobiles parked side by side.

"One's mine, one's my son's, and one's my daughter's. We can only drive two of them up to the cabin, so I'll haul my ice-fishing sled behind for all your equipment. The president can ride back with one of us. Ready?"

"Yes, sir."

"Okay, let's go."

Stowe got the two machines started and backed out of the shed. He waved to Dan to follow him as he gunned his engine and started moving down the trail. It took them a little over half an hour to travel the distance that it had taken Dan and Sydney half a day of trudging through the snow to cover.

Stowe pulled to a stop in front of the hunting cabin as the president stepped out onto the front porch, glancing between Dan Travis and the stranger driving the noisy snowmobile. Mike immediately extended his hand.

"Good evening, sir. I hope you found my hunting cabin to your liking. I'm Mike Stowe."

"Hi Mike. Don Richardson. Your cabin has proven to be very comfortable. Thank you very much."

There was an instant chemistry between the two men. They shook hands, and Stowe threw his arms around the president in a warm, welcoming embrace. In just a few minutes, Dan had explained everything that had taken place since they parted company earlier in the day.

"Sydney is fine. She was in the shower when we left, and I'm sure we'll find her sound asleep by the time we get back, or still in the shower running Mr. Stowe's hot-water bill sky high."

"I suspect that she will have taken control of the entire house and is prancing around looking like a million bucks, ready to bark orders at us when we walk in the front door," the president said half under his breath, more to Mike Stowe than to Dan Travis.

An hour and a cold snowmobile ride later, they were stomping their feet on Stowe's front porch, trying to get as much snow off their boots and clothes as possible before barging into Mike's living room. Sydney flung open the front door. When Dan saw her, his heart dropped right past his stomach all the way to his knees.

She was dressed in a form-fitting scoop-necked pullover and tailored jeans. She had put on just enough of Mike's daughter's makeup to stop him right in his tracks. He couldn't believe how beautiful she looked, as he froze open-mouthed, blocking the doorway. Mike Stowe nearly plowed over him trying to get inside.

Her father threw his arms around her in a warm embrace, acknowledging their joy at being "Out."

"You'd better slap him or kiss him back into reality before we all freeze to death with that door wide open," the president whispered to his gorgeous daughter.

It was almost dark by the time the president and Dan had showered and changed into the clothing that Mike had provided. Dan fit nicely into Mike's son-in-law's clothes, and the president fit comfortably into Mike's pants, shirt, and shoes. By the time everyone was all washed up and shaved, Stowe had a hot dinner ready.

There was little conversation around the table. However, it was clear that there were four separate minds working in high gear, digesting what had taken place in the past few weeks and planning for what lay ahead.

Once dinner was over and everything cleaned up and put away, Don and Sydney Richardson, along with Mike Stowe, collapsed into soft, comfortable chairs in the living room. Stowe had built a blazing fire that was mesmerizing them while they waited for Dan to return from the bathroom.

When Dan entered the living room, he spotted a telephone sitting on a small side table near the door to the kitchen. He looked at it for a moment, then turned back toward the group awaiting him. Only Stowe had seen him looking at the telephone. Stowe read the look on Dan's face and suspected what was racing through the mind of the young man he had come to respect almost instantly.

Stowe knew the mountains. He knew this had to be a special man to have survived and brought out two other people. His mind was on fast forward, trying to imagine what Dan and his "friends" must have experienced to get this far.

And on top of that, on top of all of that, the President of the United States was sitting in his living room, in his house, out here in the middle of God's country. Unbelievable. Un-fucking-believable!

"Need to make a call?" Stowe asked Dan. The president and Sydney turned toward the two men. Travis stood motionless. Staring at the telephone, his mind was in ferment. Sydney stood and took his arm.

"Dan, are you okay?"

Travis looked at the president. He then turned and addressed Stowe.

"Why are you doing this? Why are you helping us and not letting the rest of the world know about it? Why haven't you picked up that phone and called anyone... or have you?"

Stowe paused before he spoke. He could see the tension in the young sergeant's face and body. He wanted to ease the tension a bit before he said anything.

"Look, son, I can only imagine what you've been through to get here. I know you're tired, and you've got a lot on your plate. But think for a minute. If somebody's out to kill the president, what's ahead may be just as bad, or a lot worse than what you've already had to deal with.

"Seems to me you need help, all the help you can get. Me? I'm nobody. I'm certainly not a hero, but I am an American, a loyal American, veteran of two wars. Trust me, Dan, this is still your show. Tell me what you want me to do. I'm with you all the way."

"Who else lives here?" Dan asked.

"Nobody. My wife died a year ago. I retired from the post office. Moved up here full-time right after she died, and all the paperwork was completed. I don't mix much with the locals. Don't need to and don't have much in common with them. And I don't need any damn mob of reporters screwing up my front yard either!"

Dan smiled. He took the measure of the man, trying to read him. Trying to peer into him, to search his soul, to see what he was made of. So far, he liked what he saw, what his famous instinct was telling him. What choice did he have at the moment anyway? He was exhausted. He couldn't even think of going any farther. He looked at the president.

"Mr. President, five minutes after any of us picks up that telephone, this house will become the center of the world. Every TV network, every newspaper, every radio station, every cop, and,

God forbid, every politician within a thousand miles will be fighting for every square inch of this place. Every camera in the world will be flashing in our faces. Are we ready for that?"

"Dan, that's bound to happen no matter where we go. I'm still the president. We're coming back from the dead. There's going to be massive coverage no matter what."

"Yes, sir. You're absolutely right. I know that and I understand that. But are we ready for that? And there's something else."

"What is it, Dan?" Sydney asked.

"Somebody tried to kill you... tried to kill all of us. Do you think those grunts that I killed back there in the forest are the ones who came up with this plan: to kill the President of the United States? I don't think so. Whoever did that is still out there, and if we get the wrong person on the wrong telephone, who's to say that more of those guys aren't the first ones to show up right here? Who's to say we ever get out of these woods alive?"

The room was dead silent. The four looked at each other, waiting for someone to speak. Stowe broke the tension.

"What do you want to do, Sergeant Travis?"

Dan hung his head for a moment, then looked at each of the other three in turn. "Right now, we need to get some rest. I need some sleep to clear my mind and think. I'd ask each of you to do the same. Let's discuss this further in the morning over a hot cup of coffee. We need a plan, and we all need to agree on what we're going to do and how we're going to do it. Do you all agree?"

The three agreed. Sydney wrapped her arms around Dan and gave him a very warm, reassuring hug. The president smiled. Stowe came to him and patted him on the shoulder. A tense chatter began to spread among them as Stowe began showing where everyone was to claim a bed for the night.

"Ms. Richardson, please take my room and make yourself at home. Everything you need is in the bathroom. Clean towels are under the sink. Mr. President, the spare room is all yours. A bit small, but the bed sleeps just great. Dan, I'll pull out the sleeper couch for you."

"What about you?" Sydney asked.

"I'll take the other couch in the living room. That'll give Dan and me a chance to talk about what he wants to do tomorrow and when he wants to get going. We'll be roomies for the night."

Sydney stood and stretched. "I'm going to call it a day." She leaned over and kissed her father on the cheek. Dan and Mike respectfully stood. She stepped around the coffee table, put her arms around Dan's neck, and kissed him warmly on the lips, holding the embrace for what seemed to Dan a lifetime. "Good night, Dan," she said as she turned and left the room.

He couldn't speak. "G, Good night, Sydney," he finally got out. He was beet red.

She leaned over and kissed Mike on the cheek. "Good night, Mr. Stowe. I don't know how to thank you for all you've done for us today."

"Well, for starters, you can kiss me good night the way you kissed that young fellow."

She laughed. "Sorry, that's reserved. Good night, Daddy." She turned and disappeared down the hallway. The two older men eyed each other with knowing grins painted on their faces.

"Well, young man," Mike said, "Seems you might come out of this little camping trip of yours with something more than sore feet. That gal's got her eye on you." As the president flashed his usual grin of approval, Dan was desperately looking for a place to hide.

"Guess I'll turn in too," the president said. "Mike, thank you. We owe you. I owe you. And I fully intend to pay you back."

"Thank you, Mr. President. But you're just being here is an honor. A real honor. Just wish it was under different circumstances."

"Good night, gentlemen," the president said as he turned and followed in his daughter's footsteps.

"Good night, sir," Dan managed to say.

By nine o'clock, the president and Sydney Richardson were asleep, safe and sound under Mike Stowe's roof. Dan was stretched out on the sofa bed, and Mike was sitting on the other sofa across the room.

"Well, Sergeant, what's the plan?"

"I've got to get him back to Washington, but if I take him to an airport, the game's over! If I call any authorities, same thing, game's up. I've got to get him there without the world knowing it."

"No planes. No trains. No buses. How about by car... or should I say by truck?" Mike asked.

"What?"

"By truck! My truck! I'll drive. We'll all drive to D.C."

"Drive? Are you serious?"

"Sure!" Mike continued. "If we spell each other, we can be there in less than twenty-four hours, including gas and pee stops. I can go into any fast food place and get our meals, and we can eat in the truck."

Travis was grinning from ear to ear. Mike had provided the obvious, simple solution.

"What about money? We'll need food and gas money.

We're not carrying any cash or credit cards."

"Don't worry," Mike said.

"I've got enough right here in the house to get us there. I'm sure I'll get paid back one way or the other. Just think of who I'll be driving and with the 'good faith of the U.S. government' behind me, what's a few bucks' worth of gas and sandwiches? The real question is, how do you get him into the White House once we get there?"

Dan sat silently for a few minutes. "I think I've got the answer to that," he said as he lay down and pulled the blanket over his shoulders.

"Well, are you going to share it with me, or what?" Mike asked.

"Yeah, but I've got to sleep on it first. I've got to work out a few rough spots in my mind. I'll have it straight by morning."

"I'll bet you will," Mike said. "I'll just bet you will."

Chapter Two

By 9:00 a.m., they had Mike Stowe's Dodge Ram 2500 pickup with four-wheel drive all loaded and ready to go. Mike had found additional clean clothes, shaving gear, and beauty supplies for his three house guests. He even found a hair dryer for Sydney. They loaded all the portable food and water into the rear of the truck to keep their stops along the way to a minimum. Mike climbed in behind the wheel with Dan alongside. The president and his daughter took the rear seat.

"Where to?" Mike asked Dan.

"West, head west, and stay off the interstate if at all possible."

"West? What the hell is to the west? I could find a route and stay off the interstate if I knew where I was going! How about you share your plan with us, and I'll tell you how we can best get there."

"I have two plans. First of all, we are not going to D.C. We are not driving into a trap or into enemy territory. So that's out.

"The second plan would be for us to head to Fort Drum. I've never driven there, but I'm sure we could find it. Or, we could drive to Fort Bragg. I know the entire route and I know the base very well. I was stationed there for three years, and I have a lot of friends who are still there. But that's too far and would take us too long. The longer we are on the road, the more our chances of being seen."

The president leaned forward to listen to Dan's plan. "I say we go to Fort Drum. It's much closer and doesn't get nearly the attention of other military facilities. I say Fort Drum."

"I agree." Travis chimed in. "I know a lot of very loyal people who live and are stationed there. I served with a lot of guys from the 10th Mountain Division, and with one telephone call, I can assure you that your personal safety will no longer be an issue for us to worry about. When we get close, I'll make a call to Fort Drum to let them know we're coming. I know exactly who to call, and I know exactly who will be at the gate waiting for us, and I can assure you we'll be welcome and safe."

"I agree, Mr. President," Mike jumped in. You need to know who is making up your welcome party and if they are going to greet you with a biscuit or a bomb. From the story you guys are telling me, we need to be safe first and foremost."

"Mike, do you know where Fort Drum is and how to get us there?" Sydney asked.

"Yes, ma'am," Mike responded. "It's right next to Watertown, New York. We can get on I-95 south to I-90 near Boston. Take that all the way to Rochester, New York, and then take I-81 north up to Watertown."

"No!" Dan yelled. "No interstates."

"Why not, Dan? It's the fastest route," Mike jumped in.

"One word: cameras. There are toll booths all along that route, and every toll booth has a camera looking for toll violators, terrorists, and wanted people of every kind. No interstates! We've got to find a route using back roads."

"Well, that's not difficult. I'll drive us south until we hit Route 7 and take that all the way across New Hampshire and Vermont to Albany. There we can pick up Route 5 to Amsterdam, go a little ways south, and get on Route 20 all the way to Syracuse. There we get on Route 11, and take that up to Watertown. How's that? No tolls and no cameras."

"That sounds good," Dan replied. How long do you think it will take us to make the drive?"

"I'd say pretty close to twelve to fourteen hours. Maybe a little longer. We will be going through a lot of little towns. It will depend on what time we hit each one and what the local traffic is like," Mike clarified. "When do we leave?"

"We just did!"

It took them every bit of the fourteen hours to reach Syracuse. All of the routes Mike took were two-lane highways, and it seemed like every little old lady, every school bus, and every traffic light were put in front of them to slow them down. By the time they turned north on Route 11, it was time to think about getting some rest. Four people crammed into a pickup for that many hours made for an exhausting day, and nerves were getting frayed.

Sleeping in the truck didn't seem like a very good idea. It was decided that Mike would go into a motel and see if he could rent two rooms for "Him and his wife and kids." They looked for an old hotel with outdoor ground-level entrances to all the rooms. It wasn't hard on this route. There were dozens of old motels bypassed and left to die by the construction of I-81.

Mike was able to rent two side-by-side rooms for only $69 each. It was decided that Sydney would use one and the three men the other. Once they were all in one of the rooms, Mike walked across the parking lot to the other side of the street and came back with a bucket full of Kentucky Fried Chicken and enough iced tea to bust a bunch of bladders, particularly four that hadn't made very many pit stops during the past fourteen hours.

After stuffing their faces, Sydney stood to excuse herself. "Good night, gentlemen. I'm going to shower and go to bed. I'll see you in the morning. What time do we get rolling tomorrow, Dan?"

"Not too early. We've only got a little over an hour or so up to Watertown from here, and I have to wait until I'm sure that my contact is in his office before I call. I'd like to call him about 8:30, and that should put us on the road by nine or shortly thereafter."

"Got it. See you in the morning." And off she went without another word or her usual round of good-night kisses. She was tense and worn out, and it showed.

Once the three men were all alone, Mike spoke. "Dan, I've got to ask you a question."

"Shoot!"

"How did they find you? Both helicopters. How did they find you?"

"I don't know, Mike. I've been asking myself that question for days and days."

The president listened intently. "Glad to hear you say that, Dan. I've been twisting that around in my head as well."

"Let me ask you, Mr. President. Before I got back to the crash site, when did you first hear the chopper approaching? Did you hear it for a while before it landed, like it was flying around searching? Did you hear it circling overhead for a while before it landed on the lake?"

"No! It came straight in. No circling. No searching. It flew right in like it knew exactly where it was going."

"Okay. When you first saw it, did you notice if it had wheels along with the pontoons or just the float gear?"

The president squinted his eyes in reflective thought, trying to bring back his first sighting of the aircraft. "No wheels! Just pontoons. Why?"

Dan continued. "If they didn't have wheels... if they had only pontoons...

"They knew exactly where they were going to land. They knew they were going to land on water," Mike interjected.

"Exactly!" Dan said.

"They knew, but how?"

"What about the second one?" Mike asked.

"Can you recall that one, Dan?"

"Skids. Only skids. They were expecting to land on a dry firm surface or not land at all. And," he continued, "They flew right to me. There was no searching, no circling, no nothing. They flew a straight path directly to where I was in the water. I heard them for the first time only seconds before they cleared the trees right on top of me."

"I'll be damned," the president muttered.

"Yeah! Me too. I'll be damned. Someone knew where we were the whole time. They could have come in and rescued you and Sydney any time they wanted to. Except... they didn't want to."

"They wanted me dead! I'll be damned. But who? Why? And they were willing to either kill Sydney or let her die with me. I'll be a son-of-a-bitch." Donald Richardson's mind wandered off, his eyes blank, trying to think back. Think of who would want him dead, why someone would want him dead. His body was in the same room as Mike and Dan, but his mind was off somewhere else, searching for answers.

Mike jumped in. "Sarge, I have another question. If they wanted to kill the president right from the get-go, why didn't they just go out and do it before you got involved? Why didn't they just fly in there and kill everybody? If, on the off-chance that you found them, and they didn't even know about you until after you had already started, well, then if you found them, they would have said the president and his daughter were both killed in the crash."

Both the president and Mike Stowe looked at Dan, waiting for him to respond.

"Don't know, Mike. Let's think about that. If they went in and killed everybody they found alive, they couldn't shoot them on the chance that someone, me or some hiker or hunter, would come along a month from now or a year from now and find them with bullet holes in them. They would have to be more creative than that.

"Secondly, they didn't come in early because they didn't know where they were. They didn't know until I got there. Somehow, I led them to the crash site. They followed me in. Somehow, they were able to follow my whereabouts, and when I became stationary for a few days, they must have assumed that I had found them. Someone planted a homing device on me. I'll be a son-of-a-bitch. Someone used me! Now, that pisses me off."

"But who, Dan?" the president asked.

"Who, besides Denny Carson, even knew you existed. I can't believe he had anything to do with it."

"I don't know. I can count the number of people I talked to after leaving the White House on the fingers of one hand. I'll make a list of everyone. But man, I'm having a hard time with this. That's why we have to be careful getting back to D.C. Whoever wanted you dead still does and is still out there. We can't just walk into a trap. We've got to plan every step from here all the way to the Oval Office and know who is with us every inch of the way.

"Right now, there are only three people in your life: Mike, Sydney, and me. The four of us have no one else except you, Mike. You still have time. You can leave us here, turn around, and go home. We'll be fine if you do. We can get a bus up to Fort Drum, or I could get them to come down here and pick us up. But once you are seen with us, that's it. You're with us, like it or not. It's up to you. Beyond that, every other person is a traitor, or an enemy."

Mike looked at him for a second and said, "I'm in, young man. Let's get the president to Fort Drum, and then we can figure out who's behind all of this and nail the bastards."

Chapter Three

"Sergeant Drake speaking. How can I help you?"

"Sergeant Drake, would you please connect me to the Office of the Adjutant General in the post headquarters."

"Yes, sir. Please hold."

"Office of the A.G. Sergeant Gard speaking."

"Sergeant Gard, I'd like to speak with Sergeant Major Fields, please."

"Can I tell him who's calling?"

"Tell him it's his old gatekeeper from Fort Bragg."

There was a very brief pause, and then, "Where the hell are you?"

"About five miles from the post's front gate, George. Can you be sure I can get to your office without any problems?"

"Give me fifteen minutes. I'll be there with some old friends of ours."

Exactly fifteen minutes later, Dan, along with the President of the United States, pulled up to the main gate of Fort Drum with no dignitaries, no politicians, no banners, no ceremony, and with little notice from anyone within sight of the guard station. Mike pulled up and stopped to be greeted by the Post Sergeant Major George Fields, who looked into the truck. His face dropped damned near to the ground when he saw who occupied the vehicle.

"Follow that staff car. I'll be in it, and there will be a couple more behind you." He made eye contact with Dan, glanced at the president and the woman sitting next to him in the back seat, and said, "I'll see you in a couple of minutes."

Mike nodded and pulled up close behind the army staff car. As soon as Sergeant Major Fields got in, the car pulled away at a slow, steady pace. Within a few minutes, the lead vehicle pulled up to a canopy that covered the sidewalk leading to an impressive building. The sign announced that this was the headquarters of the post. It sidewalk was lined with twenty men in uniform, who were blocking either side of the walkway from the view of anyone who just happened to be close by and curious to see what was going on.

Sergeant Fields jumped out of the staff car and made his way quickly to the pickup. Mike pulled up and stopped within a foot of the car. Sergeant Fields pulled open the door where the president was sitting and simply motioned for him to follow.

"Quickly, please, sir. I don't want to stir up too much interest just yet."

Maintaining silence, everyone followed Sergeant Fields into the building, down a short hallway, and into a large conference room whose doors were guarded by four well-armed MPs. Once inside, he reached his hand out to the president and said, "Welcome, sir. Needless to say, this is an honor, and a shock!"

Then Fields turned to Sergeant Travis and threw his arms around the much younger man. They embraced each other, two old friends exchanging a warm hug.

"What the hell is going on?" he asked his new guests collectively.

Dan stepped up. "Sergeant Major George Fields, let me introduce Mr. Don Richardson, President of the United States, his daughter Sydney, and Mr. Mike Stowe from Back-bumba-woods, Maine." He turned to the others and added, "This is Sergeant Major Fields. We served together at Fort Bragg and a couple of other places in the world before that. He's an old friend whom I trust with my life... and yours."

"You're alive! You crazy shit, you're alive, and you found the president alive. Damn! When I heard what you did and the story started to go public, I couldn't believe what I was hearing. Then I said to the post commander, 'Of course. If anyone can do it, it would be Dan! I can't believe you're actually here. I've got to get my boss down here. If I don't get him, he'll raise all kinds of hell and have my ass."

"Understood," Dan replied. Go get him and send in some coffee, if there is any in this sorry-assed place you call home."

He grinned at Sergeant Travis, slapped him on the shoulder, turned to the president, and said, "We go a long way back, sir. Please excuse me while I get General Thompson. He's a good guy, and you can trust him. Damn, he's going to crap his drawers when he hears what I have to tell him. Be back real quick. And I'll get some coffee in here, too."

With that, he dashed from the room, leaving the others standing there, taking in all of the excitement they were causing. Within a couple of minutes, a young woman appeared with a tray of mugs and a large pot of coffee with all the fixings. And then the door burst open and in walked Sergeant Fields, followed by Major General Robert Thompson, Commander, 10th Mountain Division.

"Mr. President! My God, what a pleasure to see you alive and well, and what an honor to have you here in our building. How do you want me to arrange for you to get back to Washington?"

"I don't, General Thompson! Before we continue, please let me introduce you to my daughter, Sydney." They warmly shook hands. "And to Mr. Mike Stowe, who so graciously and courageously provided the transportation and funds to get us here from a long way off." More handshakes.

"And this General is Master Sergeant Dan Travis, who saved us and brought us home alive."

"Sergeant Travis," the general reached out and took Dan by the hand. "You are quite a mystery to a lot of people, civilian and military. I can't wait to hear your story."

"Thank you, sir," was all that Dan said. He and the others had agreed that it would be the president who would lay it all out for the General. The entire story and description of what was needed would have much more authority coming from the president to the general, rather than from a sergeant.

The president took over. "General, we have a lot to tell you. But first, we need to be sure that this is a totally secured area and that no one is privy to this conversation, except those absolutely necessary. I want everyone involved to hold a top-secret security clearance. They must understand that this is to be treated as a national emergency. If they violate this trust, I will see to it as their Commander in Chief that their career is over and they will serve time in a federal prison for treason. Do you understand?"

General Thompson stood agape, listening to his ultimate boss, not believing what he was hearing. "But, sir, I have superiors I have to report to, and the entire world is waiting to hear that you are alive and well."

"General," the president's volume increased a notch. "I am your only superior, and you will follow my orders, and my orders only, from this moment forward until I tell you otherwise. There will be no communications with anyone outside of this room. Period! Do I make myself clear?"

"Yes, sir, Mr. President. I am, as is my entire command, at your disposal."

"Good! Once you hear the story of the past few weeks, everything will become clear, and you will understand the need for total security.

It took the president, assisted by his daughter and Sergeant Travis, almost two hours to give the entire story to the general, from the time of the G11 conference until the very moment they now shared at the headquarters of the 10th Mountain Division. The general and all others in the room remained totally silent as the story unfolded, not sure how to absorb and digest what they were hearing.

"Now I hope you can understand my earlier instructions, General," the president said, as he ended the presentation.

"I'll be damned, Mr. President. Who could possibly be behind all of this?"

"That's what we have to find out, but first I have to get back to Washington. I've got to get back to the Capitol and resume my office."

"Yes, sir. We will contact the White House and"

"No," interrupted Dan Travis. The general looked at him with the displeasure typical of a senior officer tolerating an underling. "Excuse me, Sergeant. You're out of line here."

"No, he isn't, General. I've given Dan the right to say whatever he wants whenever he wants. If it weren't for him, my daughter and I would be dead and rotting away in the woods. As far as I'm concerned, this is his mission and he is still in command."

"I'm sorry, sir," Dan continued, addressing the General. "We can't contact anyone. We have no idea who is involved with this mess and who isn't. Until we find that out, we contact no one."

"But how do you intend to get the president back into the White House?"

The president spoke to the general. "I want you to put together a unit of your best-trained men, fully armed and equipped to provide protection for all of us. Then I want you to organize a convoy and escort us from here to Washington."

"But Mr. President, that will be something very difficult to keep from being on the nightly news. Everybody in the country will know something is going on, and my superiors will demand an explanation of what the hell I'm doing."

Mr. President, " Dan said and was ignored.

"That, General, we will deal with when it happens. For now, "

"Mr. President?" Dan tried again.

"...your job is to plan how we will get this done and to keep us safe and secure."

"Yes, sir, I, "

"Mr. President," Dan demanded. "What is it, Dan?"

"We don't have to go to Washington."

"What? Of course, we do. I have to, "

"No, sir, you don't. Wherever you are is the center of the country. Not some city or some building. We are here now. Safe and sound, surrounded by a huge military installation with a top-notch military division, thousands of soldiers guarding every gate and every person here. And you are here. Therefore, this is the center of power. We don't have to go anywhere. Everything has to come to you. All I have to do is pick up that telephone and call the vice president's private number and use the code word he and I agreed upon. Within minutes, the world will be on its way to Fort Drum. This will become the focal point, and we won't have to drive a single mile or risk any exposure. This will become the Capitol."

"He's absolutely right, Daddy," Sydney injected.

"No question, Mr. President," Mike Stowe added. "Just think about the reaction to a convoy of hundreds of trucks, containing thousands of soldiers, driving down Interstate 81. The whole world would know something was going on, and it would create a world-class mess of a traffic jam between here and D.C. We would never get there to get to the bottom of this mess."

"And besides," Dan added. "We don't know what we would be driving into. We don't know who is behind all this. We could very well drive right into the middle of an armed camp. Remember the helicopters and weapons those guys had? They didn't come from Walmart. They came from someone, somebody who has power. Here, you are protected, already established. Once the word is out, once the world knows you're here, you will be much safer, much more secure."

The president silently scanned the faces looking at him and considered every word spoken by the three people he had come to trust the most. His daughter. Mike Stowe. And Dan Travis. And now he had a general and a complete army division. He paused in thought, feeling the weight of his office returning to his shoulders.

"General Thompson, now you know why I trust this man." He hesitated for a moment before looking at Dan Travis. "Make the call, Dan."

"Yes, sir." Dan turned to the small table next to the wall, where there was a telephone waiting. He looked once more into the eyes of Sydney and the president. He took a small wallet containing his driver's license from his back pocket. It had his military ID and a couple of other items, including a small piece of paper with a telephone number written on it. As he dialed, he looked again into the eyes of the woman whom he suddenly trusted more than any other. He listened to one ring tone... two... three...

Hello?"

"Mr. Vice President, this is Sergeant Dan Travis."

Part VIII

Nemesis

Chapter One

He felt the vibration against his chest. He knew immediately it was coming from the cell phone in his shirt pocket, the cell phone he had been carrying for weeks, no longer expecting it to ever ring. He managed to control his excitement as he casually retrieved the device while he sat at the conference table in the White House briefing room with a dozen other officials.

"Hello."

"Mr. Vice President, this is Sergeant Dan Travis."

Shocked and startled. Not believing his own ears. His emotions scrambled like a bowl of spaghetti. "Hold please," was all he could manage to say as he cradled the phone in his hand and turned back to those at the table.

"Clear the room, please!" he said. He was met with blank stares. "Clear the room," he shouted. Those around the table seemed frozen in disbelief, acting as if their feet were stuck to the floor. "Clear the fucking room and do it now!"

That worked. A little shouting and the F-word always seemed to do the trick. That got things moving. All those present began moving toward the door with a new sense of urgency until finally he was alone.

He raised the phone back to his ear. "Sergeant Travis, is that really you?"

"Yes, sir, it is."

"Where are you?"

"Sir, we need to hold all of that until later. Right now, I have someone here who wants to speak with you, and I'm sure he will fill you in on a lot of things."

Dan handed the telephone to President Don Richardson. "Denny, it's Don. Sydney and I are alive and in one piece thanks to the remarkable young man you sent looking for us. I have a lot to tell you, but first, are you alone?"

His mouth agape, head spinning, Vice President Dennis Carson heard himself speaking as if his voice were coming from another body. "Mr. President! My God! I can't believe it. Yes, yes, I'm alone. I'm in the Situation Room and I kicked everyone else out."

"Good. We have a lot to do and a lot to discuss. First of all, am I still the President of the United States?"

"Yes, Mr. President, you are. I refused to take the oath of office until your death was confirmed. And somewhere deep inside me, something told me that Sergeant Travis would do what he said he would. But I still can't believe I'm talking to you."

"Okay, Denny. I've got a lot to fill you in on, but right now we have to get things moving. There's a lot I can't say right now, particularly on the phone, so I'm asking that you, and you alone, take the lead until we can meet and make some decisions. First, I need you to get on a plane and head to Fort Drum. Come alone. Don't tell anyone where you are going or why. Do you understand? As soon as possible, without raising too many red flags or tipping off the rest of the world. I'm looking forward to seeing you no later than tomorrow morning. Can you do that?"

"But I'm afraid trying to do that will only create a lot of questions."

The president considered that comment for a moment and then responded to his loyal friend. "Okay, Denny, bring Bob Wilson with you, along with a small unit of Secret Service guys, the smaller the better. That will look more normal. Bob's still working with you, I presume?"

"Yes, he is, and I think that approach will be easier to justify. Bob and I will create some sort of excuse for the trip. We'll be there in a matter of hours. I'll cover it here somehow. Don't be concerned. I'll get it done immediately."

"Good. Tell your pilot not to file a flight plan. Use national security as an excuse and then tell him where to fly to only after you're airborne. Have him radio ahead, and we'll arrange to have a car waiting to bring you to us."

"But, why all the precautions, Mr. President? What's going on?"

"That will have to wait until you get here. Please trust me. Please just do as I ask right now. You'll understand when we have the chance to talk. All I can tell you is that this entire event was no accident."

"Yes, sir. I understand, but Mr. President, you said to us.

Can you tell me who us is?"

"Sydney and I. The two agents didn't make it home with us. Dan, I mean Sergeant Travis, and I will explain when we see you. Tell no one, Denny. No cabinet members, no FBI or CIA. You haven't heard from me. As far as the world is concerned, I'm still missing, and this conversation never took place. You'll understand once we talk. In a day or two, everything will be back on track. We'll deal with the whole mess and the press once we get things under control a bit. Right now, it's important that we keep to ourselves and that you get up here ASAP."

"Yes, sir, I'm on my way."

The call ended, and Vice President Dennis Carson found himself holding his phone, wondering if the conversation he'd just had was real or a product of his imagination. He opened the door of the Situation Room to find a crowd of very confused people standing around, not knowing what to do.

"Our meeting is over, ladies and gentlemen. Something has come up that I need to attend to immediately. Please excuse me. We will meet again in a day or two. Mr. Wilson, will you please join me in the Oval Office?"

Once the two of them were secured in the Oval Office, the Vice President sat on the sofa, head in hands, trying to collect his thoughts. His world was once again about to shift out from under him.

"Bob, I need a small jet fuelled and ready to go immediately. I can't tell you where or why. I will give the pilot our destination once we are airborne."

"Yes, sir. I'll pack a bag and we'll be out of here in thirty minutes."

"Bob, only you are coming with me. No other staff. We'll be gone for a day or two. And I want only two agents with us. Is that clear?"

"Yes, sir, but you know they will question that request."

"It's not a request, it's an order. Now, please get things moving. I want to be airborne within the hour.

When the call ended, the president handed the receiver to his daughter, who replaced it in its cradle. He sat silently with his chin cupped in his hands, contemplating what lay ahead. Minutes slipped by with no one willing to break his meditation. Then the least expected voice brought the room back into focus.

"Mr. President," said Mike Stowe.

The president slowly raised his face, revealing the strain of recent events and challenges facing him in the days ahead. "Yes, Mike, what is it?"

"Sir, I've been thinking a lot in the last couple of days," the mountain man from Maine began. "From everything you and Dan, and your daughter have told me, this isn't over. Someone, some group, is trying very hard to not only kill you, but to keep you from returning. Dan and I have been sharing some ideas."

Sergeant Travis jumped into the conversation. "We've got to go back, Mr. President. We've got to go back to the crash site and find out what the hell happened. Sydney's plane didn't just lose power and crash. The radios didn't just decide to quit working, and the transponders didn't just decide to stop sending out a signal, so you couldn't be located. Not everything all at once. That's too much of a coincidence. A lot more took place, and we need to get to the bottom of it."

"And," Mike added, "Those guys in the helicopter weren't just flying around out there looking for lakefront property to build a log cabin. They were out there looking for you to be sure you didn't come back alive."

"What are the two of you suggesting?"

Dan jumped in. "I've got to go back, sir. Now. Before anyone tries to cover this up. As soon as the world knows you are safe and alive, whoever sent in that second chopper is going to go back to that location and try to destroy everything there that might lead to them."

"I agree, Dan, but why you?" Sydney injected. "Haven't you done enough already?"

"Because I know everything that happened out there and where it took place, and because this mission isn't over. My mission isn't over," he answered with a passion and determination she hadn't seen in him before. "These people tried to kill the President of the United States. My President. That's treason, Sydney.

Treason! I swore to protect and defend against treason. I can't tell you how pissed off I am. I can't tell you,

His face was red, his teeth clenched. Sweat glistened across his forehead. His white knuckles pounded against his knees as he fought to control himself. The president sensed the man's state and came to his aid. "What are you proposing, Dan?"

It took a few moments for Travis to regain his composure before he answered. "I'd want a helicopter. I want Mike and two CID investigators from General Thompson's 10th Mountain Division. The CID guys have the knowledge and equipment to perform a technical search of the sites, while Mike and I look around for other clues. I don't think it will take us more than a day to complete the search. And I want to bring home the bodies of the two agents and as many of the others I buried as we can transport. We might need two choppers to carry the load. When we return, we'll report directly to you with the information."

"Sounds like a plan."

"No!" Sydney blurted out, her feelings for the young soldier now seemed in command of her life. "No, Daddy." She grabbed Dan's arm. "Dan has done enough. It's too dangerous. Have the Army do it. Have the Army guys go back in there and check things out. If whoever is behind all of this finds out what's going on, they could send in another helicopter and."

"Sydney," Dan responded, gently placing his hand on hers. "I am the Army. And I was there. I know where everything is, where we camped, the trails we took. I have to go, and Mike knows those mountains as well as anyone. We'll be fine. Don't worry."

But worry was painted all over her face. Worry and deep concern. Even she was surprised at the depth of emotion that was surfacing in her. She felt it coming from deep within her, from a place she didn't recognize. She was having difficulty holding back the tears, fighting to spill over from her eyes.

She released her grip on Dan's arm and bolted off to stare out the window, not to see what was there, but to hide from those in the room, to conceal her confusion, to examine the feelings bubbling up within her.

The silence was broken when the door opened and General Thompson's aide walked in. He whispered something in the general's ear and then exited the way he had entered.

"Mr. President, your quarters are ready," the general said. "I've ordered meals for the four of you to be served in approximately thirty minutes. Would you like to retire to the house to freshen up? We can continue there and wait for the Vice President to arrive."

"Yes, general. Yes. I think that's a good idea. We all need a break right now. But before we go, you heard the Sergeant's plan?"

"Yes, sir."

The president turned to Sergeant. Travis. "Dan, when would you like to leave?"

"Right away, sir."

"Don't you want to wait until Denny Carson gets here?"

"I'd rather not. The fewer people who know what's going on, the better."

Sydney joined in. "But he's going to want to know where you are. He's going to want to talk with you and hear your side of the whole mess."

"I know, Syd. But there are too many questions that need to be answered before I talk to anyone, including him."

"And the press," she continued. "Once my father is back in the public eye, they're going to go nuts wanting to talk with you. You're going to be a hero. They're going to want your picture and your story. What will we tell them? They're going to want to know where you are and what you're doing."

"I know, Sydney. You'll just have to make up some sort of a story."

"Like what?"

"He's in the base hospital," General Thompson broke in. "He was injured and is being treated here in the base hospital. Nothing serious, just enough to need attention. Just enough to keep him in bed for a few days and out of sight. I'll get with one of our doctors and come up with a cover story."

"Great idea," said the president. "Dan, how long do you think you'll be gone?"

Sergeant Travis glanced at Mike Stowe. "What do you think, Mike? Two days, maybe three?"

"That should do it easily," Mike replied.

"Good! That should be easy to cover with the doctor's story. In the meantime, Sydney and I have to prepare ourselves to return to D.C. and face the nation... for that matter, the whole world. It's going to be absolutely chaotic!

"Okay then," he continued. "General Thompson, I'd like you to arrange for your two best CID crime-scene people to be ready to join Sergeant Travis and Mr. Stowe within the hour. I'd like you to have two helicopters fueled and equipped and standing by as soon as possible. Be sure everyone is armed and prepared for the worst. Get with your doctor and create the cover story without telling him any of the real details. Tell him the request comes directly from me. Thank him for his trust. Say that I will explain it to him when the time is right. Now, let's go eat. We've got a lot to do. I've got to get ready to return to Washington and become President again. God help me!"

Chapter Two

After a hot shower and a good meal, and dressed in a change of clothes provided to them by the U.S. Army, Dan and Mike Stowe were standing on the tarmac of Fort Drum's airfield with two fully-fueled and equipped helicopters waiting for them to climb aboard. Joining them were two senior investigators from the Criminal Investigations Division, plus two additional soldiers to assist in excavating and recovering the bodies waiting for them in the mountains of Maine. Sydney Richardson was there as well, her eyes red from crying as she prepared to say goodbye to the man who was now the center of her emotional life.

"Syd," Dan said as he handed her a piece of paper. "This is the address of my ex-wife. It's where my daughter lives. Her name is Lucy. Her mom's name is Helen, and her new stepfather is Chuck. Lucy will be worried when I don't come back with you and your father. Could you please go see her and tell her that I'm okay? That I'll be home real soon."

"Of course I will," Sydney said, choking back tears. "Is there anything else I can tell her?"

"Yes. Tell her that I love her and miss her and that I will be bringing someone to meet her very soon, someone I care a great deal about. Tell her I hope she will like this new person as much as I do. Tell her I hope that we'll be seeing a lot of this person and that I... that I'll tell her all about this person as soon as I get home."

Sydney looked up into his eyes. Their eyes locked as they shared feelings without words. She stretched her arms around his neck and kissed him gently.

"You coming with me, Danny boy, or do I need to get you two a room somewhere?" Mike Stowe yelled at them over the roar of the two choppers.

Dan gently broke the embrace. Looking into Sydney's soul, he kissed her lightly one more time. "I'll be back. I promise." Finally, he turned and strode to one of the choppers and hoisted himself in. Both aircraft immediately lifted off and began banking toward the northeast, leaving Sydney with an aching heart full of fear. Would they come back? Would he come back?

As the two choppers faded from view over the western peaks of the Adirondacks, she heard another aircraft approaching. The Vice President was about to land. Perfect timing.

As she watched Denny Carson's executive jet approaching, she felt a change overtaking her. Her mind. Her body. Everything about her. She could feel the tension and expectation of her old life returning. Her Washington, D.C. life. Her life was the daughter of the President of the United States.

The phony persona of political and public life, the acting skills demanded by her father's position, and the fact that there was no First Lady to fill the role she was forced to play were in poignant contrast to the quiet and beauty left behind in the mountain wilderness of Maine. Her heart ached for the solitude lost, the sense of adventure and excitement she'd felt, even during the tense days of fighting for physical survival, a longing for it, for him, to return.

As she watched the jet taxi to where she was standing, she became aware of the scramble of military personnel waiting for the vice president to deplane, so they could escort him to her father. She knew what lay ahead: the meetings, the interviews, the questions. The rush and the noise. The grasping and groping, and posturing of all those whose existence depended upon being seen by the world as a close friend to the president. The trumped-up importance each played in the efforts for their safe return. The fake smiles. God, how she hated the fake smiles!

She knew that the next few days would be a living hell, that their return to Washington would be crammed full of interviews and photographers and reporters sticking microphones in their faces. She knew it all too well, and she could feel it creeping into every pore of her being. For the first time in her life, she felt each and every one of those pores filling with the grime of her life. Each pore wants to erupt into a pimple filled with the pus of politics.

"Mr. Vice President. So good to see you," she said, greeting Dennis Carson as he descended from the plane.

"My father is waiting for you." The Vice President embraced her. And so it begins, she thought.

While Sydney dealt with the days of transition, Sergeant Dan Travis dealt with the issue of uncovering the cause of all she was facing. The two helicopters flew across Adirondack State Park, passing over Lake Champlain into Vermont and New Hampshire, and landing briefly at Waterville, Maine, to refuel. They then proceeded north toward the wilderness the locals called the Northern Kingdom, the forests of northern New England and Maine.

It took most of the day to reach the approach to their targeted area. Darkness was coming on. After a brief conversation with the two pilots, Dan decided that they should wait until morning to attempt flying into their target. They landed in the parking lot of Baxter State Park in central Maine. The park was now closed in anticipation of the winter season. Here, near Mt. Katahdin, the northern terminus of the Appalachian Trail, they would spend the night camped quietly out of sight of the world.

At first light the next morning, the two helicopters lifted off and headed north with Mike Stowe and Dan Travis leaning over the shoulder of the pilot at the controls of the lead aircraft. Both were providing visual directions as they flew toward the map coordinates Sergeant Travis had provided. The objective was to locate the lake where Sydney Richardson's plane had crash-landed and set the two choppers equipped with pontoons down on the same waters that now hid the helicopter that Dan had brought down.

Most of the early snow had melted away except in heavily shaded areas and atop some of the highest mountains. It would be easy to locate the shallow graves and trails left behind.

Shortly after the sun had fully risen, Dan spotted the familiar valley where his supply skids were located. He directed the pilot to fly directly over them so he could get a good bearing toward the lake. Within minutes, the early morning sun, glistening off the mirror-smooth water, led them to a soft landing with a clear view of Sydney's plane tucked up under the low-hanging evergreens. Both aircraft landed safely on the still, quiet water.

Once the side doors were opened, Dan and the others stood absorbing the surrounding quiet while taking in the view of the area they were about to examine. Each crew tossed out an inflatable raft. The two CID investigators and one member of the security team loaded into one while Dan, Mike, and another team member loaded into the other.

They paddled cautiously to shore in the misty, eerie morning silence. Dan felt as if they were paddling back in time to a prehistoric era. He would not have been surprised to see a wooly mammoth step out from beneath the trees, trumpeting to announce its presence.

Once all the men were ashore, Sergeant Travis took the lead. "That's where the president and his daughter were lying when I first arrived," he pointed. "And that's the area where I buried the men I shot."

The second inspector said, "I'll start by examining the plane to see what I can find."

"Okay, Mr. Stowe and I will kind of roam around to see what we can discover. If you need us to assist in any way, just shout out."

Pointing from one spot to another while addressing Mike Stow, Dan said, "Mike, that's the direction I came from when I first found them and when I returned from the supply skids. I was back along the shoreline when I first saw the men surrounding the president. And I was over by that big rock when I first used my bow to bring down the man about to hit the president with his pistol."

Mike took in everything Dan was saying while he scanned the area around the crash site. "Where was their helicopter?"

"Sitting out in the lake, right about there," Dan pointed. "About 50 yards from where our two choppers are sitting."

"So you nailed the guys on the ground before you fired at the chopper?"

"Yeah! I don't think the pilot saw what was happening over here, or he didn't believe his eyes if he did. It was a couple of minutes before he tried to start the engines, which gave me time to run down by the shoreline and get a bit closer to them. The engines barely turned over before he tried to lift off. They surely weren't warmed up properly. I don't know if that's what brought them down or if I actually hit the crew when I started shooting at them."

"Don't matter much. Comes out the same," Mike said. "Feds are going to want to get it out of there sooner or later, and then you'll know for sure. Let's see if the guy from CID has found anything in Sydney's plane."

They slowly walked over to the downed twin-engine. Dan could see, off to his left, that there were already two dead bodies being wrapped in body bags. It wouldn't be long before the others were found and ready to be loaded. Mike stuck his head into Sydney's plane to see the inspector pulling the controls out of the front panel.

"Find anything?"

"A lot. This plane didn't come down on its own, and it wasn't pilot error. It'll be a while before I know for sure, but give me another hour or two and I'll have some hard info for you."

"Okay, we'll go see if we can lend a hand to the other guys."

By noon, most of the work had been completed. All the bodies had been loaded onto one of the helicopters. The CID inspectors were examining the airplane, having already taken parts of the engine and communications systems out for return to Fort Drum. The two flight crews had joined Dan and Mike and were preparing to break into some MREs for lunch.

The entire group gathered around a fire. Mike was heating up some water for the MREs when the two inspectors joined them.

"Are you done?" Dan asked them.

"Yes, Sergeant," the lead inspector answered. "What can you tell us?"

"Well, Sarge, it will take us some time back at the base to be sure, but we can tell you for certain that this plane didn't come down by itself, and the communications were definitely tampered with. Somebody wanted this plane to crash and didn't want any distress calls going out. We found evidence that there was some kind of slow-acting acid poured over the wiring to the radios and transponders. It was only a matter of an hour or two before everything would be out of commission. And we have some idea why the engines quit."

"And what was it?" Dan wanted to know.

"Well, our initial thought is that it seems like someone poured sugar into the gas tanks."

"Sugar?"

"Yes, sir, Mr. Stowe. We found that the spark plugs have been fouled with a hard substance that appears to be caramelized sugar. Can't be totally sure until we check it out in the lab, but I'd bet this gourmet lunch we're about to enjoy that that's what did it."

"Sugar!" Mike exclaimed.

"Yes, sir. Works every time. Car... lawn mower... ATV... or airplane. Just pour it into the gas tank and give it a while. The old way of getting even with your neighbor and his noisy vehicles. Kids have been pulling this as a Halloween prank since way back in the '50s. Like I said, it works every time."

"Well, I'll be damned," Mike continued. "So it would be your conclusion that the plane was sabotaged. When would you estimate that all of this was done?"

"Can't say for sure," the inspector added. "But my best guess at this point would be about two to three hours before the plane went down. Takes about that long for the sugar to dissipate and get through the gas lines."

Dan and Mike exchanged knowing glances. Two to three hours. Backing up the timeline that put the plane on the ground in Nova Scotia, that meant that the plane was tampered with while Sydney was waiting for her father to complete his meeting in Halifax. Tampered with by someone who knew she would be there. It had to be done just moments before she took off. Someone who got to the plane only after she talked her father into flying with her, instead of on Air Force One.

But who? Who fits this timeline? Who could act that quickly? Who was close enough to them to know the change of plans? And who could pull this off in a foreign country? Okay, it was only Canada. It wasn't Russia. But still? It was foreign soil. Who had the punch to get this done in a matter of minutes?

All those questions would have to wait to be answered. But it didn't erase the puzzle that the two men found themselves dealing with at the moment.

"Dan?"

"I know what you're thinking, Mike. But we've got more to do before we can try to crack this nut. Let's wait until we have all of the information before we stop looking for all of the missing pieces."

Sergeant Travis turned to the two inspectors and the two flight crews. "Gentlemen, that's a lot of information we need to confirm and consider. But right now, we have to move on. We have another site to examine. How long before you can wrap things up here? We need to go down to the site we flew over this morning, where the two supply skids are. A short way from them is where I had a camp set up when the second attack took place. We won't be done until we check out that area."

"We're done, Sarge. We're ready to go," said the lead inspector.

"Ready when you are, Sergeant Travis," the lead pilot chimed in.

Twenty minutes later, the helicopter carrying Dan and Mike was in the air, headed down the mountainside toward the site of the supply skids. The other aircraft was headed to an area slightly to the west of that to find the site Dan had described to them in an attempt to locate and recover the body of Secret Service Agent Black.

Whether they were successful or not, the plan was for the two aircraft to meet up in the parking lot of Baxter State Park later that evening. Dan felt sure that the examination of the second site would be completed in only a couple of hours.

The pilot located the supply-skid site with ease. The problem was locating an open space large enough to set down his helicopter. He finally found an area about a half mile southwest of the site. The flight crew stayed with the aircraft while Dan, Mike, the two inspectors, and one well-armed soldier took off toward the skids.

They located the site within half an hour. Sergeant Travis showed the inspectors where the skids were located, as well as the actual campsite he, Sydney, and the president had occupied. He and Mike then began to roam the area looking for whatever might jump up at them and provide some clue as to what the hell was going on.

Dan described what took place just prior to the arrival of the second helicopter sent to kill the president.

"I was hunting over there, across the stream," he pointed out to Mike Stowe. "I killed a deer and gutted it out at the edge of the creek. While I was dragging it across to this side, I got covered with blood, so I decided to strip down and take a bath in the creek. I was already soaking wet anyway. As you can see, the creek is about thirty yards across, so I figured I'd wash my clothes at the same time I washed myself. So, I jumped in and waded out to the deep pool by that big rock.

"I flipped the deer up on the rock and stripped down to my birthday suit. I scrubbed my clothes and tossed them up on the carcass and began to scrub myself. That's when I heard, no, I felt the chopper approaching from the west before I heard it. The change in air pressure caused by the rotor blade can be felt before the sound gets to you.

"I looked up and saw it coming over the tops of the trees. I knew right away something was wrong. Then I saw the heat-seeking pod under its belly, and I ducked down behind the rock. I got down into the water. It was cold as hell, and I knew it would shield me from the pod.

"Then the shooting started. I thought it was aimed right at me. But it wasn't. They were aiming at the deer carcass. My uniform was draped over it, and it was still warm, so I guess the pod picked it up. It must have looked enough like me lying there on the rock, so they opened fire.

I was covered with meat and blood in seconds. And before I knew it, the helicopter had disappeared behind the trees.

"But it didn't leave. I figured they were checking out the area, so I took off running down the creek toward the campsite where the president and Sydney were. He was sitting in the water cooling down his hips, and she was standing on the bank of the creek looking up into the sky, trying to figure out what all the noise was about.

"I shouted for both of them to get into the water. Sydney hesitated, so I grabbed her as I ran by and pulled her into a deep pool next to where her father was cooling down. A minute later, the chopper came toward us, and I pushed both of them under the cold water to disguise their heat signature. It must have worked, because the chopper kept right on going and disappeared. It never came back."

"And that's when Sydney saw you standing there in all your glory?"

"Yeah, Mike, but that's not the important thing."

"Yeah, I know it's not, but I still would have liked to have seen your face when you realized you were naked in front of the daughter of the president," he said, with a deep and broad grin stretching across his face.

"Look!" Mike pointed. "Your clothes are still on top of the rock. I can see the deer hide and your OD fatigues lying there.

"I'll be damned. You're right, Mike. I'll go out there and get them just in case the inspectors want to look at them for some reason."

Dan took off his boots and waded out into the stream to retrieve the remains of his shot-up uniform. When he returned to the creek bank, he dried his feet with his shirt and put his boots back on. He then began to search his old uniform to see if there were any personal items in the pockets. He found a few coins and his military I.D. card in the pants. Then, in the breast pocket of the jacket, he found the hand warmer the governor had handed to him just prior to his setting out on the search mission. The present was sent from the vice president.

Only now it had a bullet hole right through the middle of it. A bullet hole that changed everything. A bullet hole that changed the course of everything that lay ahead of him.

"What's that, Dan?" "We've got to go!"

"What?" Mike asked, puzzled.

"We've got to go. We've got to go now." "What's up, Dan? What did you find?" "I know what we have to do next."

Chapter Three

Mike Stowe and the CID investigators had a hard time keeping up with Sergeant Travis as he raced back toward the waiting helicopter. He was clearly wired with a new level of energy. Whatever it was that he discovered was driving him full speed ahead. When they reached the aircraft, he instructed the pilot to take off and head back to the parking area at Mount Katahdin State Park.

Upon arrival, Sergeant Travis instructed the captain of the aircraft containing the recovered bodies to return to Fort Drum as quickly as possible and to get the bodies to the base hospital for examination. He then instructed the pilot of the helicopter he and Mike were riding in to fly them directly to Washington, D.C., with necessary refueling stops along the way. Both pilots were ordered to maintain radio silence, or at least not to identify their mission, any names, or their destination. Anyone, civilian or military, friend or not, could be monitoring radio traffic, and Travis did not want anyone made aware of his movements until he could meet with the president.

It was approaching 10:00 p.m. by the time they lifted off from central Maine, one helicopter headed west and the other south. It would take hours for them to reach the

D.C. area, and Travis had to get his mind wrapped around the information now flooding his brain. He was simultaneously confused, pissed off, and excited! He now knew where to begin unraveling this whole mess, but he didn't know whom he could trust. There were only three people he could talk to and share what was going on in his head: Mike Stowe, Sydney Richardson, and the

President of the United States. Pretty heady stuff for a mere Army sergeant.

He was betting that by this time, the president had returned to Washington. If not, he was wasting precious time. En route, he decided to find out the only way he knew how. He borrowed a cell phone from one of the helicopter crew members and dialed the phone number shared only by himself and the vice president. Denny Carson answered on the third ring.

"Mr. Vice President, it's Sergeant Travis."

"Sergeant, how are you feeling? Are you still in the hospital on Fort Drum?"

"No, sir, but I can't explain right now. Is the president back in Washington?"

"Why, yes, Dan, he is. He and his daughter are back in the White House. We all got here earlier today. It's a mess! The press is going crazy. The whole country is going crazy. His return has turned the world upside down."

"Yes, sir, I can imagine. I hate to interrupt you, but I need you to clear something for me ASAP."

"What is it, Sergeant?"

"I will be approaching Washington in an Army helicopter within the next couple of hours. I need you or the president to clear the way for us to land at the White House. Can you do that? It's extremely important. And tell the president that I'm coming and need to meet with him as soon as I arrive."

"Clearance is no problem, but it's the middle of the night. I'm sure the president is trying to get some sleep by now."

"Sir, please tell him I'm coming. I'm sure he will understand and want to meet when I get there."

"I'll take care of it, Sergeant. Have your pilot contact the military for clearance. I'll see you in a few hours."

Less than two hours later, the helicopter began its approach to land on the White House lawn. The pilot had contacted Andrews Air Force Base and received the proper clearance to do so and was given the proper landing instructions.

Once on the ground, the aircraft was immediately surrounded by military and Secret Service personnel who escorted the two men into the White House and into the Oval Office. President and Sydney Richardson were both waiting when they walked in. The president greeted both men with a handshake and an embrace. Sydney wrapped herself around Dan Travis in a bear hug as if she would never let him go.

"Okay, young man. What have you got to report?" the president asked.

"Sir, I think it best if we discussed this with just the four of us in the room."

Puzzled, the president looked at Dan and, with only a moment of hesitation, dismissed everyone else from the room, leaving only Sydney, Mike Stowe, and himself to hear what Sergeant Travis had discovered. It took about thirty minutes to digest what Dan had to say.

"Wow!" the president exclaimed. "This is potentially much worse than I wanted to believe." He paced back and forth with his head lowered, trying to come to terms with what his trusted protector had just reported.

"Are you willing to lead the effort to get to the bottom of all of this, Dan?"

"Yes, sir. But, I'd like Mike to be there with me."

The president paced some more and then reached for the telephone on his desk. To whomever answered at this ungodly hour, he ordered, "Get hold of Bob Wilson and have him come in here immediately. And please have a fresh pot of coffee and some bagels brought in as well."

Within a few minutes, the White House Chief of Staff entered the room. "Bob, let me introduce you to Mr. Mike Stowe. He is the gentleman from Maine I've told you about. And I think you know Sergeant Travis."

Wilson reached out and warmly took Mike's hand, then turned to Dan and did the same.

The president continued to address his aide. "Bob, I need you to get the Director of the FBI and the U.S. Marshals Service in here ASAP and tell them each to bring two agent badges with them. If they are not available, get their top deputy in here in their place. And Bob, you are about to be exposed to some very sensitive information that must be kept strictly limited to those of us here in this room. If anyone finds out what is about to take place, lives will be at risk, including your own. I'll be asking a lot of you in the coming days. I need your trust and loyalty more now than ever."

"Yes, sir. I understand." "No, I'm afraid you don't."

When the two agency directors arrived, the president gave them orders to swear in Mike Stowe and Sergeant Travis as agents of their respective forces. He further ordered them to provide unquestioning support to both men and to assign a trusted agent to Dan to facilitate any and all requests he might have during his coming investigation efforts. He gave them only enough of an explanation to gain their full support and make them understand that this could be a widespread effort on a national basis.

"Gentlemen, do you understand what I'm asking of you?"

"Yes, sir," was the only reply and all he needed to hear.

He then turned back to Bob Wilson. "Bob, Sydney will be the primary contact in the White House. She knows these men, and they trust one another, and I'm afraid you are going to have your hands full handling everything else that will be coming our way, including my return to office. Are we clear?"

"Yes, Mr. President."

"Good. One last thing: contact Andrews and make one of our executive jets available immediately and indefinitely to Sergeant Travis. Have it ready to go by noon today." He then addressed the two Directors and his Chief of Staff. "That will be it for now. Good morning gentlemen, and thank you for your support."

The circle of four once again found themselves isolated inside the most powerful room in the world, the silence in the Oval Office clearly rooted in the physical and mental exhaustion common to all. The president finally broke the stillness.

"Okay, you two. You have your work cut out for you. This is not going to be easy, you both know that. You are going to have to operate right on the edge of the law to get the job done. Maybe even beyond the law." He paused. "I want you to know that I'm here. All you have to do is call. Sydney has unlimited access to me. That goes unsaid. And through her, you have the same. Use it. If you get in a jam anywhere, at any time, I'm here and I'll put the full weight of this office behind you.

"You are both now sworn law enforcement agents of the United States. Use all the power and authority that implies, but use it wisely. If you need access to state or federal facilities, or if you need any kind of assistance, call Sydney. If you need access to private homes or offices, call Sydney. I'll see to it that she gets whatever you need, including subpoenas and search warrants.

"Dan, this is going to be tricky. You are going to have to get to the bottom of this mess without the world knowing about it. Without the people involved knowing about it. That means being sneaky and deceptive. Use the agents who are going with you; they are trained in this kind of investigation. Just remember, we've got to clean this up. Not just because it was directed at me, this is not the way this country works."

Dan Travis stood up and stepped toward the president. "Mr. President, you can be assured we will do our best, no matter what, no matter how long it takes or where it takes us."

"Okay. Now let's all get some rest. I've had two guest rooms set up for you here in the White House until you are ready to leave. Let's all meet again for a minute or two to cover any last-minute stuff before you head for Andrews."

Dan, Mike, and Sydney were headed for the door when the president called his daughter back. "Sydney, stay here for a minute, will you please?"

Dan and Mike left. Sydney turned back to her father. "What is it, Daddy?"

"Sweetheart, this is not going to be an easy task. I know Dan has become important to you. Just be careful. He's a good man setting out on a very dangerous mission. Whoever, whatever he finds, it's clear that the people involved are ready to kill to get their way. I don't want you to get hurt."

She threw her arms around her father's neck and hugged him tightly. "It's too late, Daddy."

Chapter Four

Just after 2:00 p.m. that afternoon, Sergeant Dan Travis and Mike Stowe once again entered the Oval Office. The president was seated behind his desk, talking on the telephone. Sydney Richardson was seated on one of the two couches, looking rested and refreshed. She stood and went to Dan immediately, embracing him and kissing him on the cheek.

The president completed his call and came around to his desk. The four of them sat facing one another. The president spoke first. "Well, I hope you got some sleep. It's been a rough morning around here. The press is screaming for information, and I haven't quite figured out what to tell them."

"Mr. President, may I speak?" Mike Stowe asked. "Certainly, Mike. Of course you can."

"Thank you. Sir, I would suggest you play dumb."

"What do you mean, Mike?"

"Play dumb, sir. Act as if nothing happened out there. You crashed. Cause not yet known. Dan found you. Both agents died in the crash. You survived. He got you home alive, and he's now recuperating in the hospital from some injuries he sustained in the effort. That's it!

"If you say any more, if you go public with any of what we think we know or what we are doing about it, whoever is responsible will dig in and pull the hole in over their heads. And put our lives in danger.

"If you don't say any more than that, they will be totally confused. They'll wonder why. They'll start to second-guess themselves and try to figure out what you are up to. You'll be putting the monkey on their backs to make a move.

"They will have to make a move to figure out what really happened out there. Where is the first helicopter? What happened to it? Did the second chopper really succeed in what they reported? And Dan and I will be sitting out there waiting for them to screw up. To reveal themselves. That's what I would do, Mr. President. Play dumb."

The room went silent again. The president looked at this quiet man from the woods of Maine, contemplating the wisdom of his words. "They're going to want to see Dan. Interview him. We can't hide him forever."

Sydney jumped in. "Daddy, he's in the hospital. He has a serious infection from his injuries. We're flying his daughter up to New York to be with him while he recovers. You know how this town is; in a week, they'll forget about him or at least calm down until he and Mike get back. Then we can set a time for him to address the press. That will be our story. I'll handle this part, and I'll take his daughter on a trip to Fort Drum to add to the show."

"What about Mike?' the president asked.

"Me?" Mike responded. "I'm nobody. I'm invisible. No one even knows I exist or that I'm a part of this whole thing. And they won't know until we get done and back here. I'm good to go, Mr. President."

The president paced his office. "Okay. I'll arrange a press conference for later this afternoon. We'll use it to cover your leaving here and any action observed at Andrews. Sydney, I'm going to need you to help me with the story and to field some of the questions from the press."

"Don't worry, Daddy. I'll lie like a teenager on a Saturday night."

"That's it, then," the president said. "Let's get this show on the road."

Sergeant. Travis and Mike Stowe gathered themselves and prepared to leave. The president shook their hands and wished them well and a safe return, and they exited the Oval Office. In the hallway, Sydney Richardson grabbed Dan's arm and spun him around to face her. Their faces were only an inch apart, and their eyes locked.

"You come back to me," she said. "I'll be back."

"I know you will."

"Please be here when I do." "I'll be here, Dan. I will."

They stood holding each other. "I've got to go."

"I know," Sydney said as she stood on her tiptoes and kissed the man in her arms with all the tenderness in her heart.

"I'll be back."

"I'll be here."

Tears rolled down her cheeks. She turned and went back through the doorway to her father's office.

The press conference went well. The president resumed the reins of power and authority and thanked the vice president profusely for his service and loyalty. He gave very few details of their ordeal, stating that a complete accounting of events would be provided to the country in the near future, but, right now, he and his daughter were to be examined by the White House medical staff.

Sergeant Dan Travis had suffered some injuries during his heroic rescue efforts and was recuperating in an Army hospital. He would be introduced to the press once his doctors felt he was able to travel to Washington. His daughter would be visiting with him in the hospital as soon as arrangements could be made with her mother and her school.

In the meantime, the president's plans were to work with the vice president to sort out and get caught up on all the events that had taken place in his absence. He asked that he be given a week or two to complete the process, and then he would again address the people of the United States. Meanwhile, all was well.

While the press conference was taking place, Dan Travis, Mike Stowe, and the two federal agents had quietly slipped out of the White House and traveled by unmarked van to Andrews Air Force Base east of the Capitol. They boarded a government-owned business jet and took off without notice. First stop: Maine.

For twenty-seven days, the charade continued. Sydney Richardson and Lucy Travis flew to Fort Drum to fake a visit to the base hospital. Lucy was told that her dad was on a very secret mission. She and Sydney had an instant relationship. After all, they loved the same man.

For twenty-seven days, Lucy played her role to a tee. She got a real kick out of traveling by jet plane to the base in Upstate New York and charmed everyone she encountered, most of all, Sydney Richardson.

For twenty-seven days, Sydney talked with Sergeant Travis almost every day, getting updates and lending requested assistance when needed. She kept her father informed the whole time and got his support as required.

For twenty-seven days, Dan and Mike crisscrossed the country, working day and night, dragging the two federal agents along with them. The four of them worked their way across eleven states, opening doors that did not want opening. Each door was intended to be a barrier, a shield hiding treachery.

Unwelcomed phone calls, twisted arms, threats, picked locks, hidden microphones, stolen files, all began to pave a road toward those who Dan and Mike knew existed. They began to be able to see them, touch them, smell them, and feel them. One piece led to the next, one office visited in the middle of the night led to yet another. One tip, one piece of paper, a single word, all began to connect.

A frightened aide or a secretary afraid of going to jail, a false promise revealed. A twisted mix of dates, meetings, and telephone calls lit the way. A sketch became a photograph that then became a mosaic. A mosaic of lies and deception, and treachery.

What they found was staggering. The mass of evidence confirmed that a plot had been laid. The evidence confirmed who had participated. The circle grew fast, and all those within it were slowly, but indisputably revealed.

The four were puzzled and dumbfounded by what they had uncovered. And they were exhausted. Night after night. Endless hours. Endless miles. It was time for them to return to D.C. and present their findings to the president. They had all they needed and more. Much more! Anything missing would be found by the coming massive federal investigation that was now inevitable.

On the twenty-seventh day, Sydney's phone vibrated in her pocket. She answered to hear a one-word message: Jackpot! She knew immediately what that meant. Dan had found the key to the mystery and was on his way back to Washington.

Chapter Five

Sydney sat next to Dan, not wanting him to be away from her again. She needed to feel his presence. To be reassured that he was back safely and in one piece.

The president, vice president, and Chief of Staff Wilson sat across the room and learned what had been discovered in the past twenty-seven days. They were shocked. The extent of the treachery of those involved stunned them. The degree to which these people had gone to conceal their plan was beyond anything they could have imagined.

Dan provided the oral presentation, with Mike supplying the factual and statistical support. Dates, places, and names. The sequence of their travels and searches. The accumulation of documents that supported their conclusions in detail. When and where were federal and state agencies were involved in their efforts? Names, ranks, and assigned stations of each officer are included to support and verify all the information being provided.

The presentation took over two hours. The three men trying to absorb the information were speechless. None had said a word during the entire time that Dan and Mike were speaking. They were riveted by the scope and volume of information being put before them. The president hadn't noticed the tears streaming down his daughter's cheeks. She, too, had been betrayed and threatened.

When Dan and Mike had finished, the minds of the three men listening were in turmoil. They had privately speculated on what Dan would find. They had expected bad news, but nothing like this.

They had considered many of these people friends, political allies, and supporters. People close to them. People within the

White House inner circle. They had been betrayed by so many in so many ways. The president's life was jeopardized, along with that of his daughter, who held no office, no power. Who had no influence beyond being a loyal and loving child. His child!

The president stood and walked across the room to the window overlooking the city, silently staring out into the darkness. His eyes saw nothing. His senses could not absorb anything more. His mind was flooded with information beyond reason. Emotions beyond reach. The others in the room watched him, not knowing what to say or do.

After what seemed a lifetime, he turned back to them. They could see from his expression that he had come to grips with all that he had heard and the situation that lay before him. His mind had organized the data and was in gear once again. He had an idea. He had a plan.

He walked across the room and sat on the edge of the table in front of Dan Travis. He was only inches away from one of the few men he now trusted completely. He reached out and placed his hands on his daughter and on the man she had grown so close to in recent weeks.

"Dan, listen to me, and please listen carefully. The press is all over the place. They follow me everywhere, asking about you. Where and when will you make an appearance? They're waiting for you and your story. They're chomping at the bit, waiting for you to be released from the hospital and return to D.C.

"Like it or not, you are a national hero. You saved the president's life, and they want to elevate you and praise you. That's their job. As a result, you have to accept that your life will never be the same again. That goes for you as well, Mike. Once your part of this story gets out, you won't be able to just pick up and go back home to Maine.

"They want you. They will want both of you as soon as they find out about Mike and his role. So here's my idea, if you two approve. We'll give them what they want. We'll give them their story. You two will leave D.C. later tonight and return tomorrow after we announce that you are coming. You have suddenly and miraculously recovered from all your injuries and will land on the White House lawn to the warm embrace of a thankful president and his daughter. And your daughter will be here with us to add to the welcome.

"But that's just the beginning. Dan, this whole mess is too big to hide. Too big to be cleaned up behind the scenes by the FBI or the Attorney General's office. There are too many people involved. We could never put them all away without the whole mess being exposed. We've got to go public with this.

He continued, both talking to those in the room and thinking out loud, organizing his thoughts and plans as he went along. "It's also obvious that this is highly political. If I go public on my own with the whole story, there will be many who will doubt it's for real. There will be doubts and questions about the facts and the motive. It will be insinuated that I manipulated the story and the facts for political gain.

"We can't have that. It can't be me who goes public. You've got to be the one who lets the world know. You've got to be the person who informs the world of what you have found. You would have been killed too. It was you who stopped them. It was you who brought us back alive. It was you who dug out all the facts and uncovered the plan. You were there. It's got to be you.

The president's mind continued to race ahead of his words. He was talking to Dan, but his mind was working elsewhere, thinking as he spoke. His ideas were forming fast and furious. He continued, "It's got to be done swiftly, cleanly, and completely, in one dramatic sweep. Everyone in the world has got to know that they can't get away with this kind of thing, not here, not in the United States of America.

"Dan, American hero, savior of the President of the United States of America, with special guests and dignitaries from all over the country in attendance, along with a whole bunch of slimy, conniving bastards, how would you like to follow in the footsteps of another American hero, General Douglas McArthur, and address a joint session of Congress?"

Chapter Six

"Mr. Speaker, the President of the United States."

With that traditional announcement, the Sergeant at Arms of the House of Representatives ushered Don Richardson and his entourage, including his daughter Sydney, into the hall of lawmakers, into the 'People's House.'"

They entered through the ancient wooden doors and began the slow walk down the aisle toward the Speaker's chair. Hands attached to nothing reached out from the wall of blue and gray suits and dresses, patting the president on the back or shoulder. Each fleshy paw reaching out to touch him for no real reason except to be able to brag to totally unimportant people that they were once close to the president. To touch 'The Man.' None dared touch Sydney except to shake her hand.

Don Richardson had to fight back his repulsion. He knew that some of the same hands held daggers aimed at the soft spot between his ribs. Some of these daggers had already been flung at him and Sydney, and Dan Travis in the mountains of Maine. These daggers had been aimed at taking their lives and leaving their bodies to rot in the wilderness, far from the manicured fingers and fake smiles now surrounding them.

Once he reached to podium, the formality of uproarious applause continued until he raised his arms asking for silence. Finally, the chamber came to order, and everyone focused on the man standing at the center of world interest. He turned to the gathered power brokers, the merchants of evasive double talk. He looked out over the five hundred and thirty-five overblown egos, the self-inflated, the self-important, each one knowing in their deceptive hearts and minds that they should be the person standing on the podium.

The president completed all of the necessary greetings required by protocol. He began, "I promise you all one thing, make that two things. First, I promise you I will be brief, and second, I won't be political."

All the gathered dutifully delivered their exaggerated laughter, heads bobbing, while curling their lips to reveal their lower teeth and broaden their smile just in case a television camera should be panning in their direction.

The president continued, "I'm not here tonight to fill any constitutional requirement of my office. I'm not here tonight to make any political statement. I'm really not here tonight as the president. However, being president gives me the opportunity to take advantage of my office and to ask all of you to come here and listen to me for a couple of minutes. I guess you can accuse me of abuse of office tonight, which I'm sure all of the press in the chamber will be more than happy to headline their newspapers with in the morning."

Laughter from the chamber. "I will ask you to forgive and indulge me, and I would hope that by the end of the evening, you will understand why I have asked you all to come here tonight.

"I am here tonight as a citizen of this fantastic country we get to call home. And I'm here as a grateful man and father. I'm here as a tiny man, humbled by the recent events in my life, by the majesty of nature, and by my God. I've also been humbled by a man. One lone man. One single citizen of this great country. A soldier whom I think of as a hero.

"You all know who I'm talking about. You all know what he has done for me and my daughter. Oh, you might say, 'well, Don ol' boy, why don't you just take him out to dinner, give him a big fat cigar, a medal or two, a big slap on the back, and say thanks. Why are you dragging all of us here tonight?

"Simple! This House, this place, has been used as a gathering place for us to present to the government and to the people of the United States, certain persons we wish to recognize and to honor for their contribution to our country. We gather here to recognize those we would characterize and honor as heroes. People who qualify themselves for praise and distinction.

"You all know what he has done for me. You all know what he has done for Sydney. But you don't know him. And you don't know what he has done for our country.

He paused, letting his words fall silent within this massive chamber. He continued, "Some call me a great man. No, not me. I'm just a man who holds a great office. No, I'm not a great man. But the man I will introduce to you is. You see, what I've done, I've done for a reason. I had a selfish purpose. I wanted to be important. I wanted to hold high office. I wanted to be president.

"But him: he's great because he had no purpose. He did not seek fame. He did what he did simply because it needed to be done. There was no other intent in his actions. Pure and simple. Clear and unselfish. He saw a need, and it became his goal, his only goal.

"You, me, each and every one of us who holds or aspires to high office do so, at least in part, for our own selfish needs. To fulfill our own desires, our own rewards. And in that process, we are often so blinded by our own ego and need for attention that we lose sight of ourselves. We get caught up in ourselves and the business of obtaining a lofty position. We forget the real purpose of the job we seek.

"Our target is lost, we become blinded by the light of our own halo. Drugged into a euphoria that dupes us into believing that our office is designed to serve us, instead of us serving it. How delusional we've become. How misguided and selfish.

"But not this man. His motives are simple. To many of us, they might seem hokey, old-fashioned, or out of date. We might chuckle or sneer because of their simplicity. Yet, to him, they are his guiding light. A beacon he must follow without regard to the consequences, even if it requires risking his own life. His principles are simply this. Duty! Honor! Country!

"Sneer at me if you wish. Chuckle under your breath at my use of these words if you need to. But do not dare to diminish, dishonor, or disgrace Dan Travis because you do not share his values."

He paused again to allow his words to blanket the audience. He also needed to gain control of his own emotions, as he realized what the words meant to him.

"Enough said by me. But before I step aside, I wish to introduce three other people to you. First is a man whom we had to drag here kicking and screaming, however much we wanted to recognize him. He lives a quiet life in his home at the edge of the mountains of Maine. Without hesitation, he volunteered to put his life on hold to help three smelly, grubby strangers who accidentally stumbled into his backyard one day and asked for a ride to Washington, D.C. Not exactly your everyday request.

"So he drove us instead to Fort Drum in Upstate New York, spending his own money on gas and food to get us to a military base where we could find help and medical attention. You will learn much more about this man in the coming days and the extent of assistance he provided to us. Ladies and gentlemen, sitting up in the gallery, may I present a man I now call a friend, Mr. Mike Stowe."

Everyone in the House rose and soundly applauded the man who stood to acknowledge the president's introduction. He was visibly uncomfortable dressed in a suit and tie, tugging at his neckline, and waving nervously.

"The next person I'd like to introduce to you," the president continued, "is truly very special. Over the past weeks, I've gotten to know this person for myself and learned much more about her from others, most of all from my daughter, who has been with her almost constantly since our return. Her love, her devotion, and her loyalty measure far beyond her years. When you get to know her, be careful. She will charm your socks off, and she will win your heart while she picks your pocket if you dare challenge her to any online game."

More laughter. "I only wish that I could take the credit for having raised such a fine young woman. Ladies and gentlemen, sitting in the gallery next to Mr. Stowe, I'd like to present to you the daughter of our guest of honor, Ms. Lucy Rose Travis."

Again, the entire house stood and applauded. The clapping, hoots, and yells for this young person were deafening. Lucy stood and waved to the entire crowd and to the president. She then made eye contact with Sydney Richardson and, to the absolute delight of everyone present, she blew her a kiss and silently mouthed the words, 'I love you.'

"Lastly, I'd like to introduce a new face to you. This one, you might think, looks familiar to you. You could even say you know this person. But trust me, you are wrong.

"Even I thought I knew her. But I've learned so much about her during our recent ordeal that I didn't know before; I'm ashamed of myself. Her bravery, her devotion, the depth of her character, her love for me, and her ability to love others.

"I have come to see her as much more than the woman I thought I knew. I see a person thrown into a situation where her strength became a vital part of our survival, especially because I was unable to contribute to the effort. I watched her grow, and I saw her mature, literally overnight. I now add to the love a father has for a daughter, the love and respect and affection for a woman I have gained as my best friend, one who would like to share some of her own remarks with you. If you please, by daughter, Ms. Sydney Richardson."

For the third time, everyone stood to applaud. Everyone in the chamber either respected or feared the young woman now approaching the podium. Each knew her power and influence over her father. She and she alone was the final confidant. No one was closer to the man, the office, and the power.

"Thank you... Thank you...Thank you..."

The House finally quieted and took its seats.

"Thank you," Sydney began. "It's truly an honor and a pleasure to be here before you tonight. Quite frankly, after my last effort at flying an airplane, it's a pleasure to be anywhere tonight."

There was polite applause and laughter across the room.

"And I'd like to thank all of you for the warm welcome and expression of love you have extended to my father and me since our return. I know I speak for both of us when I express our thanks.

"That is a reason I asked to speak tonight. Before I go on, however, there is one more thing I'd like to say." She looked up at the gallery, clearly fighting back tears. Her voice choked. "Lucy Rose, I love you."

This time, there was a warm, respectful ovation, with all eyes riveted on the two young women. Tears were wiped from cheeks, emotions peaked at the sharing of love between these two who had grown so close so quickly.

"And let me thank your Grandma T. for bringing you here tonight and allowing you to become a part of my life.

There are a few things I'd like to add to my father's comments, and I, too, promise to be brief.

"Master Sergeant Daniel J. Travis, United States Army. That's the way he would introduce himself. Dan. That's the way I've grown to know him. I'll not take your time to tell you what he did to bring my father and me back to Washington. That's up to him to share with you. What I will tell you is what he has done for me.

"My father used words that he felt applied to Dan. Important words. Duty. Honor. Country. Those are the guiding words that describe Dan's life. I'd like to add my own. Strength. Humility. Dignity. Dedication. Determination. Respect. And I must repeat one of my father's: honor.

"Day after day, I watched this man deal with our situation. Each day, I watched him deal with the challenges of injuries, food, water, shelter, weather, and mile after mile of rugged country. And most of all, two people who didn't know a pine tree from a tulip. Two people who would have difficulty finding their way out of Central Park on a rainy day. Two people are completely dependent on him for everything, and I mean everything. Two people who would have died out there if not for him and his skills. No small burden for anyone to carry alone.

"Dan is a very modest man. He will have difficulty sharing things with you tonight. But he will tell you things tonight that will help you understand why my father and I use these lofty terms to describe him. Once you have heard his story, you will better understand why we feel as we do.

"His presence in my life has affected me greatly, and what he did. The way that he did it. His judgment and his performance as a soldier and as a man all affected me. How? Let me explain.

"Many of you consider me to be a brat. You're right! I gave you every reason to consider me, to treat me, and to reject me as the typical spoiled little brat. Daughter of the most powerful man in the world, who took every advantage of her father's position. And just imagine, it took me less than thirty years to perfect it."

A nervous trickle of laughter buzzed across the room. Everyone knew Sydney was pretending to poke fun at herself, but they knew she actually wasn't.

"Now, I want you to imagine this. Here I am, the daughter of the president, jet setter, unemployed, flying around in my own airplane, lounging around on the shore of a remote lake, waiting for my Prince Valiant to come and rescue me. Hair all done up. Fresh make-up. Fragrant perfume masking a week's worth of body odor without a bath.

"And suddenly, out of nowhere comes this handsome young soldier. Pitter pat, pitter pat goes my heart. And I'm saying to myself... Fresh meat! The Lord provides game in the forest."

A slightly more relaxed laughter hummed across the aisles. Still mocking herself, Sydney continued.

"And what to my surprise, I'm almost totally ignored. Ordered around and told to march myself down to the lake and take a cold bath. Well! I huffed and I puffed, and then I huffed and I puffed some more before I knew what hit me. And then, I had a .40 caliber pistol stuck under my nose and Prince Valiant is telling me that if I don't quit huffing and puffing, he would be happy to put me out of my misery and his, right then and there."

Lots of laughter. "And if you think I'm kidding, you're wrong. That's exactly what Master Sergeant Daniel J. Travis, United States Army, did. He said, 'Ms. Richardson,' and here Sydney drew her chin in to her chest, puffed up her shoulders, and talked in a deep voice, trying to sound masculine, 'there's only one important person out here who needs to get home and it ain't you. Get in the way of me getting him back home, and I'll shoot your butt.' Well, that's the cleaned-up version of what he said for prime time television."

More and louder laughter, now that everyone understood that Sydney was genuinely trying to be funny and doing a pretty good job of it.

"Why do I tell you this? It should be obvious. For the first time in my life, I realized I didn't count. I was expendable." She paused for a long moment, hearing her own words for the first time. "I believe the word is humbling. I thought and acted my whole life as if I were the queen of the world's homecoming parade. And in a blink, Dan Travis reduced me to a human being.

The entire audience was now riveted on her. Hanging on every word she spoke. "Ever since that moment, I've seen things differently. I watched and learned from this man. I watched as he taught and led without trying. He led without even knowing he was doing it. It came completely natural to him. I learned from a man who could survive by eating raw berries and raw meat and bugs, and roots. A man who listens to classical music and writes love stories in his spare time.

"I learned about a man who has fought and killed to defend his country, using everything from modern weapons to a stick with a stone stuck on the end of it. A man who could do all of this and still be brought to tears by the mention of his daughter's name, who could be melted by the sight of her face.

"Dan Travis is his name. Master Sergeant Daniel J. Travis, United States Army."

She turned toward her father, and tears were running down her cheeks. The entire assembly slowly, one by one, stood and clapped. They clapped both for her tribute to Dan and for her courage to stand before them and reveal herself. Her words and tears stripped away the stone-cold façade she had built around her for so many years to protect her from the very people she now addressed. Sydney Richardson stood naked and alive for the first time in her life.

Her father held her while the applause continued. Finally, she stepped away and stood at the edge of the platform below the Speaker's chair. The president stepped back up to the microphones. He stood there until the room finally quieted.

"Sergeant at Arms," the president shouted. "Would you please escort our honored guest into the chamber. Ladies and gentlemen, I need not, I cannot say anything further. May I present to you Master Sergeant Dan Travis?"

The building exploded with clapping and shouting and whistling. Hoots and howls of every description engulfed the entire building, shaking the dust from the rafters.

Dan was led down the aisle, intermittently blocked by outstretched arms in blue, gray, and even a few in brown, grasping, slapping, and patting. The noise continued unabated.

As Dan approached the podium, he came before the Joint Chiefs. He turned and saluted each and each returned the sign of respect to the young soldier, each reaching out to shake his hand. Their pride in him and in his uniform shone on each of their faces. Their chests expanded as he passed before them.

Dan turned and stepped onto the platform. The president greeted him, took his outstretched hand, and pulled him into a bear hug. A big grin of pride flashed onto the president's face. The men looked squarely into each other's eyes, sharing much more than anyone looking on could fathom. They hugged again, and the president whispered something into Dan's ear as the ovation continued.

Sydney Richardson approached them. Dan turned and embraced her as he had her father. He lifted her off the floor and held her close to him, whispering something in her ear before setting her back down on the floor. She looked up at him with a startled expression and flung her arms around his neck.

He gently let her down a second time and turned toward the waiting audience. After a long, almost embarrassing interval, the Congressmen, Senators, and all the invited guests began to quiet and return to their seats. Dan approached the microphones.

He looked up into the gallery toward his daughter and Mike. He gave her the thumbs-up sign, and she immediately seemed to understand what her father was signaling. She let out a high-pitched shriek and jumped into Mike's arms.

Dan surveyed the faces all around him and began to speak. "Please forgive me. I'm a bit nervous, and if I try to remember everyone I'm supposed to acknowledge, I'll surely screw it up."

He was interrupted by applause and laughter.

"All of you on this list I'm holding, please consider yourselves properly greeted and recognized. My name is Master Sergeant Daniel J. Travis, United States Army. That young lady up there in the balcony is my daughter Lucy Rose. She is sitting with my friend Mike Stowe. Those two I will remember until the day I die."

More applause. Then Dan turned and pointed at the president. "That man back there is Mr. Don Richardson. He's also my friend and just happens to be the President of the United States."

Applause. Laughter. Applause. "The pretty woman with him is Ms. Sydney Richardson. She's his daughter, and as of just a couple of minutes ago, with the permission of her father, she agreed to become my wife."

The uproar was deafening. Everyone was on their feet. Lucy was jumping up and down, clapping and hugging Mike Stowe. Everyone now knew what the thumbs-up signal was all about a moment ago. Dan turned, and Sydney threw herself into his arms. They hugged each other tightly and shared their first public kiss, much to the delight of all present, especially Lucy Rose.

The president and proud father beamed with delight. The audience of dignitaries voiced their approval. All was well, for the moment. Dan returned to the microphones.

"I guess that's a historic first." He paused briefly. "I'm not a politician. Thank God. I'm just a soldier who has to work for them."

Laughter and applause. "My most recent duty assignment was as a staff aide in the White House. Part of my duties was to deliver documents to the Oval Office when necessary. Well, one afternoon a couple of months ago, it became necessary. The president and his party had decided to take a ride in Sydney's new airplane when suddenly and quite unexpectedly, they disappeared while flying over the great northern forests of Maine." He turned to look at Sydney, "And the answer is no, you will not be flying us to places unknown for our honeymoon."

Lots of laughter and applause. "It's not the flight I'm concerned with, sweetheart, it's that hike home that's the killer."

Laughter and applause.

"So, anyway, as I was telling you, one evening I had to deliver a message to the Oval Office, and who do I bump into but the vice president. While he was reading the material I had brought to him, I stood by in the event that he had a response he wanted me to carry to someone. As he was reading, he said something about the contents of the message I had given him. I don't remember exactly what he said, but I made some sort of a comment in return.

"He heard it, grabbed me by the arm, stuck me in an airplane, and sent me off on an all-expenses-paid government camping trip to the beautiful backwoods of Maine. As I was leaving the White House, he said that should I stumbled upon a spare president while I was off enjoying my adventure, would I mind bringing him back with me. So, here I am. That's my story, and I'm sticking to it. So can I please go home now?"

Another eruption of laughter and applause burst across the audience. Dan had won them over. The toughest group of people in the world was now in the palm of his hand, and he was just getting started. His presence before this group made it clear to all watching, in person or on television, that this was no ordinary man. He was not your prototypical G.I.. He was something special.

Dan continued. "Well, maybe it wasn't quite that simple, but I'd still like to go home now. I have two young ladies I'd like to be with.

Brief applause. "I really did mumble something under my breath, and the vice president did hear me, just like I said. He asked me what I thought of the search effort being conducted to find the president. I was somewhat threatened by his tone. He is, after all, the vice president. But I told him anyway.

"I told him I was only a Sergeant in the United States Army and that the search effort was being directed by every general and every admiral in every branch of the military. That they were utilizing hundreds of thousands of men and women, hundreds of aircraft, ships, submarines, police, forest rangers, boy scouts, girl scouts, and every high-ranking politician in Washington, and of course, I could do a better job!"

One more time, the capacity crowd burst into laughter and applause. When they were again quiet, Dan looked down at the

Joint Chiefs sitting all in a row in their place of prominence and gestured toward them. "Only kidding, sirs.

Honest, I am. I'm going to be married soon, and I'll need my retirement in a couple of years."

Laughter again. Even the usually grim, stone-faced military brass were caught up in the personality of their subordinate. They couldn't help but laugh at his remarks and at themselves.

Dan knew he had everyone in the chamber riveted to his every word. Everyone except the president, Sydney, and Mike Stowe wanted to know what he was going to say next. What the audience didn't expect was the instant change in Dan's tone and presentation. His demeanor changed instantly. It was time to get down to business.

"I told the vice president where I thought Sydney's plane might have gone down. I told him it was a wild guess based on my knowledge and experience in the mountains, as well as from the weather charts I had seen since the plane was first lost on the radar aboard Air Force One.

"Apparently, what I said made sense to him, but he certainly couldn't order the entire effort to be redirected, based on the idea of a lone Army sergeant. He asked me if I had enough faith in my theory to put it, and my butt, on the line and go look for the president and his missing party. Well, it's pretty tough for a lowly Army sergeant to say no to the vice president.

"He told me that he would arrange for everything. And he did. The next thing I know, I'm in a jet fighter on my way to Augusta, Maine, where I'm met by the governor and the commanding officer of the Maine National Guard. At the governor's direction, the Guard, along with the local Walmart store, gathered all of the supplies that I had requested.

"Later that day, two supply skids and I were parachuted into the northwestern wilderness of Maine exactly where I had asked to be. Once on the ground, I got everything secured, loaded myself up with enough supplies to last about a week, and off I went on my search.

"A few days later, while searching a valley from up high on a rocky cliff through my binoculars, I spotted what I thought was a body. I made my way toward it and found one of the two Secret Service agents assigned to the president. Apparently, he was trying to find me. He had seen the aircraft that dropped me into the woods and thought that he could reach me and lead me back to the president. He was wrong, and he died trying. He died doing his duty. I buried him in the mountains."

The house was totally silent. Every person present was locked on Dan's every word and anticipating the next. They were mesmerized by his unfolding story. The seriousness and the emotion with which he delivered it demanded their attention, and they gave it to him.

Dan continued. "The agent, although he didn't live to know it, had succeeded in his mission. His inexperience in the woods, his stumbling and slipping around in dress shoes, cost him his life. But it also left an easy trail for me to follow. I knew it would lead me to the president, or at least to what was left of him and his party. So, I began to backtrack along the agent's trail. It led me directly back to the president and greatly shortened the time it would have taken me to find the crash site, if in fact I was fortunate enough to succeed.

"The wreckage of Sydney's plane had skipped across the surface of a lake and slid up under the trees, preventing a sighting from above. It was a testament to her flying skills. She later told me that both engines lost all power in flight, forcing her to crash-land the aircraft. Landing on the lake with dead engines would explain why there was no fire. No spark, no fire. Had there been, sighting from above by aircraft or satellite would have been easy. However, it would probably have killed everyone on board as well.

"She told me how she had to nose up her plane prior to contact with the water to slow it down enough to bring it to a reasonably slow touchdown, slow enough that when it reached the tree line, the trees would not tear the plane and its occupants to pieces. Had she not done what she did, the plane would have landed in the trees and surely killed everyone on board. As it is, one of the Secret Service agents was killed by a tree branch that penetrated the cabin.

"I have flown hundreds of hours during my military service, in all types of aircraft all over the world, and I've had my share of close calls. So when I tell you that if it hadn't been for Sydney's flying ability and cool thinking, had she not done what she did to soften the impact, we would now be addressing Dennis Carson as Mr. President. I may have brought them home, but it was Sydney who saved their lives."

Dan turned to face Sydney and began to clap. Without hesitation, the entire audience followed his lead.

He continued. "When I reached the president and Ms. Richardson, they were in pretty rough shape. The president was lying up against a tree covered with moss and wet leaves in an attempt to stay warm. When I examined him, I quickly realized that both of his hips were dislocated from the impact. As serious as that was, it wasn't nearly as bad as it would have been had they been broken.

"Sydney had some minor injuries, but for the most part, she was in reasonably good condition. Medically anyway.

Wet, dirty, hungry, a bit scared, and suffering from the worst hair day she'd ever had in her life."

That comment brought the first sounds of laughter from the riveted audience in quite some time.

"We got her cleaned up and into some dry clothes, and she then helped me reset both of her father's hips. That was fun and exciting. We then established a campsite, got a fire going, got the president comfortable inside the tent I'd been carrying, and began to prepare a hot meal. That night, they slept warm and dry with full bellies for the first time in over a week.

"While all this was going on, I slipped down to the smashed airplane for a little inspection. I removed the body of the impaled agent and buried him nearby. Had he been six inches to the left or right, he would be here with us now.

"It was obvious that the president wasn't going to just jump up and take a leisurely walk with me back to the mountain meadow where the two supply skids were. So I decided to leave all my supplies with them, hike back to the skids, and return with as much as I could carry. I estimated that it would take me three to four days.

"You are probably wondering why I'm telling you all of this in such detail. Why the blow-by-blow account of what happened? Well, I understand that over the past few weeks, while I was away, Ms. Richardson has given the press some information about our time together. There's a lot more she could have told you, and some of what she did was false. Some of it was true and some was not. By design, she lied to you."

A murmur rippled across the crowd. It was about to get worse, far worse. Dan turned to the president, who stood and approached the microphones. He called out, "Sergeant at Arms, would you please completely seal the chamber and prohibit anyone from entering or exiting until further orders."

The audience went nuts, bordering on revolt. The volume of noise increased. Men and women stood looking around, trying to determine what was going on. Some glared at the podium with fear in their eyes, as if they were trapped. Others remained in their seats with a stoic expression, waiting to see what was coming next. Armed guards moved toward every exit, blocking all doorways. Finally, after letting the group vent their emotions and concerns, the Speaker rapped his gavel to regain order and quiet.

The president stepped to the podium. "Ladies and gentlemen, I know this is highly unusual and threatening to some of you. But please be patient. You will soon understand the necessity of this action. Please remain calm. No harm will come to any of you." He waved for Dan to continue.

The audience settled down. "As I was saying, Sydney lied to you. Why? Let me explain. What I'm about to tell you, none of you has heard before. It might be hard for you to believe. Some of you will be shocked. Others not. Believe it. It's all true, so listen up.

"I was a couple of miles away from the campsite on my return from the supply skids. I was feeling real good. I had managed to load up enough supplies to last a couple of weeks. I was carrying a heavy load. I was moving slowly and was almost a day overdue.

"As I approached the south end of the lake, I thought I heard a helicopter. But that couldn't be possible. This was not an area where anyone would be out taking a pleasure flight for no reason. This was not an area where anyone would risk just flying around for a Sunday picnic. So I just dismissed it, brushed it off as some weird sound echoing through the mountains.

"When I reached the lake, I realized I was wrong. I was standing on the exact spot from which I had first seen Ms. Richardson's downed aircraft when I looked across the water and saw a helicopter sitting on the lake, floating on pontoons. It was about fifty yards from the shoreline near the campsite.

"Naturally, I was excited. I figured we had been found and would be flown out within minutes of my getting back to the camp. I began to double time toward the campsite as best I could, until I realized I was carrying all those supplies. So, finally, I stopped about five hundred yards from the camp and dropped everything, except for those things that a soldier is trained never to leave behind. I picked up my compound bow and my rifle, and I began jogging toward the president.

"When I got close enough to see the men who had flown in on the helicopter, I was stopped dead in my tracks by what I saw. I had a hard time understanding what I was seeing. The men were standing over the president and his daughter with guns in their hands. They were screaming at both of them. One man, the one who seemed to be in charge, hit the president on the side of his head with the barrel of his pistol."

The room vibrated with a hum of disbelief.

"Over the course of the next few minutes, I launched an attack on the men threatening the president and was lucky enough to dispatch all of them. The two-man flight crew attempted to take off in the helicopter, and I was quick enough to shoot down the aircraft before it cleared the lake. They also died in their attempt to escape."

The House chamber was alive with the buzz from five hundred and thirty-five men and women. "Did he just say what I think he said?" "Did he say the president was being pistol-whipped?" "Did he say he killed all of the attackers and shot down a helicopter?"

The president rapped the gavel once again to bring the chamber to order. Drained, disbelieving faces with dropped jaws turned back toward the young soldier as the room quieted and returned to order. Dan hesitated for a few moments before he began again. He wanted his shocking words to sink into his audience.

"Early the following morning, we left the immediate area of the campsite. I built an Indian style drag to put the president and some food on and left everything else behind except for what Sydney could carry in a backpack. Our first objective was simply to get away from the immediate area. It had obviously become a target area. Secondly, I wanted to reach the two skids, where we would have access to food and supplies.

"It took us three days to reach that objective. The following day, we were attacked again. A second helicopter, which I believe was equipped with heat-seeking devices, flew directly to our new campsite and opened fire on me and everything around me. We escaped by jumping into the ice-cold water of a nearby stream. The cold water shielded us from the device on the aircraft. We stayed submerged until it finally left the area and flew away.

"There's no need to present a day-by-day description of what followed. We cleared the area as quickly as we could. After some very trying and difficult days of hiking, we came across the cabin of Mr. Mike Stowe, who, without hesitation, assisted in getting us to Camp Drum, where we were cared for by the 10th Mountain Division and ultimately returned to safety. The remaining details will be reported in due time.

"There are, however, three things that must be asked tonight. Three questions that must be answered. All three questions became obvious from the moment when I first saw the helicopter resting on the lake.

"First, what brought Sydney Richardson's plane down? As it turned out, this was the easiest to answer. As a part of the investigation, the Army investigators took fuel samples from the wing tanks. When it was analyzed back at Fort Drum, it was found to contain large amounts of sugar. Plain old sugar.

"Sugar dissipates in gasoline. When it runs through a hot engine, it caramelizes. It becomes solid, clogging and gumming up the entire engine and fuel lines. Sydney Richardson's plane was sabotaged. At some time within an hour or two of flight time, someone added sugar to her gas tanks.

"Second question: how did those two helicopters find us? There was an element of luck in my finding the president. The trail of a dead man led me to him and Ms. Richardson. As I have told you, the Secret Service agent made that portion of my task easy. Now, all of our military, all of our satellites, using the best technology available, couldn't locate the downed airplane. Yet those two helicopters flew right to our location.

"Third question, who sent them and why?

"Since our return to Fort Drum, it has been reported that I was injured and hospitalized until my recent return to Washington, and that my friend Mike Stowe simply wished to return quietly to his home without a lot of fanfare. Please forgive us, but all of that is a lie.

"At the president's request, Mike and I took on the task of trying to come up with answers to the last two questions. With the support of two Army investigators and two helicopter flight crews, Mike and I returned to the site of Ms. Richardson's downed airplane. We recovered the bodies of the men who had been threatening the president and, I'm pleased to report, those of the two Secret Service agents. A few days later, a Navy dive team went back and recovered the bodies of the two men in the helicopter I shot down over the lake."

"Out of the corner of his eye, Dan caught the movement of a man trying to leave the chamber through a rear door. He immediately recognized it as Melvin Adams, Governor of the State of Maine. "Sit down, Governor," he ordered. "You're not going anywhere just yet." Adams was restrained by two men and forced to return to his seat.

Dan returned to the podium after the commotion settled down. "Before leaving, Mike and I were sworn in by the FBI and the U.S. Marshals Service as officers. Anticipating what might be ahead of us and wanting to be sure we were operating within the law and with proper authority.

"Let me now answer the first of our two questions. How did those helicopters find us?" Dan glared directly at Governor Adams as he slowly and deliberately reached into his pants pocket. He extracted a small plastic bag and held it up for all to see. "This, ladies and gentlemen, this is how they found us, isn't it, Governor Adams?

"This, ladies and gentlemen, is a hand warmer. Or should I say the remains of what was supposed to look like a hand warmer? It is the casing for a hand warmer, but inside it was packed with a low-frequency radio transmitter like those used to track animals by attaching one around their necks. This was given to me as I boarded the C-130 aircraft that flew me and my supplies into the north woods of Maine.

"It was presented to me as a 'good luck' gift from Vice President Carson. Except, the vice president didn't know anything about it. So that was yet another lie, the first of many Mike and I were to discover. The man who really gave this to me, who handed it to me and lied as he did so, was Melvin Adams, Governor of the State of Maine."

There was an immediate uproar. Shouts of outrage filled the air. Fingers pointed at the governor. All eyes turned on him in disbelief. Words like traitor and treason flew across the room. The Speaker once again had to rap his gavel to regain order.

"Please!" Dan requested. "Please take your seats, I have more to report to you." Somberly, he continued. "Unfortunately, our investigation did not end in the governor's office or even in the State of Maine. It only began there. A couple of days ago, with the assistance of the Attorney General of the United States, a special grand jury was convened to receive the information that Mike and I and the two Army investigators from Fort Drum had accumulated.

"As a result of that presentation and based on the volume and merit of the evidence, thirty-four arrest warrants were issued. All thirty-four of those named in those warrants are currently sitting in this chamber." He held his arms high to maintain control of the room. "You will notice a group of men and women now moving about the chamber. Each is either a U.S. Marshal or a Special Agent of the FBI. They are here to arrest the thirty-four people I am referring to, all of whom will be removed from the chamber, placed under arrest, and brought into custody awaiting further action."

There was no way to control the room after this announcement. Bedlam erupted. Dan began reading the list of names, but no one heard him. He was completely drowned out by the mass of confusion unfolding as the agents moved through the room, taking all thirty-four into custody and reading them their Miranda rights. Each was handcuffed and led to waiting vehicles for transport to an undisclosed location.

Those sitting or standing near those being arrested looked on in shock. Disbelief reigned as their friend or associate, or maybe just a familiar face, was hauled away by a federal agent. A void opened around each of the thirty-four as if they were carrying a contagious disease. Those surrounding did not wish to be caught in a photo or television shot with the now condemned.

Thirty-four people, who moments ago were valued and influential members of the power club, were totally alone. Isolated. Abandoned. Declared untouchable. Political rats are being excised from the ship of state, while those standing nearby stood with sharp knives of righteousness, ready to cut any and all ties to the infected.

Chapter Seven

Ten minutes went by. The Speaker reached for his gavel twice to call for order. Both times, the president stopped him. He knew it would be hopeless. What had taken place had to run its course. It would take some time for the full impact to sink in. He wanted to give all those milling around the chamber time to fully absorb what was going on within their ranks.

Another ten minutes passed. The president signaled to Dan to approach the podium. He stood at the microphone without speaking. His silence, his presence alone took command. Slowly, all eyes turned to him, and seats were retaken. It was evident to all that this was not the same man who had stepped before them at the beginning of this eventful night.

Who was this man? Surely not a simple Army Sergeant. Who was this man who just shook the government of the most powerful nation on earth to its very core? Who was this man who, with a single stroke of his words, cut a traitorous cancer from their midst? Who set events in motion far beyond the room where he now stood. Surely the people watching across the country and governments around the world were stunned and would react.

"Ladies and gentlemen, I promise you I won't keep you much longer." Grave faces surrounded him. "I will, at the risk of my own life, assure you that the evidence we have collected will justify all the drama that has taken place here tonight. Everything Mike Stowe and I have uncovered with the help of both federal and state agents will stand up in any court of law. And in public opinion.

"Let me assure you. There is no vendetta here against any of those involved. No politics. No axes to grind. No one, no one, influenced what Mike and I have done. No one led us down any path to any predesignated end. The president's instructions to us were clear. Dig... dig...dig, no matter what. No matter where. No matter who.

"To the best of our ability, the only motivation that Mike and I could decipher from all of this was that those involved just couldn't wait for the next election cycle. They couldn't win the presidency fair and square. They had to eliminate all risk of giving the people of our country a choice. They had to take the office now. Why? Simple. The president has two more years in office. If he were removed, his replacement would have a real shot at being in office for the remainder of his term plus two more. Ten years in office. Ten years. What a temptation!

"The evidence we gathered will prove that not only did they plan to kill the president, but they had similar plans for the vice president. He, too, was in the way."

A shockwave of disbelief swept across the entire chamber.

So much to take in. Such a violation to digest.

"The arrogance of those arrested tonight made our task easy. Their trail was broad and clear. They never expected to get caught or to be revealed. They didn't try very hard to conceal their moves or their treachery.

"Their arrogance, pure and simple, is what brought them down. Don Richardson wasn't the target of these people: his office was. Sydney Richardson wasn't the target: her father's office was. Her flying skills were grossly underestimated. She was supposed to crash and get everyone killed. I certainly wasn't the target, I was just some jerk who came along and got in the way and foiled the attempt."

Dan paused, his head bent low over the podium, contemplating his next words. "Mr. President, that fulfills my need to be here tonight. I have made my report. All the supporting materials have been turned over to the proper authorities. I'm done. But, could I please ask you to allow me to speak freely? »

"Son, you can take all the time you wish and speak as freely as your mind requires. You've earned it. Please go ahead."

Dan turned back to face everyone assembled before him and all those watching on television. "I'll never have this opportunity again. I've put my life on the line for this country and for each and every one of you sitting here. So please be patient with me for a moment.'

He paused again, took a deep breath, and looked out over the silence. "I began this evening by saying that I'm just a sergeant in the United States Army. Well, I'm more than that. I hold an office. A very high office. I am an American citizen.

"Not many of us, and certainly not those wearing a uniform, will ever get to stand where I now stand. Here, in our House of Representatives.

"Isn't that odd! You do," he said, sweeping his across all those before him. "But how many citizens do? How many of the more than three hundred and twenty million of those you represent will ever have this opportunity? How will they be heard? How many of them do you even talk to? Do you even read their letters? No, not your staff, you!

"How many of their telephone calls do you answer? How many times have those snot-nosed puppets you call aides referred to your constituents as crackpots? Troublemakers? As the little people? The voiceless? The nobodies are back there on the farm, or in the factory, or in the office with the water cooler and coffee pots?"

He paused again, knowing that his emotions were getting the best of him and that he was way out of line. But he didn't care. Not now. Not after all that had taken place. "Mr. President, please forgive me, and please be patient." He swept a pointed finger at everyone again. "You owe me these few minutes. Each and every one of you owes me, and the more than three hundred and twenty million like me out there."

He paused again. His shoulders slumped forward from the weight of the moment. He slowly turned toward the president. There was so much more he wanted to say, but could have said. He wanted to scold them. Humble them. Embarrass them. But he knew that was not his place to do. He knew he had already overstepped the limits of welcome. He knew he had already gone beyond the bounds, standing here before the lawmakers of the land. He began again... deliberately.

"The moment I step away from this platform, I will consider this debt paid in full. My daughter and I, and my future wife, will go home. But those out there they don't have this opportunity. They can't stand here and collect on their debt. You still owe them." With a determination in his voice and a glare in his eyes, Dan looked out over the lawmakers and added, "And I intend to do everything I can to see that you pay up. That they, too, are paid in full."

Sergeant Daniel J. Travis, United States Army, looked up into the gallery. "I love you, Lucy, and I hope Daddy didn't embarrass you tonight. Thank you, Mr. President... Mr. Speaker. Good night and may God bless America."

The silence was deafening. He gathered his notes and turned to walk from the platform. Heads hung low throughout the chamber. No one spoke a word or moved a muscle. Dan descended from behind the podium and headed toward the aisle. From high above him, a single voice broke the silence. "I love you, Daddy!"

Dan looked up at his adoring daughter. She was standing, looking down upon her father. She began to clap as he walked toward the rear of the House. Another pair of hands joined hers. Then a third. Then another. Some began to stand. Others wiped tears from their eyes. The applause grew. And grew. And grew! Before Dan reached the midpoint of the aisle, everyone in the House was applauding.

There were no shouts. No whistles. No hoots. Only respectful applause. Anything else would diminish and discredit the demonstration of courage and conviction displayed by the man now passing among them. This man, they called Master Sergeant Daniel J. Travis, United States Army.

Chapter Eight

The next morning, Dan woke up lying on top of the covers in a strange bed. He was in a room at the Marriott Hotel on 14th Street, compliments of the U.S. Secret Service. On one side of him, Lucy lay curled up next to her father. On the other side, Sydney Richardson lay curled up next to her husband-to-be.

After leaving the Capitol building the night before, they were whisked away from the crowds and the press and brought here to be alone, finally alone. A late-night dinner was brought to them, compliments of room service. The three of them ate and talked, then talked some more, getting to know one another again. They talked late into the night.

Dan was about to take Lucy to her room when he realized that she had fallen asleep wrapped around one of his arms. Sydney curled up with the other wrapped around her, and the three of them soon fell asleep from exhaustion in the comfort and security of being together.

Sydney woke up within a few minutes of Dan, and Lucy stirred shortly after. Dan got them off to their own rooms to shower and dress while he did the same. Within an hour, the three of them met in the suite's living room, ready to go. There was a knock at the door, and Mike Stowe stepped in to join them.

Dan was about to summon one of the Secret Service agents to ask about where they could have breakfast when the telephone rang. They all looked at one another. No one wanted to answer it in fear of what or who was on the other end. Dan finally felt compelled to pick it up.

"Hello."

"Dan?"

"Yes, sir." He recognized the voice. "This is Don Richardson."

"Yes, sir, I know."

"Is Sydney with you?"

"Yes, sir. So are Lucy and Mike," he added, to cover his embarrassment at being caught by the President of the United States in a hotel room with his only daughter. "We were just about to go down for some breakfast."

"Good! I'd like to see all of you this morning. Could you please come by the White House? I'll send a car. I promise that I won't keep you long."

"Yes, sir. Of course. We'll come over right after we finish eating."

"Dan," the president continued.

"Have you had the television on this morning?"

"No, sir."

"Have you seen a newspaper?"

"No, sir, we all just got up and took showers. We haven't done anything else so far."

"Look outside," the president said. "What?"

"Look out of the window."

Dan walked over to the window. Sydney, Mike, and Lucy followed him.

"Oh my God," Sydney muttered. The street below their hotel window was packed solid with people, from curb to curb and corner to corner. Television camera trucks from every network lined the sidewalks, jamming the street.

"They're waiting for you, Dan," he heard the voice in the telephone say. "They're waiting for you and Sydney and Mike and

Lucy. You'll never be able to eat breakfast there. Besides, I've got plenty here. Please come. I've sent people to help you get through the crowd and into the car."

Half an hour later, they were inside the White House. The president, the vice president and his wife, and Chief of Staff Bob Wilson met them at the door. They all proceeded up to the private living quarters. Through the windows overlooking the vast lawns and streets beyond, they could see the streets full of people, arms waving and cameras and cell phones held high, trying to capture the moment.

Everyone in the White House greeted each other with hugs and kisses and two-handed shakes to emphasize their newfound sincerity and affection. The greetings were real and warm, at least by D.C. standards. Everyone dressed and behaved casually. Even the president wore jeans and a T-shirt. It was, after all, a Sunday morning.

Dan was amazed at the ease with which Lucy moved about until he remembered how much time she had spent with Sydney while he and Mike were away. A large Sunday morning brunch of eggs, waffles, country ham, biscuits, bacon, baked apples, toast, and grits with red-eye gravy had been prepared by the obviously southern kitchen staff. They all sat and ate and laughed and talked. Finally, the president brought the conversation back to the real world.

"Well, young man," he began, holding everyone's attention. "You had quite an evening last night. You made quite a splash."

"I'm sorry, sir."

"Sorry? What on earth for? You had the courage to do and say what I and God know how many other people would love to have said. Sorry? No, son, I don't think that's what you need to be. You were a hero before you stepped up to those microphones last night.

This morning, you are a double hero. Look at those people out there. Look at those television types dying to get to you. Listen to what the people are saying. You're the hottest thing since...

"Since James Bond."

"That's right, Lucy, since James Bond." The laughter around the table continued until the president resumed. "So, Dan, the question is what's next? What are you going to do with all this fame and attention?"

"Well, sir, like I told you last night, first thing is that I'd like to marry your daughter."

"Yeah!" Lucy yelled out.

"Then I've got a little over two years left in the Army before I can retire. So I'd like to return to duty as soon as I can. And I've got a little lady over here I'd like to see graduate from high school down the road. Seems that I've got plenty to do."

"Dan," the president said. "I've also got about two years to go in my term. So you and I will be out of a job at about the same time. This is my second term, and I can't run again. By the time I'm done, I'll be ready to call it quits. You, on the other hand, will still be a young man."

Vice President Carson leaned in to join the conversation. "Dan, I know this might not be the right time to bring this up, but I'm planning on running for the presidency in the next election. I'd like you to run with me. I'd like you to be my vice presidential candidate."

"Whoa! Are you nuts?" Dan exclaimed, "Excuse me, sir, but hold on here." He had been caught completely off guard. He looked over at Sydney and Lucy. Both looked stunned. Dan's mind was racing. "Hold on. That seems to be politically opportune, but remember, I'm only an Army sergeant. I'm no politician and in a week, I'll be forgotten."

"You're wrong there, Dan," the president said. "You are one now. After that speech you made last night, you are the number one politician in the country. You have no idea what a powerful impact you had last night."

"That may be so, Mr. President. I may be a hot property because I made a one-time speech, but that's it. One time!" He turned to face the vice president. "Mr. Vice President, I'm honored. Truly I am, but, sir, "

"No buts. I'm dead serious. I've gotten to know you well enough to know your character, and I want you on my team."

"Well, sir, okay, I'll run with you. I'll be your running mate, but only on the condition that you make me a promise and give it to me in writing. I want you to guarantee me that nothing, absolutely nothing, will happen to you while you're in office. An absolute, carved-in-stone guarantee that you won't die or take any plane rides over the mountains with any of your kids. Write it down and sign it right now."

"I can't do that, Dan. Nobody can. Nobody knows what's going to happen in the future. I mean, look at what we've just gone through. Nobody knows when they're going to die."

"Exactly," Dan replied. "You can't do what I ask... and I can't accept your offer. As honored as I am, sir, I can't accept. Besides, if the president and I are out of work around the same time, we can keep our date with Mike to go camping up in the mountains of Maine. There's a certain high mountain lake we would all like to see that needs some serious fishing. So you see, sir, I'm going to be a bit busy, what with a new wife, a teenage daughter to keep track of before you know it, and a cranky old retired father-in-law who's kind of used to getting what he wants. No, sir, I just don't think I'll be available."

Everyone in the room laughed. Sydney threw her arms around Dan's neck and kissed him. The president wrapped his arms around both of them.

"What do you want to do now, Dan?" the president asked.

"Well, sir, I'd like to take some time off. I could use a little vacation."

"I think I've got the authority to take care of that. As of now, you are officially on a thirty-day leave.

About the Author

Richard Totino was raised on an apple farm in the town of Marlboro in the mid-Hudson Valley of New York. His small-town roots and values have guided him throughout his entire life. Although he has traveled extensively, he still considers himself a small-town boy with small-town values. After he enlisted in the U.S. Army, he returned to college to complete his graduate degrees at the ripe old age of 34. His work in international sales and marketing provided him with an insight into many cultures and customs beyond our borders, and his extensive travel in the U.S. taught him that people everywhere are as open and friendly as you give them the opportunity to be. He likes to tell people, "I have slept in 49 states," which leads his wife to describe him as George Washington, who seems to have slept everywhere.

Together with his wife Sharon, Dick now resides in North Carolina, where they soak up the sunshine and sea breezes. Their combined family includes eight children and five grandchildren, providing them with plenty to do and all the related challenges that go with keeping up with a large family. An avid hunter and outdoorsman, his personal experiences enhance his writing. He refers to fall as "scrapbooking season," that is when he leaves Sharon at home to occupy herself with her crafts while he escapes to the wilderness of North Carolina and the Adirondack Mountains of New York. He has been active in the Knights of Columbus, the Elks, Disabled American Veterans, and the American Legion and as a crew boss with Lower Adirondack Search and Rescue (LASAR), participating in numerous search and rescue efforts throughout the region.